CHRIS

Christina va...
always game for an adventure. After all,
experience has taught her that there is no
place on earth that can't be turned into a
paradise. On the other hand, what wealthy,
beautiful, intelligent and endlessly sexy
woman in her right mind would turn down a
winter in California teaching the natives how
to make interesting home movies for the
chance to traipse through the Russian tundra
at the coldest time of year with a fortune in
stolen jewels sewn into the lining of her
coat? Well . . . there is one such woman.
And why? Is it for money? Of course not. Is
it for fame? Hardly necessary. Is it for
excitement? Not likely. Is it for love? Ah . . .
it is something like that . . .

CHRISTINA'S ESCAPADE

Blakely St. James

ARROW BOOKS

Arrow Books Limited
62-65 Chandos Place, London WC2N 4NW

An imprint of Century Hutchinson Limited

London Melbourne Sydney Auckland
Johannesburg and agencies throughout
the world

First published in Great Britain 1986

Printed and bound in Great Britain by
Anchor Brendon Limited, Tiptree, Essex

ISBN 0 09 944640 5

CHAPTER ONE

"The gentleman you were expecting is here, Miss van Bell," Miss Watford announced in depressed tones.

"Excuse me," I said into the mouthpiece of the telephone. I looked up at the tall, spare figure of the housekeeper the agency had sent me for my stay in New York. It was the Christmas holiday and temporary help was in short supply. Miss Watford was frigidly polite and extremely efficient, but during the past several days it had become apparent that, despite generous wages and easy working conditions, she viewed working for me in the same way a Southern Baptist would view employment in a whorehouse.

"I've heard he was a terrific stud," I said wickedly. "What do you think?"

"I'm really not in a position to judge, miss," she replied pointedly. "But, speaking strictly as a disinterested observer, I'd say he was quite presentable. He is apparently prepared to work, as he has a large rolled mat of some kind and a duffel bag that presumably contains his equipment."

"Well, show him to my bedroom," I said, smiling suggestively. "I'll be there in a moment and I can check out his equipment personally."

"Yes, miss," said the housekeeper stiffly. Her face registered no emotion, but the straightness of her spine as she left the breakfast room made me laugh. I poured some more coffee into my cup and went back to my phone conversation with Malcolm Gold, editor-in-chief of *World* magazine.

"I heard that," Malcolm said. "Why did you do that to the poor woman?"

"I can't help it. She's so prim and proper she brings out the worst in me."

"She has no sense of humor," Malcolm agreed, "but I'm sure she has some qualities you can admire. Give her a chance."

"She makes a great omelette," I said. "But you're right, Malcolm. It's Christmas and I should be kind to widows, orphans, and spinsters."

"You're incorrigible," Malcolm laughed. "Now, to get back to the reason for my call, will you handle that interview for me?"

"I suppose so," I said, "though I don't see why one of the staff writers can't do it."

"Princess Anna Borisovna Lyapunov is one of the last descendants of the Romanoffs, a first cousin to the murdered Czar. Today she's the undisputed leader of old-money society, a sort of dowager empress. Everything she does is news, but she never grants interviews."

"She's granted *World* magazine one."

"An exclusive, the first one in thirty years," said Malcolm with undisguised pride. "It's a real coup. I can't just send some hack writer and a couple of kid photographers over. I have to bring out our class act, and that's you, Christina."

"*I* was only a kid photographer once," I reminded him.

"And you're still better with a camera than anyone I know. If you'll just let the tape recorder run while you're chatting and taking pictures, I'll have a staff writer translate it into an actual story."

"I'll do it for you," I said, "but only as a late Christmas gift."

"You already gave me a Christmas gift," said Malcolm in a voice that made little shivers race along my spine. "Are we still on for New Year's Eve?"

"There's no one I'd rather spend it with," I said truthfully, "but you'll have to excuse me now. I don't want to be late for that interview."

"It's not for hours. What's the big hurry?"

"I'm going to give myself a Christmas present," I said. "I've been a good girl all year and I deserve a reward."

"The guy with the equipment," Malcolm laughed. "I forgot about him. Who is he, a hairdresser?"

"A masseur."

"Sorry I asked. Have a good time, Christina, but don't forget you're expected at Her Highness' apartment at four o'clock."

"I won't," I promised. We said our good-byes and I hung up the phone.

I have long been an advocate of massage. There is nothing as relaxing and at the same time as stimulating, and I have both a masseur and a masseuse who I use interchangeably, depending on my mood. If all I want is to relax, I call Annette but if I'm feeling depressed or out of sorts, it's Paul's nimble fingers that reawaken my senses.

This time, however, neither Paul nor Annette had been available and the receptionist at the massage salon had suggested that I give their new employee, Axel Corman, a try. "He was trained in Sweden," she told me. "He's been in this country only a short time, but he's had nothing but the highest praise from our customers."

I had eagerly agreed to her suggestion and when I opened my bedroom door now I was not disappointed. Axel Corman stood well over six feet with sun-bleached hair, arresting blue eyes, and a magnificently proportioned body displayed to perfection by a white turtleneck sweater and faded skintight jeans. I could hardly wait to get my hands on him, or rather for him to get his hands on me, and gave him my most dazzling smile.

He smiled back, letting his eyes travel from the burnished tan of my throat to the shapely curves of my hips and thighs clearly visible through the transparent silk of my negligee. I asked him where he would like to give me my massage, and he replied that the thick pile carpet of my bedroom would be perfect. He knelt on the floor and unrolled a white cotton-covered exercise mat, then indicated that I should undress and lie down on my back. His tone was thoroughly professional, but his eyes held a gleam of desire as I slowly unfastened my robe and let it fall to the floor. I stretched out on the exercise mat so that my head was between his knees. Axel took several small porcelain jars from his duffel bag, unscrewing the caps and sniffing the contents. He selected a pure white cream that smelled faintly of roses. Taking some on his fingertips, he began to smooth it onto my face. I gave a sigh of contentment and closed my eyes as Axel's fingers moved against the tight muscles in my neck and shoulders. His hands were gentle and he worked with practiced assurance, probing deep into my tired muscles to make my body come alive at his touch.

From my neck he moved to my chest, his fingers tracing concentric circles around my breasts. A rush of sexual heat washed over me as I felt his touch graze my nipples, which stiffened immediately. I heard the sharp intake of his breath but he made no move to touch me there again. As he worked his way along my abdomen to the soft swell of my belly, he switched to a soft stroking motion that sent shivers of excitement along my limbs. Though he deliberately ignored my pubic area, I felt a quivering sensation in my loins and my pussy juices began to flow.

Axel now changed his position, moving to the foot of the exercise mat and kneeling between my spread legs. He put more cream on his hands and began to work on my calves and thighs, first kneading briskly, then stroking lightly upward. My sighs of pleasure turned to moans of excitement as his fingers slipped between my aching pussy lips, hot and damp with wanting him.

I dug my heels into the mat and arched my hips upward as Axel's finger massaged my cunt. He leaned over me, his other hand slipping beneath my hips to penetrate the tight hole between my cheeks. My entire body was a quivering, aching mass of raw desire, sweating and straining toward orgasm. I climaxed explosively, my juices flooding his finger, crying wildly as my sphincter muscles gripped then released the finger in my asshole.

I was sated but not satisfied. Axel was still fully dressed, his expression a mask of detached professionalism. I wondered if the rest of him was as talented as his fingers, if he was as good a lover as he was a masseur.

"You have skillful hands," I said softly. "I've never experienced an orgasm quite like that before."

"I always manipulate all parts of the body when giving a massage," he replied. "The vagina is just another set of muscles. It should be exercised regularly like the hands and feet."

"There's a part of my body you missed," I said.

"Oh?"

"My mouth," I whispered, puckering suggestively. "You didn't exercise my mouth.

Axel was not slow to remedy this oversight. Stretching out beside me on the mat, he covered my mouth with his in a searing, passionate kiss. His hand fondled my ripe, firm breasts and stroked my belly as my lips yielded to his and his tongue explored the inner recesses of my mouth. I pressed my nude body against his clothed one, my arms encircling his neck and my pussy grinding against the growing bulge in his crotch.

Suddenly Axel tore his lips from mine. Gathering me in his arms, he stood up, lifting me as if I weighed no more than a child. He carried me to the bed and laid me gently down, then proceeded to strip in front of me. The way a man undresses before a woman tells a lot about him. Axel's movements were self-confident. He knew I was watching him and he performed this simple act in a way calculated to show off his hard, muscular lines to their best advantage. He had a beautiful body and obviously enjoyed showing it off as much as I enjoyed looking at it. His cock was enormous. It was long and thick, swollen with his lust.

Then he was on top of me, his firm sure hands eagerly exploring the luscious curves of my body. I spread my legs, gasping as his rigid pole pushed its way into my steaming slit. My hips arched upward and my nails dug into the hard muscles of his back. He moved with impressive power and control. His cock stretched my cunt, filling me completely. I grasped his hair, pulling his head down to mine. Our lips opened to each other, tongues snaking around each other's mouths as our bodies moved together. Though he was fully erect, Axel's staying power was tremendous. He kept his movements slow and steady. His hands gripped my buttocks, forcing my hips to angle upward so that my clit was grinding against the rock-hard base of his prick as his thrusts pounded into me. My entire body was on fire, trembling with the intensity of stimulation Axel's thrusting cock was giving it. I was on the brink of orgasm but I held back, savoring the sensation of Axel's turgid pole coring my aching cunt. We kept fucking and fucking, intent only on our own carnal lusts. The sensation of our twin control heightened our pleasure. We could last forever. Axel's hands fondled my breasts, my lips sought his, and all the time he was thrusting his stiff rod into my gushing pussy, grunting with the effort as I moved to keep pace with his rhythm. At last I could hold out no longer and with a wild scream, I let go. The waves of my orgasm washed over me as Axel's body, engulfed by his own release, convulsed and bucked on mine.

I lay for a while, half asleep in Axel's arms, admiring the way the sweat glistened on his smooth skin like diamond dust on polished amber. The smell of his maleness and the animal scents of our lust blended pleasantly. Axel's eyes were closed. My fingers lightly stroked his body, then moved to the source of his maleness. His prick was soft and limp, nestled between his hard-muscled thighs. I began to stroke the loose skin of the shaft with the tips of my nails, blowing softly into his ear and nibbling gently on the lobe as I worked. Axel's body trembled slightly and I could feel the blood begin to flow into his flaccid member. Like a snake being coaxed from its slumber by the siren sounds of its master's flute, Axel's prick began a slow but certain resurrection.

I sat up and straddled his legs. Leaning over I ran my tongue along the underside of his prick, sliding it over the helmetlike head. Moving my head up and down, I licked the entire surface of his cock, coating it with saliva. My expert ministrations were rewarded by a tremendous hard-on throbbing with pent-up desire. I considered bringing him to orgasm with my mouth but I wanted to prolong our pleasure and, rising to my knees, I grasped his gorgeous tool and guided it to the entrance of my cunt. Axel gave a low moan as I slid down the full length of his shaft, his hips arching upward to meet my descending twat.

I like the reverse missionary position. It gives me almost total control of the tempo of my lovemaking. Axel relaxed his body, his hands reaching for my breasts. I very slowly began to move up and down his slick hard pole, tightening and releasing my vaginal muscles to increase the muscular tension and sensation. Axel's hands roamed over the firm flesh of my abdomen to the rounded curves of my buttocks. As the tension began to build he moved with me, grinding his hips so that they lifted off the sheets with each downward thrust of my cunt.

"You got great moves, baby," he moaned. "I'm really hot for you."

"I want your cum," I cried, sucking him into me. "I'm ready for you."

He gave a loud groan and I held my breath as the first spurts of cream geysered upward, sending me into a mind-blowing orgasm. I cried out my pleasure as I collapsed on top of him, feeling utterly, deliciously spent.

Several hours later I stood before the full-length mirror in my bedroom making a final check of my appearance. I had dressed conservatively in a narrow, black wool jersey suit with a long, side-wrapped dolman-sleeved jacket and matching knee-length straight skirt. An ivory silk-satin muffler accented the graceful line of my neck, and my blond hair was swept into a French twist to expose the large jet button earrings that completed the ensemble.

A custom-made, black leather shoulder case contained a compact tape recorder and my Leica R/4 camera with a 90mm f2.0 lens and a lightweight flash attachment. I remembered how professional I had felt the first time I had wound my own film. The elegantly dressed, sophisticated woman in the mirror was a far cry from the leggy, naive girl in miniskirts that had lied her way into a job at *World* magazine years ago, and I smiled as I slipped on my Canadian coyote coat and picked up my gray leather gloves.

As I stepped outside, I was hit by an icy blast of northern

air. "Welcome to the deep freeze, Miss van Bell," said the doorman, closing the door quickly behind me.

"How was your vacation, Sam?" I asked as we stood under the awning.

"Wonderful. I spent Christmas with my family in Los Angeles. Nice and warm. I've spent too many winters standing out in weather like this."

"I once spent Christmas on the Coast," I said. "It was terrible. Tinsel hanging on palm trees, a traditional Christmas dinner of tacos and sangria on a huge yacht with a dozen movie producers chewing cigars and talking percentages and points. I swore that would be the last time I spent the holiday in a warm climate. It just doesn't seem like Christmas."

"I guess at my age comfort is more important than tradition," Sam laughed. "But I remember your once telling me that you were raised in Vermont."

"That doesn't make me part polar bear," I said. "I hate the cold as much as anyone. Christmas in Vermont was like a picture postcard, all silver and white and green, but by mid-March I was sick to death of hats and scarves and itchy woolen leggings and used to long for the feel of the sun's heat on my face."

"You get enough sun now," Sam teased. "I bet it takes work to keep up that tan."

"It does," I said, "and I'll be off again right after New Year's. But now I have to go to work."

"No kidding? What happened? The vault bare or something?"

"This interview calls for a class act," I told him, remembering Malcolm's words. "I'm going to see a member of the Russian royal family. It should be pretty interesting."

"I'd better get you a cab then," Sam nodded. "I wouldn't want you to be late." He stepped quickly into the street and flagged down a passing taxi, then held the door for me. "Have a nice time," he said, and I smiled and waved as my cab pulled away. I gave the driver a Central Park West address. He looked barely out of his teens with a peach-fuzz complexion and a shock of carrot-colored hair. He was wearing a blue and white down vest over a navy wool shirt.

"How about some music?" I called to him through the Plexiglas shield. The driver nodded and snapped on a small portable that was hanging from the meter. From the speaker poured an electronic blast the likes of which I had never heard. Mixed somewhere between the lines of synthesizer strings and pounding drums, I could hear a nasally blocked adolescent bawling what sounded like the chorus to an old standard.

"What the hell is that?" I yelled.

"That's Christmas carols, baby," the driver replied. "Don't you recognize 'White Christmas' when you hear it?"

"I thought I did," I called. "Who's doing the hatchet job on it?"

"New group from Long Island called the Bilious Gorillas," he replied, sticking a cigarette into his mouth and lighting it with one hand as he swerved around some pedestrians at breakneck speed. "All New Wave."

"I think I prefer the old wave," I moaned. "It's Christmas, for God sakes!"

"That's the sound of today. We got Christmas music by Dead Droppings, Cut My Wrists, Polished Bayonette, and my personal favorites, Lost Patrol."

"When I was a kid, Elton John was pretty big."

"Not anymore. You ought to update your record collection."

"I'll have to do that," I said, thinking I was too young to feel old. A few moments later we pulled up in front of my destination, and I wished him a merry Christmas and watched him speed away, wrapped in electronic bliss. I promised myself I would never again complain when someone put on Johnny Mathis singing "Silent Night."

I gave my name to the doorman, who told me that the Princess had left word to send me right up, and, following his directions, I took the ancient elevator to the third floor.

The door was answered on the fifteenth ring by a tiny wizened old woman in a maid's uniform.

"My name is Christina van Bell," I said. "I have an appointment with Princess Anna Borisovna Lyapunov."

"What?" the old woman demanded, her cloudy gray eyes scanning my face.

"I have an appointment with the Princess," I said, raising my voice slightly. "My name is Christina van Bell."

"What d'you want?" she demanded, scowling. I resisted the temptation to lift her up bodily and move her aside.

"Appointment!" I shouted, leaning down and speaking directly into her ear. "I have an appointment with the Princess!"

"You don't have to shout," the old woman snapped. "I'm not deaf. Come in. Her Highness is expecting you." I followed her into the foyer, closing the door behind me.

She shuffled along at an agonizingly slow pace, giving me plenty of time to take in my surroundings. A wide hallway ran the length of the house with highly polished wood floors and gold-hued marbled walls. I caught a glimpse of the dining room, painted a bright tangerine and furnished in the cluttered Victorian style fashionable in the late nineteenth century. The chairs were covered in lime velvet and a lime-and-tangerine rug covered the floor. We entered the garish lemon-tinted drawing room with its lemon rug and bright yellow flowered chintz sofas and chairs. I could not repress a smile, for despite the expensiveness of the furnishings and antiques it was plainly an old lady's room and an old lady's apartment, with parfait-sundae colors and memories of the past. Everywhere were small lacquered boxes, porcelain figurines, and clusters of photographs in silver and gilt frames. One wall was decorated with baroque festoons, carved by Grinling Gibbons, she explained to me later, which surrounded a portrait of a beautiful young woman with a high-bridged nose, a swanlike neck, and a profusion of honey-colored hair.

"Miss van Bell?" said a voice behind me. I turned and found myself facing the aged mirror image of the portrait I had just been admiring. The Princess' hair had grown white and there were fine lines about the eyes and mouth and she used a cane, but her body was still erect, her slim figure elegant in a lilac wool challis dress. It was hard to believe she was close to ninety, but I could understand even now the envy and love such beauty must have excited. I blurted out this appraisal and she laughed delightedly.

"You are very kind, my dear, and most correct, though I

won't admit to more than seventy for the record." She took my coat herself and we sat together on the sofa.

"Do you mind if I take a few pictures before we begin?" I asked "The light is at its best just now."

"Of course not. I will ring for refreshments. In Russia there was always a lavish *zakuska*—you Americans call it a buffet—set out on a table in the hall or in an alcove. Guests and family members served themselves at any hour, for the table was a permanent fixture, constantly replenished, always available."

"That's a lovely custom."

"It was. In some ways the Russians, at least the nobility, raised gluttony to a fine art. It made for thick waistlines and double chins but, then, in the Russian winters it did not pay one to be too thin." She picked up a small silver bell from the table and tinkled it gently. Several minutes passed and the maid still did not appear. "She's a little hard of hearing," the Princess said, shaking the bell more vigorously.

"So I noticed," I said, checking my light meter and taking a few casual shots of the room.

The Princess turned toward the doorway and cupped her hands over her mouth. "Natasha! Come here, please!" she bellowed in a surprisingly loud tone.

A moment later the ancient maid shuffled into the room. "You don't have to shout like a peasant, Your Highness," she said waspishly. "That's what the bell's for."

The Princess ignored this remark. "We would like our tea now, Natasha," she said politely, "and some *zakuska*. I believe you have it all prepared?"

"It took all morning," the maid whined, "and we were out of tea. Not that it matters. You can't get decent tea anymore. Even when the Mongol hordes took over our village, you could still get good Russian tea. Now all they have is pencil shavings and horse manure bound into little bags with strings at the end and they call it tea! Piss-water is what it is," she said, glaring at me.

"I'm sure it will be delicious," I said soothingly.

"Bah! What do you know," she muttered, wobbling to the window and wheeling over a large serving cart with a beautiful gold and silver samovor and a delicate Sèvres china tea service. Her hands shook slightly as she set the cups and saucers on the table, making the china rattle dangerously.

I had never seen tea prepared this way and watched in fascination as Natasha filled the samovar with cold water and put burning coals in the draft chimney. An extension was placed on top, and when the water was boiling, the extension was removed and the samovar was placed on the table in front of us. The china teapot was then placed over the top opening.

The Princess served the tea herself, first pouring a little of the strong tea essence from the teapot into a cup, then adding hot water from the spigot of the samovar. There was cream on the table and a silver dish containing ice-blue sugar cubes, but I noticed that the Princess drank hers black.

"That's a beautiful samovar," I said.

"Our family has made tea in this very samovar for generations," she nodded, obviously pleased that I had noticed. "It was one of the few things I brought with me when I fled Russia, and even when times were rough I couldn't bear to part with it. It belonged to my grandfather, who was a collector of beautiful things. He died quite young . . ."

"He was a whoremonger," Natasha snapped, placing a tray of food on the table. "He died of the pox, as he deserved."

"Really, Natasha," the Princess admonished. "You shouldn't say such things. Your family benefited from his profligacy, after all."

"My grandmother was raped by His Royal Highness on her wedding night," Natasha recounted. "We were serfs but her baby, my mother, was taken from her and brought into the palace to be raised. She worked in the kitchens when she grew up and when I was born I was trained to be a lady's maid to Her Highness, as we were near the same age."

"It was Natasha who helped me escape," the Princess said. "We sewed some jewels into the linings of our clothes and took the samovar and some gold plate in a bag. We were dressed as peasants and I had to pretend to be mute. My accent would have given me away."

"Then, Natasha saved your life."

"She did, and has taken care of me ever since," the Princess said, smiling fondly at the old woman.

"We've taken care of each other, Your Highness," Natasha said gruffly, but her cheeks were pink with pleasure at the compliment.

"She's a bit outspoken sometimes," the Princess confided when the old woman had shuffled from the room, "but she means no harm. We were all alone when we fled Russia and we've grown old together. I could not imagine life without her."

"What happened to the rest of your family?"

"Many were killed. The rest . . ." She shrugged expressively. "I had a sister only two years younger than myself. We were especially close. She was in the country the night I fled St. Petersburg. A large part of the family jewels were kept on that estate and I always hoped that my sister had escaped. The jewels were never found." Her voice trembled slightly and she poured herself some more tea, keeping her eyes lowered.

"It must have been difficult for you, alone in a strange country," I said, tactfully changing the subject. "How did you manage? Did you pawn the jewels?"

"Of course not. A beautiful woman can always manage," the Princess said, looking directly at me. "I was young and pretty and titled. The Jazz Age was beginning and I wanted it all, love and freedom and good times. I had them too. Wait, I will show you something." She stood up and walked over to a marble-topped console, returning with a large leather-bound album which she handed to me.

I turned the pages, scanning the contents. The book was filled with newspaper and magazine clippings, all of them about the Princess. There were mentions in the society columns of all the major newspapers as well as tabloid exposés that hinted of romantic liaisons, wild parties, and other social and sexual improprieties.

"You were quite a sensation," I said, studying the yellowed clippings with great interest.

"Your generation didn't invent fun," she replied. "I've had my share of love and adventure. But no one ever took advantage of me, I assure you. I've lived my life as I wanted, my dear. I have no regrets."

"Did you ever marry?"

"No, though I had a great many offers, I never felt the desire to give myself exclusively to one man. There were so many to choose from and they all seemed so eager to make my life comfortable that I didn't want to disappoint any of them." We both laughed at this.

We spent the rest of the afternoon exchanging stories with the ease and intimacy of longtime friends. It was late when I finally got up to leave, and the Princess saw me to the door herself.

"You're a charming young woman," she said, taking my hand. "You remind me very much of myself at your age."

"I hope that's meant as a compliment," I teased.

"It is. We live life to the fullest, you and I. I hope you will come and see me again."

"I will," I promised, kissing the old woman on both cheeks. "I'll come again soon."

I took a taxi to the Madison Avenue building that houses the offices of *World* magazine and pushed the elevator button impatiently. Though the office was closed, the next issue's deadline was fast approaching and I knew that Malcolm would still be at his desk. He was a meticulous worker and always checked every final detail himself.

As usual, I pushed open Malcolm's door without knocking. I always hoped to catch him in flagrante delicto, but so far I'd had no luck. Malcolm was seated behind a desk littered with sheets of copy paper and piles of page mockups. He was bent over a small lightboard, studying alternate designs for the next issue's cover. His suit jacket and tie hung on the coatrack in the corner and his yellow shirt was open at the neck. His brown hair was tousled and there were frown lines between his brows, but he looked up and smiled as I banged into the room.

"Vice squad, darling," I said authoritatively as I walked across the room toward him. "Drop your cock and grab your socks! This is a raid!"

"As always, a tasteful and modest entrance," Malcolm laughed. He stood up and took me in his arms, giving me a warm kiss of welcome. From the first time he had kissed me I had wanted him, and even after all this time, the touch of his lips could make my knees grow weak.

"I've just spent a very unusual afternoon," I told him as he helped me off with my coat and took my shoulder case. "Very inspiring, very uplifting. I've had my whole life-style reaffirmed."

"I assume you mean the Princess," Malcolm said, going to the refrigerator/bar and pouring out two glasses of chilled white wine. I flopped into his chair and he handed me my glass, then sat on the edge of his desk facing me.

"She's really something, Malcolm. She spent the entire afternoon telling me all sorts of stories about her life. She's done things that are as outrageous as anything I've done. Well, almost as outrageous. I mean, times being what they were she couldn't hope to actually match me, but I was too polite to point that out. We had a wonderful time together and I got some great pictures."

"I'm sure you did," Malcolm smiled. "I'll send the film to the lab first thing tomorrow. Why don't you give me the interview tape now and let's see what we have."

"Oh, I never did turn on the tape, darling," I said, sipping my drink. Malcolm's face dropped.

"What do you mean, you never turned on the tape? You were supposed to turn on the tape, Christina. You were there to get an interview."

"It would have been so awkward, so gauche, just sticking a microphone into her face from the start. And once we got to talking, I forgot all about it."

"That interview took weeks to set up," said Malcolm, obviously controlling his temper with difficulty. "I've been holding a great deal of space open for that article and I have covers prepared and press releases already mailed."

"I don't know what you're so worried about," I said. "I can do the article. I remember everything that was said."

"I planned to have a staff writer do the article," Malcolm sighed. "You know, one of those drudges we pay huge salaries. I need it tomorrow."

"Well, you just order two pastrami sandwiches on rye with

mustard and cole slaw and a double order of french fries and I'll go into the next room and whip up something on the word processor."

"Like a cake, huh?"

"Precisely. You can go over it for organization and spelling and punctuation and all those other details you Columbia graduates think are so important."

"You're too good to me."

"I know. Get some pickles too. You have to trust me more, Malcolm. Have I ever let you down?"

"Frequently, but this time I'm stuck. Okay, go to work in the next room and try to stick to the subject." I gave him a hard look but I could see that he was only teasing. Malcolm liked playing the gruff metropolitan editor, but I knew that he trusted me to do a good job. No matter how turbulent my life became, Malcolm was always a safe port to which I could retreat, a sturdy anchor to hold me down.

I blew him a kiss and went next door to start typing.

CHAPTER TWO

I learned an important theory in behavioral science one night while sleeping with the head of the anthropology department of a well-known Ivy League college.

"You see, Christina my dear," he mumbled as he undid the zipper of his trousers, "in the days of the caveman, people spent the long, cold days of winter huddled in their miserable drafty shelters waiting for the weather to get warm. Then one day, some wise man developed the calendar and he stuck New Year's Eve smack in the middle of the worst days of winter so he'd have an excuse to fill his belly, drink quantities of liquor, and engage in the kind of behavior that only large parties give license to." With that, he threw himself on me and our conversation was, of necessity, terminated. His theory was published in an important academic journal several months later, and as the years passed I have come to agree with it. Accordingly, I always spend New Year's Eve having the wildest time possible. It's the least I can do for science.

I also make it a point to spend the evening with someone who is more than a casual acquaintance. Though Malcolm and I do not have an exclusive relationship, he occupies a very special place in my life.

This year, as always, I had invitations to more parties than I could possibly attend. Everyone who was anyone in New

York's upper crust wanted me to attend his or her little soiree, to add a touch of class or perhaps to get a mention in the society columns. I never attend the same party two years in a row and always try to make an appearance at at least two affairs before midnight, which was why I was dressed and ready to start out just before eight o'clock. Malcolm had cheerfully agreed to accompany me to any of the affairs I wanted in return for my promise to see in the New Year in a place of his choosing. "I want to be totally alone with you at midnight," he said, "so I will be assured of the first kiss."

"Don't you want a bit more than a kiss?" I teased.

"I do, but I'm romantic enough to want to woo you a bit first."

"I won't spoil it," I promised. "I'll pretend it's the first time."

I laughed, remembering Malcolm's expression and was still smiling when I answered my doorbell a few moments later.

Malcolm stood framed in the doorway, his black cashmere overcoat open to reveal a classic black dinner jacket with a stiff shirt and bow tie. It has recently become fashionable in some circles to wear all sorts of grotesque and colorful variations on standard evening dress, but fortunately Malcolm turns up his nose at such idiocy.

"Hello, handsome," I purred, grabbing the lapels of his coat and pulling him into the room. "Goin' out tonight?"

"With the prettiest lady in New York," he answered, taking me in his arms. "Have you decided on our itinerary?"

"I have," I said, "and I hope you managed to arrange some sort of transportation. This is the worst night of the year for cabs."

"Don't worry," he assured me, helping me into my full-length sable coat. "I have just the thing for a holiday evening. Wait till you see it."

When we stepped outside, he took my arm and steered me down the block, stopping before a large silver Mercedes 300D sedan with gray leather upholstery and diplomatic license plates. It was parked blatantly in a no-parking zone.

"We should have no trouble parking," I said. "Did you rent it or steal it?"

"Neither. The Swiss Ambassador owed me a favor. Where to?" he asked as he steered the car into traffic. I gave him the address of our first destination and a look of surprise crossed his face. "Is that Wiltshire Pendleton, the publisher?" I nodded. "I always thought you considered him and his wife pretentious boors. Why go to their party?"

"They're dreadful people," I agreed. "But I've heard marvelous things about their new chef, and since we haven't eaten yet, I thought we'd go there for appetizers and see if the stories are true."

"That appetite of yours will be the death of me," Malcolm groaned as he headed the car downtown.

"We won't stay long," I promised. "Most people party-hop on New Year's Eve, and no hostess expects her guests to stay more than an hour or two."

Poole Pendelton was the sort of woman who could easily give being rich and idle a bad name. She had spent her adolescence sleeping through several exclusive finishing schools until one had become embarrassed enough about taking her tuition and her father's lavish endowments and worried enough about the increase in venereal disease among the male faculty to grant her a degree and thus rid themselves of her presence. Poole's father bought her a pink Cadillac and a co-op in New York as a graduation gift and, bolstered by a large trust fund, she set out to make her way in the world. Poole had an itch to write that she insisted on scratching frequently, despite a complete lack of talent. After having her initial literary efforts rejected by every agent in town, she finally managed to seduce an impoverished and impressionable young publisher whom she married, then browbeat into publishing her soppy, witless romances. There being a mysterious power somewhere in the universe which pities and protects the hapless, she shot to the top of the best-seller lists her first time out and has been the darling of the pseudoliterary set ever since. She always sends me signed first editions of her annual assault on literacy and I find them very handy when I run out of toilet paper.

The Pendeltons lived in a duplex apartment in the newest and most expensive high-rise luxury building in the city. Malcolm parked in a no-standing zone, pausing as we left to pull out his white handkerchief and grandly polish the gleaming DPL plate on the rear of the car.

By the time we arrived, the party was in full swing. The decor could be described as space-age chic and the living room was jammed elbow to elbow with garish, overdressed people all three sheets to the wind and bent on having a good time. I had deliberately worn black, a slinky long-sleeved silk jersey shaped to my body and slit for a real show of leg. A sunburst of sequins accented my breasts and hips and a thin diamond garter encircled one black silk-clad thigh.

A huge buffet had been set along one wall and the tantalizing smell of the food made my stomach juices begin to flow.

"Christina *dar-ling*, how wonderful to see you!" Poole, a symphony in blood-red silk and diamonds, lumbered across the thick white carpeting to embrace me. Her momentary peck on my cheek told me that she'd started drinking early. I quickly introduced Malcolm.

"Thank you for inviting us, Mrs. Pendelton," Malcolm said, smiling politely. He did not shake hands, something he avoids when he doesn't like someone. "Looks like the party is off to a rousing start."

"Oh yes, we're having a *love*-ly time," she gushed. "I was just talking to Mr. Blagdon over there. Do you know him, Christina darling?" I shook my head. "He's a wonderfully innovative film producer, and he wants to make a movie out of my latest book, *The Pirate and the Peasant Girl*. He says we can get that new Spanish actor, Domingo Velez, to play the part of the pirate. Perhaps if you go over and talk to him, Christina, he'll cast you as the peasant girl. You'd look terrific in a torn dress, all beaten and bloody, lashed to the mast of a ship."

"Thank you, Poole, but the honor of being rape-queen of the seas isn't worth being assaulted by some actor with clicking dentures," I said, smiling brightly.

"Not Mr. Velez," she gasped. "It isn't possible. Those gleaming white teeth are his fortune!"

"They certainly cost a fortune," I said solemnly. "His dentist swore me to secrecy, but I know it's safe to confide in you."

"Of course, Christina darling, my lips are sealed," stuttered Poole, looking around nervously. "But I must mingle with my other guests now. Why don't you two get a drink and make yourselves at home." She turned and bowled her way toward the tight little knot of sweating pates and large cigars that marked the nesting place of the Hollywood contingent.

"Really, Christina, you have the most awful nerve sometimes," said Malcolm, taking my arm and steering a path for us through the crowd.

"She deserved it," I replied. "Imagine thinking I would have anything to do with bringing that dreadful bilge to a larger audience."

"We didn't have to come," Malcolm reminded me. "But you were right about her chef. The food looks wonderful." He handed me a plate and, knowing my dislike of overprotective escorts, left me to satisfy my hunger in my own way.

I spent several minutes sampling bits and pieces of each dish, finally settling on baked chévre, cold shrimp pâté with dill sauce and a large helping of roast breast of chicken with lemon-mustard sauce. I sat on the fuchsia modular couch, placing my plate on the long black plastic table in front of me. The food was so good that I made a mental note to corner Poole's chef sometime before I left and offer him double his salary to abandon the Pendelton pirate ship and swim over to my kitchen where I could stuff myself and sneer at Poole.

My dinner companion was a sallow-faced young man with a crew cut and thick, black-framed glasses. He was staring at me intently but I ignored his lack of manners since most men have that reaction when they first see me.

"You're Christina van Bell, aren't you?" he said suddenly.

"Yes, I am," I said politely. "Have we met?"

"No. You were pointed out to me. My name is Richard Latham and I'm the head accountant at Pendelton Press, the company that publishes Poole's books."

"Lucky old you," I said dryly.

"Poole wanted to know if I thought you'd look right as the female lead in the movie they're making from her book, *The Pirate and*—"

"I've already refused her offer," I said.

"You should reconsider. They're always mammoth hits. I should know—I keep the books. Pendelton never had a best-seller before he met Poole. He was practically bankrupt."

"I'd heard that," I said. "What did he publish?"

"Highbrow novels, books of poetry by graduate students of writing programs at Ivy League colleges, books about unpopular causes like environmental protection or socialized medicine, the kind of stuff you need more than a sixth-grade reading level to appreciate and that never makes a dime. Poole changed all that. She has more nerve than talent, but her money and Pendelton's reputation for intellectual integrity made her book a best-seller overnight and Pendelton a wealthy man."

"Is he pleased with his success?" I asked. "Has it made him happy?"

Richard gave me an odd look. "What difference does that make?" he said. "He has more money than he can possibly spend. He can *buy* anything he wants."

"I can see that," I said, nodding toward the window where Wiltshire Pendelton was fondling a girl of about eighteen who was seated on his lap.

"If they weren't rich," said Richard defensively, "Poole would be called a drunk and Pendelton a dirty old man. This way, they're respected members of the community." He rose abruptly to his feet. His fists were clenched and there was a nervous twitch in his cheek. "Nobody's *happy*, for Chrissakes," he said in a choked voice. "Nobody!"

"He's right, you know," said a voice to my left as Richard walked angrily away. I turned and saw a tall morose-looking man nursing a very large scotch. He was wearing a rumpled leek-green suit that did not quite reach his wrists and ankles, making his thin body appear even more wraithlike.

"Right about what?" I asked.

"About being happy. God, I hate New Year's! It's so depressing. Look at those poor bastards." He waved his hand in the general direction of the room. "Talking too loud, drinking too much. They're trying so hard to have a good time, it makes me want to cry."

"Some of them may really *be* having a good time," I

pointed out. "Personally, I've always been an optimist. I look forward to each new year as an exciting adventure. You have to make good things happen."

The man looked at me as if I had leprosy. "What are you, some kind of Pollyanna?" he snapped. "Or are you just weirded out on drugs? No, don't tell me," he said as I started to speak. "I don't want to know. Look, why don't we go upstairs and get it on together? Perhaps it would cheer me up."

"Do you mean you want to make love?"

"Who said anything about love? I want a quickie. You don't even have to undress."

There are times when the idea of being used in this way might have tempted me to accept his offer, but I'd had enough of angry, empty, self-centered people. Having fulfilled my reason for attending Poole's party in the first place, namely to get a good meal, I decided it was time to effect my escape. Making the briefest of excuses to the young man next to me, I went in search of Malcolm. Being the only man in black, he should have been easy to spot, and it quickly became apparent that he was nowhere in the room. Perhaps he had met someone and gone upstairs for a bit more privacy. There is no jealousy between Malcolm and me when it comes to enjoying relationships with others and, in fact, watching others make love when they don't know they're being observed can be a fantastic sexual turn-on. Thinking Malcolm might have provided me with just such an opportunity, I trailed upstairs to see if I could locate him.

The five rooms on the second floor were all located off a center hall. The thick carpeting muffled my footsteps and, holding my breath, I softly opened the door nearest my right hand and peeped inside. The bedroom was deserted but there was a pink silk dress on the floor and the sound of voices came from the private bath just off the main room. Flushed with triumph, I tiptoed across the floor and secreted myself behind the drapes.

A few moments later, the bathroom door opened and a young girl came out. She was totally naked and had obviously just showered, for her dark hair clustered in damp ringlets around her face and drops of moisture glistened on her smooth bronze skin. She had a beautiful body, without an ounce of extra fat. Her breasts were small and uptilted, the nipples already pinched and hard. I could see the faint outline of her rib cage as she stretched luxuriously.

I heard someone moving in the bathroom and my pulse raced excitedly as Malcolm's figure appeared in the doorway, a towel tied modestly around his waist. He moved toward the girl and took her in his arms. His mouth covered hers as he pressed himself against her. Their lips were open. I could see the interplay of their tongues and hear the faint whisper of their sighs. I touched my own lips as I watched, then let my finger trail along my neck to my breasts. Malcolm knelt before the girl, flicking his tongue over her engorged nipples. She put her hands on his head to draw him closer, urging him to take her breasts into his mouth. My breathing quickened as I watched, and I massaged my own breasts through the thin material of my dress. The girl was moaning now, totally involved in the ministrations of Malcolm's tongue on her eager flesh. She closed her eyes and arched backward as Malcolm grasped her ass cheeks to prevent her from falling. His mouth fastened on the full black bush of her mound of Venus and she cried out, her fingers tightening on his shoulders as she swayed her hips back and forth.

The tension between the couple was electric and I felt a stirring in my own loins as Malcolm lifted her in his arms and laid her gently on the bed. With a casual movement, he undid the towel still covering his hips and let it drop to the floor. I saw the girl's eyes widen and heard the sharp intake of her breath as his cock was revealed, already swollen with desire. By this time my panties were soaked and I felt a familiar tingling between my legs. My evening dress was slit to midthigh on both sides and instinctively my hand slipped inside to fondle my aroused pussy through the thin silk of my bikini briefs. I could not take my eyes from Malcolm's cock, hard and throbbing with lust, and I groaned as the young girl opened her legs and spread her pussy lips with trembling fingers. A moment later Malcolm was between her thighs, guiding that gorgeous hunk of maleness into her welcoming slit. She moaned as it slid inside her, wrapping her thin arms around his neck and arching her hips to allow him maximum penetration. Her eyes were closed, her groans and cries audible above the creaking of the bedsprings as Malcolm's hips rose and fell with his rhythmic thrusting movements.

I stood transfixed, aware only of the scene taking place in front of me and a feeling of heightened sexual excitement as my fingers crept under the thin silk of my panties and entered my sopping cunt. My knees were trembling so hard I had to lean against the windowsill to steady myself as my plunging fingers stroked the fire of my lust. As Malcolm's thrusts became faster and more powerful, my own hand speeded up so that the tempo of our excitement was perfectly matched. Then suddenly the young girl cried out, digging her heels into the bed and arching her back. I saw the muscles in Malcolm's buttocks tighten, then relax. As he shot his cream deep inside her, I started to come also, choking back the scream of pleasure that threatened to burst from my throat.

They changed position. Malcolm lay on his back and the girl bent over him. Her fingers wrapped around his flaccid prick, coaxing it to life. She rubbed it over her breasts, then along the indentation between her ribs to the flat hardness of her abdomen. I could almost feel that cock on my own body as I touched those sensitive areas with my fingers.

Malcolm spread his legs and the girl crouched between them, cupping his balls in her hands and licking the entire length of his penis before taking him into her mouth. Her blue-black hair swirled around her face as she moved up and down his shaft. Her hair obscured my view, but I didn't have to see. I could hear Malcolm's moans of pleasure as she sucked on his cock. Her ass bobbed deliciously in the air and one of her hands strayed to the juncture between her legs. My own pussy was tingling now, my breath coming in short sobbing gasps. Once again my fingers plumbed the wetness between my thighs. I had never been so turned on. Watching the lovemaking of my own lover had brought me to a new level of excitement.

Suddenly, with a loud cry Malcolm's hips arched upward. His semen shot into the girl's eager mouth and I could see her body jerk convulsively as she fingered herself to orgasm. The girl raised her head, brushing her hair away from her face. There was a drop of cum on the tip of Malcolm's prick, which she still held in a gentle embrace. I held my breath as she bent over and lazily licked it away with a flick of her pink tongue. The sight of that tongue lapping up that last drop of cream drove me over the edge and, with a violent shudder, my own climax washed over me.

I waited until Malcolm and the girl had dressed and left the room before coming out of my hiding place and going to the bathroom to straighten my clothes and comb my hair. It was just after eleven o'clock and, remembering my promise to Malcolm about seeing in the New Year, I hurried downstairs to find him.

When I reentered the living room, I saw that more people had arrived and the noise and cigarette smoke had reached dangerous levels. Richard Latham was discussing projected interest rates for the next quarter with several men in banker's pin-stripes and the morose young man had passed out on the couch. Poole was gaily handing out paper party hats and noisemakers, and Malcolm was sipping a drink and looking anxiously about the room.

"Where have you been?" he asked as I stepped up to him.

"Upstairs looking for you," I replied, giving him a wide-eyed stare. "I got a bit sidetracked. Did you just take a shower, Malcolm? Your hair is damp."

Malcolm gave me a hard look but refused to rise to the bait. "The room is too warm," he said evasively. "Are you ready to leave? We have a bit of a drive."

"As soon as I get my coat," I said, taking his arm. After what I had just witnessed, the thought of Malcolm's lips on mine made my blood pressure soar. I could hardly wait to be alone with him.

Brushing off Poole's protests that the fun was just about to start, we said our good-byes and took the elevator downstairs.

The fresh air smelled wonderful and despite the cold I was glad to be out of Poole's stuffy apartment. I kept the windows cracked open as Malcolm inched his way through traffic. As midnight approached, more and more people crowded the streets, showering confetti and waving noisemakers, but

Malcolm didn't seem inclined to stop the car and join the merrymaking. He drove over the Brooklyn Bridge and onto the Brooklyn Queens Expressway, heading away from the city.

"Why are we going to Brooklyn?" I asked suspiciously.

"What's wrong with Brooklyn?"

"Nothing. There's nothing wrong with Ames, Iowa, either but I have no desire to visit it."

"One of the most breathtaking views in the world is right here in Brooklyn," Malcolm explained. "The Verrazano is the second longest expansion bridge in the world. I swiped two glasses and a bottle of Poole's best champagne and I thought we'd toast the New Year in the middle of it."

Though I personally thought that taking an hour's drive to stand in the middle of a freezing bridge at midnight for the sake of a view was carrying romanticism a bit too far, I did not say so. I am not usually so diplomatic, but I could see that Malcolm had planned this moment carefully and that it meant a great deal to him.

It was 11:55 when we arrived at the nearly deserted bridge and stepped out of the car. The night was crystal clear and I forgot my uncharitable thoughts as I looked across the water at the New York skyline, a mass of light against the blackness of the midnight sky. Malcolm handed me a glass and we saw in the New Year in fine style, our champagne-coated lips clinging together in a promise of delights to come.

We drove back into Brooklyn, and as the night was still young, we decided to stop for a drink before returning home. There are some well-known night spots in Bay Ridge but we perversely chose a bar with an unpretentious facade and the unimaginative name of Casey's. I had had enough of the rich and dreary for one evening.

The main room was crowded, and I gathered from the verbal exchange going on between tables that most of the patrons were regulars. There was no maître d' and no place to sit, but before we could leave, two couples, seeing us standing uncertainly at the door, waved us over and made room for us at their table.

Michael and Bridgett were in their midthirties. Their neighbors, Tim and Mary, were a few years older. There was a bottle of cheap vodka and several empty cans of domestic beer on the table and all four people seemed pleasantly lit.

Malcolm went to hang up our coats and returned with a bottle of twelve-year-old scotch and half a dozen clean glasses.

"I didn't know old Tom Casey had anything this good," said Tim, looking at our bottle, "or maybe it's just nobody could afford it." He seemed a bit embarrassed.

"He did have to dust it off a little," said Malcolm. "But I wanted something special," he added, covering his faux pas. "This is a special night." He gave me a look that made me flush and Tim, catching his glance, laughed and accepted a glass.

"This calls for more food," said Michael. "I bet you two have been too busy cooing at each other all night to eat."

"You're right," I lied, realizing our table companions felt the need to return Malcolm's generosity. "We're starved."

"It's corned beef and cabbage all around, then," said Michael. "Come and help me with the trays, Bridgett."

They moved away. Michael had his arm around Bridgett's shoulders, and I noticed that he seemed to have difficulty walking. Malcolm started to go to his assistance, but Mary put a hand on his arm to stop him.

"Don't," she said. "Mike doesn't like to be thought an invalid. He has Lou Gehrig's disease and he's had a bad time these past months. He was a construction worker and they laid him off. Can't blame them really, but Bridgett had to go to work and she can't make near the money Mike did. He's had to stay home and take care of the kids—they're not school age yet. He won't get better," she added in a choked voice, "but you never hear him complain. I asked him if the New Year made him unhappy, you know, like it does some people, but he just laughed. He said he had his wife and kids and that he looked forward to seeing the tulips he planted come up in the spring."

"Well, I agree with him," Tim said. "You can't dwell on the bad stuff. You have to make good things happen."

"Hear, hear," said Michael, returning with the trays. He served out the corned beef and cabbage while Malcolm poured another round of drinks.

"To the New Year," said Tim, raising his glass. "To good neighbors and new friends."

We all drank to that sentiment. Tim asked Bridgett to dance, and they made their way to a small clear area near the bar. The jukebox was playing "Love Is a Many Splendored Thing."

"That's my favorite song," said Malcolm, taking my hand. "Let's dance, Christina."

"Liar!" I whispered as he pressed me against him. "I saw you pushing the food around on your plate."

"I can't help it," Malcolm groaned. "I've already eaten. I don't know how you do it, Christina. You took seconds."

"I'm insatiable," I said, giving him a wicked look. "I can never get enough."

"You'll get enough tonight," Malcolm growled, nibbling playfully at my neck. "I'm going to eat you."

"I'll look forward to it," I assured him, tightening my arms around his neck.

When the music ended, we returned to our table.

"So, young fellow," said Tim amiably to Malcolm. "What line of work are you in that allows you to dress up like a penguin?"

"I'm Editor-in-Chief of *World* magazine," Malcolm said. "Have you heard of it?"

"You mean that's your magazine?" said Tim, obviously impressed. "I read it all the time when I go to the dentist. He has them all over the waiting room. I especially liked the story you did on the dirty pictures."

"Malcolm, did you run dirty pictures in *World*?" I laughed, causing him to blush.

"Not really dirty," Tim stammered, correcting his statement. "You know, those naked women. The fat ones."

"I think you mean the coverage of the Rubens exhibit at the Metropolitan last summer," Malcolm suggested.

"That's right. You don't see women like that anymore. They all look like broomsticks now. No offense, Christina," Tim apologized, looking me over, "but some men like a bit more meat on their bone."

I looked at Mary's ample proportions, then over at

Malcolm. A muscle twitched in the corner of his cheek and he took a hasty sip of his drink. "I've often told Christina the same thing," he said solemnly. "She has potential, though, don't you think?"

"She does that," Tim agreed heartily. "You just keep eating, honey. You'll fill out in time."

"Have some more corned beef and cabbage," Bridgett urged. "Nobody makes it like Casey's."

"I've never tasted better," I agreed, refilling both my plate and Malcolm's. He paled visibly.

Malcolm ordered another round of drinks, and we drank and danced and laughed together like old friends. The saying, money can't buy happiness, is a cliché that is often quoted but seldom believed. It was refreshing to see that this is sometimes really the case, and I could not remember enjoying a New Year's Eve party more.

It was well into the wee hours of the morning when we parked the car and took the elevator to my penthouse. Malcolm knew his way around my apartment, and after hanging up our coats, he headed for the kitchen. I flopped in a chair, kicking off my shoes and massaging one foot with the other. I was tired and a bit stiff, but I was excited too. The sexual tensions between Malcolm and me had been building all evening. I was hot and horny, but I knew that Malcolm often enjoyed creating a mood, setting the stage, before we made love. I liked this romantic side to his nature and was content to follow his lead. Whatever form our lovemaking ultimately took, I felt sure I would not be disappointed.

A moment later Malcolm's long lean body appeared in the doorway. "Would you like some Irish coffee?" he asked. "I noticed some heavy cream in your refrigerator and I managed to find your whisk."

"I'd love some if it's not too much bother."

"It's not, but it'll take maybe fifteen minutes to prepare. Why don't you relax in a hot tub while you're waiting. I'll bring it to you there."

"Will you scrub my back when you come in?"

"With the greatest pleasure," he said softly. The look in his eyes made my body grow warm and I felt a rush of dampness between my thighs.

I couldn't wait to undress and had my evening gown off before I had reached the doorway of the living room. I left it in a crushed heap on the floor, then took off my stockings, garters, and bra as I moved through the rooms. The trail of clothing was a sensuous invitation and I carefully deposited my bikini briefs at the entrance to the bathroom before going inside and closing the door.

I spend as much time in my bathroom as the average housewife does in her kitchen and am constantly remodeling and redecorating it to suit my mood. I had recently torn out the sunken marble tub and replaced it with a huge Victorian cast-iron one, complete with claw feet and a high curved rim. I had the entire room tiled in white with rose and gold accents. Rose velour towels hung on heated brass towel stands and a rose silk chaise longue stood next to an antique gilded oval mirror. I poured some scented bubble bath into the tub and, pinning my hair on top of my head, I stepped into the warm, fragrant water. I leaned my head on the edge of the tub, letting my tired muscles relax as the bubbles rose around me in glistening spun-sugar peaks. I mounded the suds on my breasts, leaving only my neck and shoulders exposed. I glanced across at the mirror and smiled at the picture of placid maidenly modesty I presented, so at odds with the raging turmoil of my senses.

The door clicked softly and I held my breath as I saw in the mirror that Malcolm was now standing behind me. He, too, had shed his evening clothes and was clad in a short cranberry velour robe tied carelessly at the waist. He moved a stool next to the tub and sat down just behind my shoulder. His lips brushed my cheek as he handed me a long-stemmed glass, his hand touching mine a moment longer than necessary.

"This is perfect," I sighed, sipping the strong, whisky-laced coffee through the soft peaks of whipped cream.

"It is," Malcolm agreed, putting some of the whipped cream on his finger and holding it to my lips. I sucked it into my mouth and he slowly withdrew it, tracing a wet sticky line over my chin and along my neck to the cleavage between my breasts. He cupped one firm round orb while his other hand reached across my back for the bath sponge. He plunged it into the sudsy water and began to gently wash my back, moving the sponge in concentric circles toward the base of my spine. He took the empty glass from my hand and I shifted my position so that my head rested against his arm. I half closed my eyes as he began to wash the upper part of my chest, trailing warm sudsy water over my breasts. My nipples peaked through their soapy coating, stiff with desire. Malcolm lifted first one, then the other to his mouth, his hot breath and warm tongue sending sweet shivers over my body. Still holding the sponge, he moved his hand down over my abdomen and beneath the surface of the water to the springy bush of my pubic hair. He swirled the sponge carefully over this sensitive area and I moaned softly as he touched me there.

Malcolm's mouth closed over mine. The feel of his lips was warmly exciting as they touched mine. He traced the outline of my mouth with the tip of his tongue, then kissed me again, first my mouth, then my eyes, then my cheeks, until my face flamed with pleasure and my breath came in short, sobbing gasps.

Abandoning any pretense that I might want to continue bathing, he lifted me from the tub and, wrapping me in a huge heated rose terry towel, he carried me into the bedroom and laid me gently on the bed. Slipping out of his robe, he unfurled the towel and lowered himself on top of me. His hard chest brushed my breasts and his lengthening cock pressed against my thigh. I flung my arms around his neck and pulled him tightly against me, sucking his tongue into my mouth. Every muscle in his body tightened and I pushed myself even harder against him, grinding my hips against his rigid pole. I could feel his heart beat and hear the heaviness of his breathing. Pulling his mouth from mine, he began to kiss his way down my throat, pausing a moment where my pulse beat wildly, then moving to the little hollows in my collarbone. His burning lips seared my breasts, his tongue sending flames of fire along the indentation between my ribs and over the soft swell of my abdomen. He moved downward and every inch of my flesh begged for the touch of his sensuous mouth. I wanted to be licked, kissed, devoured, as his tongue teased and tantalized in a way that made my senses soar.

I spread my legs and he crouched between them, his lips and tongue feathering my inner thighs. Then he moved around and over me so that his cock and balls hung tantalizingly over my face. There was a drop of semen on the pink tip of his cock and my tongue flicked it hungrily. I felt his body quiver and, emboldened by this response, I drew his cock into the hot cavity of my mouth as his own lips fastened greedily on my cunt.

His hips rose then fell as I deep-throated his cock while his tongue tunneled deeper between the engorged lips of my pussy. We licked and sucked at each other's sex, our bodies trembling and damp with our lust. My hands stroked the hard muscles of his buttocks and cupped his balls, which were heavy with desire.

I was on the brink of orgasm and I wanted him—Oh, how I wanted him—but not this way. I wanted the feel of his lips on mine, of his pulsing cock skewering my aching cunt. I wanted to bring in the New Year with his hot cream shooting deep inside me.

I pushed at his pelvic bone. I didn't know how to state my need but I didn't have to. Malcolm understood my desire and quickly changed his position. His eyes burned into mine as he arched above me. I spread my legs as wide as they would go, tilting my pelvis upward. He entered me with one sure movement and I felt a surge of pure joy as his steellike shaft sliced between the moist, swollen lips of my cunt. I wrapped my legs around his hips and shuddered, crying out as the waves of my orgasm flooded his advancing cock. Aware of my orgasm, Malcolm paused. He pulled his engorged member out to the tip, then plunged into me again, deeper and deeper with each pounding thrust until my body responded again and again in a mind-blowing series of orgasms. I ground myself against him, my nails raking his back, sobbing and crying with the force of my passion. I squeezed his cock, arching my hips, wanting it never to end.

Suddenly I felt him stiffen, so deep inside me that his balls brushed my ass. I felt his cock throb, then a burst of his semen shot against my pulsing walls. He gave a loud groan, drowning my own cries of pleasure. The flood of our love-juices over-flowed my cunt, trickling along my thighs and dampening the sheets.

His softened member was still nestled inside me and I pressed my sweat-soaked body to his as his arms tightened around me. I wrapped my legs around his, relaxing at last as he pulled the covers up over us. He brushed the damp hair off my forehead and kissed me chastely, cradling me in his arms as I drifted off to sleep.

CHAPTER THREE

Two days after New Year's, the dismantling process began. The colorful lights and balls were stripped from Christmas trees which were then discarded at curbside with bits of tinsel and ribbon still clinging to the dark green branches. Wreaths and banners were ripped from doors and terraces, cards taken off mantels, and Christmas goose carcasses turned into soup. Christmas carols disappeared from the radio and January white sales were announced. A heavy snowstorm and below-freezing temperatures snarled traffic and frayed tempers, and people wrapped scarves across the lower half of their faces and stopped smiling at each other. In other words, all was back to normal.

"If you don't need me right now, I'm going out of town for a few weeks," I told Malcolm over the telephone. "Two weeks of dragging around in my winter coat are enough. I want to go someplace warm."

"Poor Christina," Malcolm teased. "Why don't you buy a down coat instead of sable or mink. They weigh a lot less."

"Perhaps, but I'd look like a hand grenade."

"Not you," Malcolm laughed. "You'd look good in a potato sack. Where are you going? Southern Italy is nice at this time of year."

"It is, but it's too staid. I'm still in a party mood. I thought

I'd fly to the Coast and check out the latest trends and fads. Want to come?"

"I'd love to, Christina, but fortunately, I mean *un*fortunately, I have a magazine to put out. We're running your interview with Princess Lyapunov. Some of the pictures were outstanding, and I wouldn't want anything to go wrong at the last minute."

"Don't be a stick-in-the-mud," I coaxed. "We don't have to eat berries and nuts or roller skate or jog if you don't want to. There's more than one way to have fun out there."

There was silence on the other end. I could tell he was weakening. "I'll tell you what," he said at last. "Call me in a week. If I have things wrapped up by then, I'll join you for the weekend."

We said our good-byes and while Miss Watford packed my suitcases, I called the airlines and secured the last available first-class seat on the five P.M. flight to Los Angeles.

The doorman hailed a taxi, piled my luggage into the trunk and gave my destination to the driver. The days of gracious, elegant taxis in New York have long departed, and this vehicle was a prime example of the yellow heaps that litter the roads these days. I settled uncomfortably on the lumpy, cracked vinyl seat and peered through the yellowing Plexiglas shield that separated me from the driver, a thin middle-aged man with thick glasses, unruly tufts of gray hair, and the latest in cabbie winter wear: an orange down jacket, a purple and black striped scarf around the neck, and a bright red wool ski cap decorated with this year's union button.

As the driver screeched away from the curb and ran a red light, I noticed that there was another passenger in the cab with us. A tremendously fat, lazy-looking black cat with white paws and stomach was cuddled against the driver on the front seat. Unlike most cats, which roll themselves into a snug ball when they relax, this one was propped upright, his front legs resting on his stomach and his back legs sticking straight out in front of him in a bizzare parody of the driver's own position at the wheel.

"I've never seen a cat sit like that before," I said conversationally through the plastic shield. The driver's eyes darted to the mirror and he looked at me.

"What's that?" he called. He seemed a little deaf.

"I've never seen a cat sit like that," I yelled.

"Don't worry. He went before we left the house. He's my cat." He scratched the cat affectionately on the top of its head.

"I figured that," I said. "But why is he in the cab with you? Wouldn't he prefer to stay at home?"

"Nah, we're friends. Besides, my wife doesn't like him. She says he sheds on the furniture. Says I shed on the furniture too, that we're two of a kind. She has plastic covers on everything so you stick to the seats in summer. But cats don't shed on plastic. Everyone knows that. Cats don't shed on plastic."

"Everyone knows that," I agreed, having no idea what the hell he was talking about.

"So I take him to work with me," the driver continued. "He's no trouble. He just sits there on his ass. Never seen a cat do that." He gently tickled its belly and it purred loudly.

"What do you feed your cat?" I asked.

"How's that?"

"What do you give the cat to eat?" I repeated, raising my voice.

"The seat? No, he don't go on the seat. He goes before we leave the house."

"Not seat! Eat!" I yelled, frustration starting to build.

"No thanks, we already had breakfast. Bacon and eggs. I don't know what to feed the cat so I just give him a few dollars and let him order what he likes. Corn's his favorite, though. Mine too. We eat corn every night."

"What's his name?"

"Irving. Irving Cohen. That's me right there on the hack license. I call the cat Bastard. Named him after the mayor. They both spend the whole day sitting on their asses. Only the mayor don't like corn. He likes Chinese food. It's a great place, Chinatown, but you can never find a place to park. It's all the goddamn mayor's fault. He . . ."

By the time we got to the airport I had received a long lecture on the reason the mayor should be shipped in a crate to Mars, and I had the beginnings of a tension headache. As I exited the cab, I gave the driver a generous tip.

"Take your cat to The Four Seasons for lunch," I told him. Bastard looked at me in supine splendor and belched majestically.

An hour later, I was reclining in my seat in the first-class cabin of a 767, watching the lights of the city fall away beneath me as the plane gained altitude. I ordered a triple scotch on the rocks but declined the flight attendant's kind offer of a headset to listen to the in-flight movie. My current luck running true to form, the cinematic offering that afternoon was the star-splattered film version of Poole Pendelton's epic tale of blood and lust in the Arabian desert *The Sheik and the Belly Dancer*.

"Like, aren't you gonna watch the movie?" said a high-pitched nasal voice to my right. Due to the popularity of the flight and my last-minute reservation, I had been unable to obtain my customary two first-class seats. My traveling companion was a spindly, flat-chested young teenager with sun-streaked hair and a sprinkling of freckles across her nose and cheeks. She simply reeked of California health and vitality.

"I think I'll pass and curl up with *Vogue*," I said.

"Like, I never miss one of Poole Pendelton's books or movies," she said in happy anticipation. "I'm totally into heavy-duty romance, you know, and like, I can really get into all those sheiks and pirates an' stuff to the max. The boys in my school are so-o-o grody, you know, like they always want you to touch them in the movies and, I mean, barf-out, like no way, fer sure."

"I know what you mean," I said, pretending sympathy. I had always enjoyed touching boys in the movies. I still do. "When I was your age I was very fond of *Jane Eyre*."

"School books!" she squealed in horror. "Like, pure gag time, you know? They take for-*ever* to read, then you don't have time to, like, go to the mall and play the video games or anything. Listen, after the flick can I borrow the *Vogue*? I'm like really into clothes, you know, heavy-duty mall action and shoes an' stuff."

"Certainly," I nodded, turning my laughter into a discreet cough. I ordered another drink and watched as she jammed the plastic plugs of the earphones into her pink ears and gazed vacantly at the screen, enraptured at the sight of two men in sheets mauling a busty young actress.

It was seven P.M. California time when I emerged from the terminal at Los Angeles International Airport, a luggage-laden redcap trailing in my wake. The redcap loaded my suitcases into a taxi, accepted my generous tip, wished me a nice day—oh, that California ritual—and after instructing the driver to have my bags brought to my hotel, I made my way to my newly rented Corvette convertible.

Wheels are essential operating equipment on the West Coast. Whole generations of California children have grown up thinking that their feet were only good for pressing the pedals of a car.

I made my way to the San Diego Freeway, which would whisk me past Culver City and Santa Monica to the welcoming arms of Beverly Hills. Though the glory days of the movie capital, when the studio's most glamorous stars lived in slow-paced, elegant, and somewhat protected splendor, have been replaced by a harder, faster, more faddish generation, Hollywood is still a fun place to be. The eternal sunshine, the desperation that comes from always trying to be in the right place at the right time, the unnatural necessity to remain young and beautiful, create a fertile soil for fads and foibles, but I enjoy such social rituals and am always game to try the latest trend. Being young, beautiful, and wealthy, my place in the center of the social whirl is assured.

Presiding over Sunset Boulevard is the Hollywood Hills Hotel, a pink stucco palace that is one of the most outstanding luxury hotels in the world. It is more of a stage set than a real building, the cast an oddball mix of executives, starlets, and visiting royalty that blends business and hedonism in true Hollywood style. The hotel is almost always fully booked, but despite the popularity of the winter season and my last-minute phone call, the manager greeted me by name when I arrived and assured me that a corner suite had been set aside for me.

There is almost no trendy place for a late-night drink in Hollywood because in this one-industry town most people are in bed long before midnight. Though my system rebelled against this schedule, I knew I'd have to mend my ways while visiting planet Los Angeles so I ordered dinner from room service and, aided by jet lag, half a bottle of scotch, and several sleeping pills, managed to get to sleep before one A.M.

Being "in" is more important in southern California than in most places and the current "in" thing in this town is health. Everyone from well-known actors to the newest agents and producers on the Strip drag themselves out of the sack at four in the morning to jog along some godforsaken beach, then they tramp off to health clubs where they strap themselves into machines that stretch and pull their muscles into various shapes, followed by a good sweat in a sauna and a breakfast of fruit, nuts, and berries that a caveman would have turned up his nose at. These same people then spend their evenings ingesting huge amounts of alcoholic and pharmaceutical substances through their noses and throats and other points of entry. They see no contradiction in all this.

While I was prepared to get up earlier than usual in an effort to conform to my surroundings, I refused to consider any form of ritualized exercise. I wouldn't be caught dead in a striped leotard hanging by my heels from a gym bar or humming in a yoga class. It was difficult enough to get out of bed by ten o'clock.

I showered and dressed in a pair of full-cut, candy-pink velour culottes and a matching top with bateau neckline and pushed-up sleeves—very California, very in—then made my way to the famous Palm Lounge, the hotel's restaurant, for a little fortification against the ungodly hour. The menu offered tofu and alfalfa salads, frozen yogurt, and mineral water, but a sympathetic waiter brought me a plateful of sausage and eggs and a generous Bloody Mary from the bar.

I was sipping my drink when I was accosted by a table hopper. Hopping tables is the Hollywood version of saying hello. You order a meal, then carry it around the room, eating it at various people's tables.

"Christina van Bell! Baby, good to see you. How are you?" The speaker was a balding man with gray-tinted glasses, polyester clothes of the checked variety, and a wide smile. "Sol. Sol Berenger."

"Sol, how are you?" I said, forcing a smile and accepting a quick peck on the cheek. The last time I had seen Sol was at a crowded party several years ago. He had just started his own agency and spent most of the evening trying to sign up and seduce young starlets. Like most people in Hollywood he never forgot the face of someone who could do him some good, so I wasn't surprised that he remembered me.

"I'm doing great," he assured me. "In fact, I'm here on business right now. My man will be here any minute and we're going to take a meeting." In Hollywood people don't hold meetings. They take them, like aspirin.

"How's the agent business?" I asked politely.

"No more agent business," he grinned. "I'm a producer now. I created *Motor Cop 509* for television. Very hot property. Have you seen it?"

"I'm afraid not," I said. "I've been out of the country." I didn't tell him that I didn't watch television. He might have had a coronary.

"It got big ratings last season," he boasted. "It's the sensitive, yet realistic story of a Vietnam vet who becomes an L.A. cop, despite his bionic arm and his alcoholism. He has a broken marriage, a young kid he cannot get to love him, and a wacky partner for comic relief. It has everything—pathos, drama, laughs. Very hot property."

"I'm glad you're doing so well," I said, not really caring that much.

"I have a new idea that's even better," he assured me. "Very hot property. I'm meeting on it this morning. It's a mini-series set in the upper echelons of New York society. It has high finance, Wall Street competition, and two families who've hated each other for a hundred years. Lots of backstabbing and blackmail for the male viewer and some incest for good measure."

"No comic relief?" I asked.

"Oh sure, one family has some wacky neighbors. Like Fred and Ethel Mertz, only rich and beautiful. Lots of actresses with high busts and thick hair in this one for the preteen set. You'd be perfect as the spoiled and fiery daughter, Magda. Want to take a meeting and chitchat?" I seemed to be getting a lot of movie offers this week.

"No. Thank you anyway. I hope it's a success."

"If it is, I can spin off a series and go into reruns. That's where the money is. You're sure you won't consider . . . oops, there's my backer, I have to run. Ciao, sweetheart, have your people call my people and we'll get together and talk." With that he was gone, glad-handing two executives and their money across the room.

I spent the next few hours deepening my tan, then changed and headed for Ma Maison, at the moment the most "in" place in Hollywood for lunch. As in almost all the in Hollywood restaurants, the tables at Ma Maison are set close together, the food is adequate but not superb, and the noise level is deafening. Nobody minds, however. Eating out in Hollywood serves many purposes, the least of which is food, and lunch at Ma Maison is the fastest way to let people know you're in town.

An impatient crowd was gathered at the bar but the maître d', having ascertained my name, returned in a few minutes and offered to squeeze me into an already occupied table, a common practice at this busy hour.

"I think you know these people," he assured me as I followed him to a large corner table where several men and women were sipping Perrier and lime and devouring platters of green salad garnished with carrot shavings and sprouts. I recognized Dale Trell, a prominent film director whom I had met several years ago at an East Side party in New York.

"Christina van Bell. I thought I recognized the name," he cried, leaning across the table to kiss me on the cheek. He was a man in his midforties, with strong yet sensitive features, thick dark hair and eyes like liquid chocolate. He wore a white silk shirt open at the throat, and, looking at him, I was reminded that when we had been introduced, I had made a mental note to take him to bed. The opportunity had not presented itself that night but fate has a way of making all things work out in the end.

Dale introduced me to his table companions and convinced me to order a shrimp and avocado salad for my lunch. Not wanting to flaunt my vulgar East Coast inclination to order a drink with my meal, I bribed the waiter to fill my Perrier glass with vodka.

"I loved your last film, *Summer Fantasy*," I told Dale. "I thought the problems of the main characters were sensitively yet realistically handled and your use of black-and-white sequences in a color film were brilliant. The ending made me cry, it really did."

"An artistic success but a box-office failure," Dale sighed. "I really lost a bundle on that one. I have to make money on my next film or I'm dead in this town."

"Any ideas?" I asked.

"Outer space," he nodded glumly. "Aliens land in a pond in a Midwest town and turn all the kids into zombies."

"I thought all kids already were zombies."

"No one notices," Dale agreed, "except the basketball coach at the local high school. He convinces the English teacher of the takeover and they fall in love and single-handedly fight to save the Earth. What do you think?"

"Sounds salable to me."

"The problem is capital," he continued. "For five million dollars we make a two-dimensional film that sits in Southern drive-ins. For thirty million, we get an hour of special effects and stereo music, we open in New York, and we get tie-ins with cable and the major TV networks. But with my last picture such a financial failure, it's hard to raise the cash."

"If that's your only problem, you can count on me to invest a few dollars," I said. "Just send my lawyer the details."

"Give me his number. I'll have my people call your people," said Dale, smiling happily. "Christina, you're a life-saver."

"Anything to further the cause of art," I said grandly, and we all laughed.

"If things work out, I'll cut you in for the merchandising," Dale promised me. "Record albums, zombie T-shirts, the works. Listen, as long as you're in town, why not drop out to my place this evening? I'm having a little get-together, just a few friends, nothing formal. I think you'd have a good time, meet some people. How about it?" His invitation was casual but the look in his eyes promised something more intimate. I promptly accepted. It was pure kismet.

Dale lived in a large Spanish-style mansion set on an acre of manicured landscape at the crest of Beverly Hills. Appearance is all important in the film industry, and I could see that Dale's decorator had a fascination with nineteenth-century Oriental design. The first-floor rooms had straw-covered ceilings, green latticework over white walls, and Oriental-patterned fabrics on low-pillowed furniture. The atmosphere was cozy and informal and no expense had been spared to make it so.

California parties start early and I was one of the last guests to arrive. A maid took my wrap and I lifted a glass of fruit punch from a passing tray. It had an unusual flavor and its alcoholic content, if any, was completely disguised. I looked around the room. There were about twenty other people at the party, most of them young and good-looking and all of them thoroughly looped. Thai-sticks and marijuana were being passed around the room, and several men and women were inhaling a communal plateful of cocaine. The conversation was of contracts and early-morning cast calls, and, feeling slightly bored and out of place, I wandered over to the buffet. There was more fruit punch and I took another glass. Lemon juice, that was what gave it its unusual flavor. I refilled my glass, beginning to feel more mellow. The chef must have come from the Philippines, for the dishes were a mixture of the Spanish, French, and Chinese influences prevalent in the cooking of that part of the world. I had seconds of baked spareribs in honey sauce and Chinese-style fried rice and made a pig of myself on mango cake with mango icing.

Dale spotted me sitting on the couch between two glassy-eyed young men and came over to greet me.

"I was beginning to wonder if you'd show up," he said. "Are you having a good time?"

"The punch is delicious," I said. "But two pounds of snow couldn't loosen some of these people up. All I've heard is shop talk."

"Never fear," he said, holding up his hands. "I have the perfect entertainment all planned. I was just waiting till you showed up before I started."

Dale called for attention, then asked that we all assemble in the screening room. The crowd was ready for some diversion and they cheerfully followed him through the house, carrying plates of food, tins of drugs, and glasses of punch with them. I took two glasses of punch and followed somewhat unsteadily along with the rest.

The screening room, a standard feature in most Hollywood homes, was a large windowless room decorated with sofas and floor pillows and dominated by a large white screen at one end.

"Our presentation tonight is a package put together for theatrical release by my good friend Bret Beaumont here," Dale announced, pointing out a tall handsome man sitting near the projector at the back end of the room. He stood up and bowed as the crowd cheered his generosity. "Bret never managed to sell this turkey and he took a severe bath on the deal, but after viewing the film, I thought of a way to rescue Bret's reputation and have some fun at the same time. So watch closely, boys and girls, because there's going to be a test next period."

Everyone laughed and Dale plopped down next to me on a sofa as the lights dimmed and the film started.

"What is this thing?" I muttered, staring into my empty punch glass and wondering if I could get a refill.

"It's a compilation of clips from bad S&M porno films," Dale replied, taking the glass from my hand and placing a lit joint between my lips. "Here, try this. That punch has got you high, but you'll be in the bathroom all night if you keep at it, and you'll miss the film."

"I wouldn't want to do that," I sighed, subsiding against his shoulder and turning my attention to the screen.

The scenes all involved some form of bondage or discipline. They were clumsily, unenthusiastically handled and were, for the most part, more funny than erotic. My favorite was *Mr. Reed Does the Deed* in which a thin young man in a silk bathrobe ineffectually spanked a partially clothed, overweight woman whom he had trouble balancing across his thighs.

"She should have spanked him," I whispered to Dale as the man now ordered the woman to strip, then halfheartedly went down on her. "He deserves it for that performance. It's not entirely Bret's fault that this turkey didn't sell. The idea is a good one but the acting and direction are terrible."

"Perhaps," Dale admitted, "but you'd never make a convincing scene out of female domination."

"Why not?"

"Men dominate, women submit," Dale shrugged. "That's what the public wants to see."

"That's your standard script," I admitted, "but haven't you ever wondered what it would be like to be sexually dominated by a beautiful, forceful woman?"

"Of course, but—"

"Well, so have other men, though it's not the kind of thing a man would easily admit to. But it's catered to in private, and I'm sure there'd be a large viewing audience for this particular form of sexual diversion."

"Hear, hear," said a male voice from the audience. "*There's* a liberated woman, and a very beautiful one too! Would you like to beat me, sweetheart?" The film had ended and all the guests were now listening to our conversation. I gave the young man a sharp look and he smiled at me suggestively.

"I'd like to beat you, Ron," said the petite redhead next to him. "You've been a perfect bore these last few weeks. Wham, bam, thank you, ma'am, without a thought for my pleasure."

"You should have told me," the young man protested, blushing furiously.

"I've tried. You just don't listen. Perhaps if I took a strap to your bare behind you'd hear me!"

"Perhaps we should both beat him," I said wickedly. "I'd like a whack at that bare behind myself. We can let Bret film the action and the rest of you can provide an audience and judge the performance."

"Christina, you're a genius," Dale said. "I had something similar in mind myself so I gathered some costumes and equipment in the next room. Why don't you and Trixie go and change while Bret and I set up the film."

Everyone applauded this idea except Trixie's friend Ron,

but I sensed that though he was apprehensive about his coming ordeal he was intrigued at the same time. Trixie and I hauled the boxes containing costumes and equipment into an adjoining room, leaving the others to argue about lighting and the selection and arrangement of stage props.

We stripped off our clothes as we discussed possible ways to handle the proposed scene. Trixie was an elfin-looking young woman with a trim, almost boyish figure and pertly uplifted breasts. I found myself attracted to her and when she eagerly confessed to similar feelings, we agreed to incorporate an exploration of each other's treasures into our drama. We agreed on our roles, then looked over the available costumes.

I selected a black satin corset that was laced up the front so that it pushed the ripe fullness of my breasts upward. It was cut high on the sides, exposing the golden mound of my pubic hair and the roundness of my buttocks. I attached black silk hose to the garters and stepped into three-inch, spike-heeled shoes.

Trixie slipped into thigh-high black leather boots, a skimpy black lace bra, and bikini briefs.

I confess to almost opening-night jitters as we took a final look at ourselves in the full-length mirror, but the round of cheers and applause that greeted our entrance restored my self-confidence.

There was a table with two chairs, a sofa, and a double bed arranged to simulate an apartment. Trixie and I sat down at the table and I nodded to Dale to indicate that we were ready to begin.

Ron approached the table in an attitude of wary submission, aware, as we all were, of the camera and the audience. Trixie leaned back in her chair and began to lecture him on his recent sins—his sloppiness around the house and his lack of consideration of her needs both in and out of bed—and as she spoke she played with herself in a blatantly erotic way. I heard Ron's breathing quicken. He brushed off her tirade with a brusque, half-hearted apology, then moved to take her in his arms. Her hand cracked across his face and he stopped, startled by her reaction.

"Stay right where you are," she demanded before he could

reach for her again. "I've had enough of your insincere apologies and boorish macho behavior in bed. I intend to wear the pants from now on and my pleasure will come first. Is that understood?"

"Yes . . ."

"Yes, what?"

"Yes, mistress."

"That's better. Better, but not good enough. You've insulted Mistress Christina . . ."

"I—?"

"Shut up. Speak when you're spoken to. You've intimated that she would want your puny cock in her pussy, your lips on her breasts. The way you make love is insult enough, but you'll learn. If a dog can learn tricks, so can you. Follow us. On your hands and knees," she added as she took my hand and led me toward the bed at the far end of the stage.

Still a bit uncomfortable, Ron did as he was bid. He was still acting, playing a part, but I could see that Trixie had forgotten all about the camera. She moved and spoke as if the scene were indeed taking place in the intimacy of their bedroom instead of on an improvised set.

I sat on the edge of the bed and spread my legs, and Trixie motioned Ron forward. "Come and kiss Mistress Christina's pussy," she directed him.

Ron happily smothered my bare bush with kisses and my stomach muscles tightened pleasurably. As he continued to eat my pussy, his protruding butt attracted Trixie's attention. Picking up a riding crop, she brought it down sharply on his behind. Ron flinched, though the fabric of his trousers absorbed most of the blow.

"Don't stop," I commanded. "Use your tongue. I want to feel your tongue against my clit. And don't come," I added maliciously. "You're here to pleasure me, not yourself." I leaned back, opening my legs wider and spreading my cunt lips with my fingers to allow him greater access to my love-canal. Still on all fours, his tongue tunneled between the soft, moist folds of flesh, licking and sucking at the sweet juices within.

Trixie loosened his belt. I heard the sharp intake of his breath as she pulled his trousers and briefs down over his hips to expose the rounded curve of his buttocks. He tensed and I reached down and grabbed a handful of his hair.

"Suck me, you worthless piece of shit!" I said harshly. "I didn't give you permission to stop." I yanked his head forward and he began to lick at me like a madman, running his tongue up and down the length of my steaming slit and whirling it around my now inflamed clit. I kept my hand on his hair, yanking his head up every now and then to lecture him on his poor technique, inciting him to even more creative efforts.

Trixie watched, hands on hips, every so often bringing the whip across Ron's quivering ass cheeks to remind him of her presence. Ron's eyes were closed and tears slipped down his cheeks, mingling with the juices of my vibrating pussy. His body was trembling and his breathing was a harsh sound in his throat, but I could see that the stinging pain of the whip, the verbal humiliation, and the pleasure of my cunt grinding against his face had sent his senses soaring. His cock hung between his legs, huge with lust and with a final stern warning for him not to climax, I gave way to a breathtaking series of orgasms.

I lay back against the pillows to catch my breath and Trixie, after a final swipe at Ron's blistered buttocks, ordered him to strip, then lay down next to me. He hastened to obey and I helped Trixie secure him spread-eagled to the bedposts. His body was covered with a thin film of sweat, trembling with the effort to hold back his orgasm. His eyes shone with excitement as he watched our movements, completely caught now by the sexual tension that simmered between the three of us.

I straddled Ron's chest, placing my fanny firmly on his face. I leaned over and began to run my tongue in long leisurely strokes along the length of his shaft. He groaned loudly and his buttock muscles tightened convulsively. Trixie knelt between his spread legs and began to copy my motions. Ron's groans grew louder and he strained against his bonds, begging for release. We continued to tease his pulsing tool, keeping him on the brink of orgasm without allowing him the ultimate release. Finally tired of the game, Trixie cruelly called a halt. Ron was unbound and ordered to stand at the foot of the bed.

His breath was coming in short sobbing gasps and tears of frustration coursed down his cheeks, yet so immersed was he in his submissive role that he obeyed without protest. Debased and humiliated, he stood passively awaiting our pleasure.

"I'm going to show you how to make love to a woman," Trixie told him. "It's about time you learned how useless that puny cock you prize so much really is. Now, put your hands on the footboard and keep them there. If you even touch yourself before I give you permission, I'm going to blister your bottom so you can't sit down for a week. Do you understand?"

"Yes, mistress," he whispered.

"Good!" said Trixie. She turned her back toward him in a gesture of dismissal.

She came toward me now, her features softened by desire. I was still lying against the pillows and her fingers lightly brushed my chest as she reached to undo the laces of my corset. Released from their bondage, my breasts spilled out like ripe fruit. She gathered them in her hands and pressed them to her mouth and I sighed and relaxed beneath the velvet softness of her lips. Trixie's delicate fingers stroked the satin smoothness of my skin as her pink tongue darted between ruby lips to tease my tender nipples to hard points of pleasure.

I touched her hair, which was like a bright red flame obscuring her face as she bent over me. Her hands were pulling at the stiff satin of the corset and I eagerly helped her remove the garment. I kicked off my shoes and peeled off my stockings.

"Now you," I whispered. "I want to feel your nakedness against my own."

Trixie leaned back and tugged off her boots, slipping off her bra and panties with no pretense of modesty. Her high, firm breasts were barely a mouthful, but they had a tangy sweetness. We did not linger in foreplay. We had been cruel and taunting, and like wild beasts who have tasted blood, we could not be satisfied with tender kisses or feathery caresses. We squirmed around, head to feet, and I shivered with delight as Trixie's tongue searched out the source of my womanness.

"You're like honey," she murmured, parting my trembling thighs.

I mirrored her actions, entranced by the red-gold of her closely cropped mound of Venus. I had never seen pussy hair quite that color. There was a shimmer of moisture on the exposed curve of her lips, their pinkness deepening to a darker shade of rose as I spread them with my fingers like the petals of a flower. My tongue slid along the entire length of each outer lip, then I buried my face in her fragrant juncture, my tongue searching out the hard red knob of her clit.

Her tongue was darting at my sex like an eager kitten lapping at some cream and my entire body responded with an upsurge of desire. The rounded curves of our bodies melted against each other, fused by our passion. We might have been lovers for years, so easy was it to please and be pleased. Trixie's tight little pussy opened to my tongue, the muscles of her buttocks tightening convulsively.

"Oh, Jesus," she moaned. "You're so wet, my darling. Open your legs a little wider."

I did as she asked, then gasped as she pushed her thumbs into my quim, forcing the lips apart. I felt her hot breath on the exposed walls of my cunt and I gave a scream of pleasure, arching my hips as her tongue plunged into my aching void. I felt myself approaching climax as the tempo of our lovemaking increased. Trixie's juices were flowing freely now as I sucked avidly at her squirming pussy.

And then I was coming, and Trixie was coming and we held each other tightly, our tongues lapping at the juices of each other's sex.

We rolled apart and, as my senses slowed, I became aware once again of the trembling, sweating man watching us. Ron's cock was swollen to its full length, a monstrous shaft of desire. The sight of so much maleness made my mouth water and my body grew warm as I pictured its enormity cleaving my pussy. Trixie saw the direction of my glance.

"You've been a good little slave," she told Ron, "and you shall have your reward. You can come inside Mistress Christina's pussy. After you've made her come," she added as I bent my knees and spread my legs, parting my pussy lips in a lewd invitation.

Ron climbed on the bed and, positioning the swollen tip of

his shaft at the entrance to my canal, he entered me in one smooth, clean motion, his prick so long and thick that I felt as if the tip were at the entrance to my womb. I was hot and wet, primed from Trixie's lovemaking. My pussy hugged Ron's thrusting pole and a few hard strokes were enough to cause me to explode. I cried out, my nails raking his back, my spasming cunt still clasping his rock-hard shaft. He froze for an instant, every muscle tensed, his passion rubbed raw with waiting. Then, with an animal cry he let go, his semen pouring into my upturned cunt. I was so full of him that his thrusting, pulsating cock triggered a second, then a third orgasm in me.

Now Ron knelt at our feet and confessed that by putting himself completely at the mercy of his mistresses, he had discovered a new avenue of sexual expression, one that was personally, intensely satisfying. It was the perfect end to our fantasy drama and the round of cheers and applause that greeted this final speech told us how well we had all played our parts. The lights were turned on and the other guests surged enthusiastically around us. Many were eager to duplicate Ron's experience or to play out a dominant or submissive fantasy of their own. By the time everyone had been satisfied, the sun had come up and eleven reels of film had been shot and were now waiting to be revised and edited.

Too emotionally charged for sleep, someone suggested a jog along the beach and breakfast at Charmer's Market. Everyone who could still stand began to gather up their clothing, but I'd had enough of group games. I had a much more intimate activity in mind, something horizontal. Dale was still fully dressed. He had spent the night behind the camera instead of in front of it, but as I leaned naked against him, casually watching the flurry of activity in the room, I felt the swell of his cock against the rounded curve of my ass. He reached around me, his hand cupping my breast.

"I hope you enjoyed the film party," he murmured. "They're really in now. Everyone is having them."

"Mmmm, it was fun. What will you do with the film, Dale?"

"It depends. Most of these films end in the garbage. But Bret is a really good cameraman and with proper editing we might even have something salable. Want to stay and watch the rerun?"

"Just us?"

"Just us," he nodded. "Do you know, Christina, the first time I met you I wanted to take you to bed, and I was mad as hell at myself for months afterward for not creating the opportunity to do so. Then when I saw you at Ma Maison this afternoon, it was like fate had dealt me a winning hand. It was pure . . . what's the word I'm looking for?"

"Kismet," I said, turning and throwing my arms around his neck.

CHAPTER FOUR

It was just past dawn when I finally pulled my car up in front of the hotel. Dale and I had spent the past twenty-four hours eating, sleeping, making mad passionate love, and watching reruns of the movie that had been made at the party. Dale had an early-morning meeting and, though he had begged me to wait for him, I knew that I needed more than love and yogurt to keep me going. After thirty-six hours of health food, I was beginning to crave something more substantial. I picked up the telephone and punched in the number for room service.

"I'd like breakfast delivered to my room," I told the operator when she answered. "What's on the menu?"

"Oh, fer sure," she said. "We have avocado with cottage cheese, tofu and bean curd porridge, and sesame seed surprise, all served on a platter with pita bread, sprouts, and a selection of decaffeinated herbal teas."

"That can't be all," I said. "You haven't read me everything."

"Well, those are our recommendations, but the chef will cook anything you want."

"Good. Let me have a Bloody Mary, heavy on the vodka, a chili omelette with three eggs, six strips of fried bacon, light toast with lots of butter, and a pot of coffee with plenty of cream and sugar on the side."

"Like, gross me into the last century," she squealed. "That stuff will kill you for sure. Clogs up your arteries and stuff."

"I'm a human being," I said, rapidly losing patience. "I eat bacon and eggs for breakfast. Parakeets eat bean curd and sesame seeds. Now hop to it."

"For sure," she said. "Have a nice day."

I winced and hastily hung up the phone. It was 6:15 A.M. I kicked off my shoes and lay down on the bed, but I was still too wound up to relax or fall asleep. I wanted to talk to someone and, picking up the phone once again, I obtained an outside line and tapped in the eleven digits that constituted Malcolm Gold's home number. The circuits clicked and moments later the phone in New York was ringing. It was finally answered on the twelfth ring.

"H-h-hello . . .?" a harried voice stammered at the other end.

"Malcolm, it's Christina! Did I wake you?"

"Christina? No, I was just in the shower and I'm running late for an appointment. Why are you calling?" Malcolm asked.

"I wanted to tell you about this terrific party I went to. I had the most amazing time. You'll be sorry you didn't come with me."

"Believe me, Christina, I'm sorry I'm not there right now. Then I could strangle you for making me miss my appointment. But it's too late now."

"If you don't put a smile in your voice this minute," I pouted, "I'm not going to tell you about the movie I made."

"What movie? What the hell are you talking about?"

"I was at a film party. They're the hottest things out here. Instead of cards or charades everybody gets looped and does a bit of acting before a camera."

"You mean like scenes from old movies?"

"Sometimes. But at this party we acted out S&M scenes. There was this terrific bit where I'm dressed in leather and some guy's my slave. Dale thought I was so good that he's going to edit the other reels to flesh it out a bit and then try to sell the whole package to a distributor."

"Who's Dale?"

"Dale Trell, the director. He's going to call it *Kiss My Whip*."

"You certainly get in the swing of things in a hurry," Malcolm sighed. "You haven't even been there a week and you're already corrupting the town."

"What's corrupting about sex? It's the most natural thing in the world. It's all this jogging and yoga and pita bread that's corrupting, but now that I'm here I hope to help turn things around."

"I'll wire the good news to the *Times* first thing tomorrow."

"Have you considered jetting out here and joining me? I have a beautiful suite with a king-size bed, a marble bathroom, and a Do Not Disturb sign on the door."

"There's nothing I'd rather do than be with you," he said, "even in Los Angeles, the roach motel of the nation. But there was something I was supposed to tell you . . . Wait a minute, let me clear my head a bit . . . That's right, there was a call for you at the office yesterday. Your secretary mentioned it to me. Princess Lyapunov called."

"Probably to thank me for the terrific article I did on her for the magazine," I said.

"Apparently it's more than that. Your secretary said that she wanted to speak to you at once and that she was upset when she was told that you were out of town."

"That's strange," I said. "I wonder what the problem is?"

"Why don't you come back and find out," Malcolm suggested. "I have a fireplace in my bedroom, a sunlamp in the bathroom, and I'll take you to dinner in the finest restaurant in New York."

"New York is like a Popsicle this time of year," I complained. "Why don't you handle it? That cracked old servant of hers probably needs a ride out to the home for the terminally senile."

"As a matter of fact, I did have your secretary call back to find out if there was anything I could do but Her Highness said you were the only one who could help her and begged us to have you come and see her as soon as possible. It wouldn't hurt to be nice to the old lady," Malcolm chided. "I thought you'd taken a liking to her. Besides, if it turns out to be nothing, you can go right back to bean-curd city."

"You're right," I sighed. "I'll take the next available flight out. Have someone call the Princess and tell her I'll be there tomorrow. But I think this is all a ruse on your part to avoid joining me out here."

"I admit the thought of having you in my arms tonight did cross my mind," Malcolm laughed, "but that's your fault for being so desirable. Whether it's hot dogs at Pinks or poached salmon at The Four Seasons, I just want to be with you."

Several snappy comebacks flashed through my mind, but I didn't deliver any of them. Malcolm was the kind of man who could make the tritest lines ring true. In his own way he was pure Hollywood and suddenly I could hardly wait to get home to him.

With several hours to go before my flight, I lingered over my breakfast. I had it served on a bed tray, eating in the solitary splendor of the huge lace and satin bed. I had showered and changed to a full-length pale-blue silk peignoir edged in white mink. It was a deliciously wicked sexy confection, and I could see myself striking a Harlow-like pose in the tall mahogany-framed mirror that stood near the far corner of the bed. The color of the silk deepened the green of my eyes, and my hair, still slightly damp, was a shower of bright gold. The outlines of my body were clearly visible through the transparent gauze, and I bent one leg as I leaned back against the pillows. The material fell away to reveal a dazzling display of tan leg and a hint of gold pubic hair. I gently stroked my inner thigh and as always when I touch that sensitive area, I felt a sudden twinge of excitement. I pulled on the loose satin bow that held the edges of the peignoir closed beneath my breasts, watching my mirror image as I touched my fingers to those luscious golden orbs. I put my finger in my mouth, then toyed with my nipples, making them darken and stand erect. A ripple of excitement raced along my spine. My stomach muscles tightened and my hips curled involuntarily upward.

I fantasized that I was a silent-screen star isolated from an adoring public by the cruel whim of my agent. He controlled every aspect of my career, manufacturing a public image of mystery and silent beauty. Though my face and figure were known to millions, it was only a cold celluloid image that they saw. The warmth of my living flesh, the sound of my voice, the intimate secrets of my naked body were reserved for him alone.

I gave a face to this fantasy man, a compilation of lovers I had known. I imagined him standing before me now, his hard eyes riveted on the exposed glory of my skin, his hands on the buttons of his cream silk shirt. I spread my legs so he could see the delicate pink membrane of my pussy. I could see the pulse beating in his throat but he undressed with a calculated deliberateness, not wanting me to know how much he desired me. I imagined his long hard cock against my thigh, his hot breath against my cheek as I reached between my legs to press the hard bone at the top of my mons. My pussy tingled in response. I pressed back against the pillows, running my fingers along the outer edges of my cunt, letting a finger slip between the swollen folds, then wriggling away as if I were being teased by the head of his cock.

I did this a number of times, each time creating an answering response in the pit of my stomach and causing my buttock muscles to tighten involuntarily. My body grew warm and my breathing quickened. One hand went to my breasts, massaging them painfully, while my fingers pushed inside the slippery walls of my cunt. I heard my own harsh breathing and imagined it was his, felt my probing fingers and pictured a man's swollen shaft plunging the hot length of my canal. I ground my hips against the bed, my nails raking my own flesh. I felt a rush of excitement as my fingers found the hard knob of my clit. I dug my heels into the mattress, arching my hips and crying out as the spasms of my orgasm washed over me.

I lay back against the pillows, breathing heavily, my body filmed with sweat. Since I was a young girl, masturbation has played a natural part in my sex life and over the years I have experimented with dozens of ways to give myself pleasure. I almost never travel without a dildo or a vibrator, but in a pinch I have found hairbrushes, Coke bottles, and even phallic-shaped vegetables such as cucumbers to be excellent substitutes. Now I rummaged in the drawer of my night table and drew out a small compact vibrator with a large selection of tips. I slipped out of my peignoir, more businesslike than casual in my preparations. On my dressing table was a large rectangular hand mirror but it wasn't the phallic shape of the handle that attracted me. Placing the mirror on the bed, I knelt so that my knees were on either side of the glass and the rose-pink of my exposed pussy was clearly reflected. I enjoy watching myself when I masturbate and have used a mirror in every position imaginable. Now I concentrated on my cunt, on the dark gold curls of my pubic hair and the pink shell-like delicacy of the outer lips which deepened to a warmer rose within.

My heart began to pound as I switched on the vibrator. Using the smooth tip, I began tracing concentric circles around my breasts, rubbing the tip over my nipples till they stiffened with desire. I slowly moved downward, my eyes on the mirror image of my cunt still wet and open from my recent ministrations. I held my breath as I guided the throbbing tip of the vibrator to my parted lips. I felt a stab of pleasure as I inserted the dildo into my aching cunt, and I closed my eyes as I eased my body over its quivering length. I held my hand steady, raising and lowering my hips. My pussy juices slickened the plastic rod and I pushed it in as far as it would go, imagining it a real cock, warm and swollen. I spread my knees even wider and opened my eyes, enjoying the sight of my pussy lips sucking greedily at the glistening tip of the vibrator. The force and timing of my thrusts were completely under my control. I ground my hips, feeling my inner muscles relax as I pushed down over my own hand. My body stiffened, then relaxed, and the tears coursed down my cheeks as I creamed all over the stiff tool. I continued working it in my spasming cunt till I climaxed a second time, doubled over with my fist clamped between my trembling thighs. Slowly I unfolded my limbs, stiff and aching from my exertions. The party, the interlude with Dale, and my recent masturbatory activities were finally catching up with me. I was drugged on sexual excess, but like a true addict, I wanted one more fix.

Being a water sign, I think of bathing not as a perfunctory act but as a stimulating and at times even erotic experience, and I always check the bathroom decor in my hotel suite before deciding whether or not the room will be acceptable. Now I lay back against the side of the sunken red-lacquered fiberglass tub and let the warm water flow over my outstretched limbs, aided by the automated whirlpool device.

I picked up a hand-held spray and directed the needlelike jets of water at my partially submerged breasts. They responded instantly, the nipples swelling to a rosy hardness, the flesh tingling pleasurably. I moved the spray downward, arching my back, then tightening my buttock muscles as the water flowed over the blond triangle between my thighs. I held the spray closer, undulating my hips beneath the water. A slow heat began to build inside of me, traveling along my limbs like the lit fuse of a powerful explosive. My breathing became harsher and I moaned softly as the growing ache in my pussy began to demand attention. I narrowed the spray head to a single, hard stream of water. I spread my legs and, parting my pussy lips with the fingers of one hand, I aimed the spray directly inside. The force of the water was like a jolt of electricity. My muscles tightened but I forced myself to relax, moving the spray head until I found the swollen little nub of my clit. Years of self-love have taught me to understand and appreciate my body. I knew just how to move, the exact angle at which to aim the spray to give myself maximum pleasure. Within minutes I had teased myself to a frenzied height of passion, my entire body trembling violently. I had difficulty keeping the water centered on my clit and braced my back against the side of the tub, knees bent and heels searching for a foothold on the glassy surface of the bottom. I held my breath, my body going rigid, then I let go, exploding in staccato rhythms of orgasm.

It was with mixed emotions that I oversaw the packing of my luggage and said good-bye to the sunshine and party mood of the movie capital. Though I was anxious to see Malcolm and curious as to what Princess Lyapunov had to say to me, the prospect of New York's icy winds and leaden skies was depressing. My glum mood wasn't helped by the long and tedious flight. Despite the comforts of first-class travel, I am never able to sleep on a plane. I require a soft bed, silk sheets, lots of blankets and pillows, and other aids for a comfortable hibernation. There were no interesting-looking men in my section, only mopy children and their nervous parents who kept the flight personnel too busy to attend to more than my most superficial needs. This left me with a triple scotch and the in-flight movie, a tasteful little confection called *It's Sitting in the Oven*, about a Midwestern family terrorized by a living loaf of man-eating bread that oozes out of the oven door and slithers fragrantly through the house, probably looking for butter.

Darkness comes early in New York during the winter and by the time Malcolm had collected my luggage and commandeered a cab, the city was an icy blackness that made driving treacherous at best. I snuggled against Malcolm's shoulder, grateful for his silence, and allowed him to take me home where a hot bath and a change of clothes did much to restore my good humor. We had a late dinner at Windows on the World with its understated decor and unsurpassed view of the city. Dressed in black and diamonds instead of a gauzy Indian print and eating timbale of crayfish tails with a sauce Nantua (flavored with crayfish butter, tomato, and cognac) instead of shrimp salad with lemon wedges and grated carrot, I understood Malcolm's passionate attachment to New York. There is an elegance and sophistication in this city that can be found nowhere else, and by the time we went to bed in the wee hours of the morning, my time in Hollywood had faded to a tinsel-edged dream.

It was just four o'clock the following day when I handed my sable coat to Princess Lyapunov's ancient maid and was ushered into the lemon-tinted drawing room. The low table before the couch was laid for tea and the Princess, in a French-blue cashmere dress, presided over the big silver and gold samovar. I quickly crossed the room and bent to kiss her rouged, high-boned cheek.

"Christina my dear, it's so wonderful to see you. Please sit down." She patted the sofa next to her. "Thank you for coming so quickly and from such a distance just to please an old woman. Mr. Gold told me you were on the West Coast."

"I was, but when Malcolm told me that your message was urgent, I came right back. Is something wrong?"

"Wrong? No, quite the contrary. Things are quite right. I've just had some rather exciting news from home." She poured me a cup of black tea and laced it liberally with brandy. "It will keep out the chill," she explained, handing me the cup.

I piled an assortment of *mazurki* (small rich cakes) on my plate, waiting politely while she poured her own tea. "I'm not supposed to drink brandy," she confided. "The doctors say it will kill me. So I drink tea. If some brandy falls into the cup, accidentally of course, I try my best to drink around it."

I laughed at her remark and helped myself to more cake. "Now then, what's the big secret?" I asked, brushing crumbs from my lap. "I presume when you spoke of news from home, you meant Russia."

"I did," she nodded. "Shortly after I met you, I received a hand-delivered letter from a Nikolai Brosoff, a Soviet citizen currently hospitalized at Harrison-Sloan, requesting to see me. In the envelope with the letter was a small gold cross with the Russian letters *M* and *L* engraved on the back. The cross had belonged to my sister Marie and you can imagine my feelings upon seeing it after all these years."

"I remember your telling me about her," I said.

"Of course I went immediately," Princess Lyapunov continued. "Nikolai Brosoff is a military aide attached to Gregory Kabalevsky, a high-ranking officer in the Russian army. He had developed a rare form of cancer that no Russian doctor knew how to treat and was given just a few months to live. However, Kabalevsky had used his influence to arrange for his aide to be admitted to this specialized American hospital in the hope that with their advanced treatments, they could bring about a remission. In return for this favor, Brosoff agreed to contact me."

"I assume there's some connection between Gregory Kabalevsky and your sister," I said.

"He's her son," the Princess said. "He's my nephew."

"Then your sister escaped."

"In a way. When the violence broke out, my sister fled north, intending to meet up with her husband, a young man she had married just a few months earlier, and escape with him to the Continent. In those dangerous days, travel was slow and news unreliable. She wasted precious weeks waiting at the appointed place, only to learn of his death at the hands of an enraged mob."

"Could she not escape then? She must have taken some of the jewels. There would have been money for bribes."

The Princess shrugged expressively. "She might have tried, but she was pregnant and alone. We know only that she did not succeed. She ended in a remote village near Siberia where she lived out her days under an assumed name. She pretended to be a peasant woman and no one questioned her story. In that part of the country, the Revolution had little impact. While the names of the royal family may have been known, few photographs existed and the average peasant never left his own village. My nephew was not told of his identity until shortly before my sister's death. He was eighteen years of age."

"It must have been quite a shock," I said. "I'm surprised he didn't contact you sooner."

"As a young soldier he would not have heard of me. There is no world news available to the average Soviet citizen that the government has not carefully screened, and travel, as you know, is restricted. It is only in his present position that news of my existence might have reached him, but he would have no legitimate reason to contact me. To do so without official permission would involve a great risk."

"Yet it was a risk he took."

"It was unfortunately necessary," said the Princess sadly. "Gregory did well in school and when World War Two began, he enlisted in the army. He distinguished himself in combat and was quickly promoted, managing to hold his position even in the shifting political tides of the postwar Soviet government. He never married and now, in his midsixties, he is a powerful man . . ." She hesitated as if searching for the right words.

"You said powerful, not well liked," I observed.

"Those in the Party hierarchy seldom are," she replied. "The Revolution did not change much. It is now political position, not family name that determines access to the limited goods and services, but as always it is in the nature of those without special privileges to resent those who have them. A low-ranking clerk in the Kremlin's Bureau of Statistics has apparently pieced together enough information to prove my nephew's identity and has threatened to expose him."

"But your nephew was born after the Revolution," I pointed out, "and he has served his country well. Surely, after all these years the accident of his birth would not greatly matter."

"You are thinking rationally, my dear," the Princess smiled, "but logic has no place in political or bureaucratic decisions. The fact that a member of the deposed royal family holds a position of influence and power in the current proletarian government would greatly embarrass them, but if it became known that my nephew is still in possession of a large portion of our family jewels, even his reputation as a war hero would not save him. He would be totally disgraced, his very life forfeit."

"My God, he still has the jewels?" I whispered. "He must have taken them when he left his village to join the army. But why? He could never wear them or sell them or even show them to anyone."

"Why not?" said the Princess. "They are his, no matter what the current government decrees. Those jewels are part of the history of Russia, as we are. No matter how much the communists rewrite that history to suit their political needs, there is nothing in the past that my family need be ashamed of."

"Is the clerk blackmailing him?" I asked.

The Princess nodded. "For the moment he is satisfied with gifts of foreign goods and small amounts of cash. Perhaps he doesn't know of the jewels or perhaps my nephew's high rank intimidates him, but it is only a matter of time before he becomes bolder and his demands escalate. It is always so with blackmailers. When this chance came to contact me, Gregory had no choice but to take the risk. I am his only living relative. He had no one else to whom he could turn."

"How can you help him? You can hardly smuggle him out of Russia, and from what I can see of the situation he must be smuggled out. I doubt that even a letter from the President of the United States, should you convince him to write one, would persuade the Soviet government to let your nephew emigrate legally."

"That's true," the Princess said. "The President was not interested in helping my nephew, but he did set up an appointment for me with U.S. Army Intelligence. As a high-ranking officer in the Russian army, Gregory has a great deal of information that would be useful to them, and they have agreed to effect his escape from Russia."

"Well, that's good news," I said. "Some of our finest men are working for Uncle Sam. I'm sure everything will go off without a hitch and we can throw a grand party to welcome him when he arrives. I hope you'll allow me to arrange it."

"I will leave it entirely in your hands," the Princess laughed, "but that's not the reason I asked to see you."

"What is the reason?"

Again the Princess hesitated. She poured us both a second cup of tea and urged me to try some *kuhorost*, crisp buttery twiglets, that she said always reminded her of home. She absently fingered a small gold cross that hung on a thin chain around her neck, then slipped it off and held it out to me.

"My sister wore this all her life," she said as I turned it over to examine the engraving on the back. "There are other pieces too: a gold watch belonging to my father, the tiara of diamonds worn by my grandmother on her wedding day and then by my mother and my sister on their wedding days. Wonderful historical pieces of great sentimental as well as monetary value. The Americans will help my nephew escape, but they say he must leave the jewels behind."

"Perhaps it is too great a risk," I said reasonably. "If your nephew is caught he would be charged with theft of state property, a far more serious crime than defecting, and our government would be named as his accomplice."

"Gregory said the same thing," the Princess nodded, "but I convinced him I was right. It is not theft, and I will not let those jackals have what is rightfully ours. So Gregory devised a way to smuggle the jewels out separately," she continued, "and even the Pentagon agrees that the plan involves virtually no risk. But they will not assign the extra manpower to carry it out."

"Why not?"

"Principle, they say; stubbornness I call it. They claim that they have no interest in a private fortune no matter what the historical or sentimental value involved."

"That's too bad," I murmured sympathetically, "but I must confess that I can see their point."

"So could I," said the Princess. "That is why I proposed a compromise. Gregory's plan to smuggle the jewels out of Russia can be carried out only by a woman, someone who can secure permission to enter the Soviet Union as a tourist. This precludes any former Soviet citizen and, of course, the Pentagon has refused to allow anyone connected with the U.S. government to volunteer."

"Whom did you get?" I asked, contemplating the cookie plate.

"No one . . . yet."

I stared at her for several moments, digesting the implications of her remark. I was fond of the Princess and sympathetic to her plight, but the thought of traipsing through the frozen Russian tundra in the dead of winter with a fortune in stolen jewels sewn into the lining of my coat did not exactly appeal to me.

"I know what you're asking," I said carefully, deliberately avoiding her eyes, "and believe me I would like to help you, but I'm a very busy woman . . ."

"Please, Christina, you are the only one with the credentials and resources to carry this off. The Pentagon would not have agreed to my suggestion if they thought there was any danger. You will simply enter Russia using your own passport for some legitimate reason—Army Intelligence will set this up— and stay about a week. During that time you will be handed the jewels. Then you will leave, like any other happy American tourist on her way back home. There will be no reason to suspect you. In fact, given your social position, even if you were discovered to possess the jewels, you could claim that they were yours and easily get away with it. I am begging you, Christina, and that is something I have never done in my entire life.''

I was reminded of all the reasons I had avoided traveling into Russia in the past. The fact that they had the lumpiest beds, the coldest rooms, the leakiest, rustiest showers, the deepest snow, and the gloomiest people in the world did not exactly place them high on my must-see list. I wanted nothing to do with this harebrained cloak-and-dagger scheme no matter how minimal the risk, yet I could not bring myself to refuse outright.

"I'll have to think about it," I said, playing for time.

"I understand," she said, "but I have a suggestion. You hesitate because you do not know all of the details. Even I do not know them, but I am sure that the young man in charge of the mission would be happy to discuss them with you, perhaps over dinner. Colonel Landon is a very handsome man. No, more than handsome." Her eyes twinkled mischievously. "He has an air of sensual masculinity about him that makes me wish I were your age, just for one night."

I smiled. She had found my Achilles heel and, sensing this, she pressed her point.

"Go and see him," she urged. "If you do not like what you hear, you can refuse and I will say nothing. All I ask is that you give my request a fair hearing."

"I guess I can't say no to that," I laughed, thinking that a night in a deluxe Washington hotel with a handsome man uselessly begging for my help on a secret mission might be fun. It would also give me a polite way to refuse the Princess's request, for I still had every intention of ultimately turning her down. "All right, Your Highness, I'll meet your sexy young man and see what he has to offer."

"You won't be sorry," said the Princess happily. "I think you two are made for each other. You're a perfect match."

"Don't be a Jewish mother," I teased. "I'm not the marrying kind."

"Who said anything about marriage?" the Princess replied, and we both laughed and hugged each other.

CHAPTER FIVE

At ten o'clock the following morning I was seated comfortably in the first-class car of the Amtrack Metroliner, staring out the window at the somewhat unfamiliar field of railroad tracks that stretched for blocks under Pennsylvania Station in New York. There was a time when I would have sneered at rail travel as an uncomfortable, inefficient, and downright unsanitary mode of transportation; and, indeed, with the growth of modern airlines, the trains that had once spanned the East Coast had deteriorated to a shameful level. However, recent concerns about energy conservation had sparked new interest in the iron horse and a massive infusion of capital had made traveling by train once again a viable alternative. This was especially so when I took into consideration the time lost going to and from the various airports for what amounted to less than an hour in the air.

A solicitous waiter in the elegantly appointed dining car took my order for breakfast, and as we began to gather speed I watched the frozen landscape, fantasizing that I was a top-notch secret agent on my way to the Pentagon to discuss a dangerous mission behind the Iron Curtain, a scenario not far from the truth, if Malcolm Gold was to be believed.

"She's out of her mind," he had said angrily when I told him what the Princess had asked me to do. "There is nothing safe about that proposal. You would be smuggling out what is considered state property, no matter what that romantic old fool says. You'd have about as much right to take the *Mona Lisa* out of France by claiming to be a descendant of Leonardo da Vinci as you have to take the Romanov family jewels out of Russia. They don't play games over there, Christina. If you're caught, there is no bail or habeas corpus or expensive private attorneys. They don't read you your rights or give you fair and impartial trial. There *is* an insanity defense, but I don't think you want to spend the next ten years being rehabilitated in a Soviet psychiatric institution. Forget it. Let the professionals do their job and mind your own business."

I had assured Malcolm that I was only making this trip to Washington to comply with the Princess' request that I hear all the facts before making a decision but that I had no intention of risking my neck for a pile of old jewels. I would go to Washington, listen to the proposal, back out, and the matter would be settled to the satisfaction of all concerned. He seemed pleased with this answer, and we agreed to meet for dinner when I returned. I had never been to the capital and I planned to stay for a few extra days and perhaps take on the Congress. It would be useful to have a Senator or two in my pocket should I ever need a favor, and I amused myself by imagining which ones I might invite to bed. I was trying to decide if I should add a cabinet member or a Supreme Court Justice to my projected list of conquests when my thoughts were interrupted by an overweight, jovial-looking man with a bulging briefcase who introduced himself and asked if he could share my table. Though it was a bit early for lunch, Mr. Poplar ordered linguine with clam sauce, a bottle of the best white wine, and one each of every dessert on the menu. Not wanting to appear impolite, I accepted his offer to share.

"I'm fighting a losing battle with the old waistline," he sighed, patting his rotund midriff. "I hate to give up the sweets so I order what I like and only eat half."

"I'm a real junk food addict myself," I admitted, taking a forkful of cheesecake.

"You don't look it," he said. "You have a beautiful figure."

"I never seem to gain weight no matter what I eat," I bragged, attacking half of an eclair. "It's the exercise, I think."

"Really? Do you jog, do aerobics, lift weights . . . ?"

"It's more horizontal," I said, giving him a suggestive wink. He laughed and smiled back.

"My wife is a looker like you," he said, "but she claims it's the low-cal cottage cheese and vegiburgers she makes for dinner. I'm always starved at home, but fortunately I travel a lot in my work. Of course, I lie about what I eat on the road, but then perhaps my wife lies too. Horizontal exercise, huh? I wouldn't begrudge her an affair if it made her happy just as long as she didn't tell me about it. Honesty is a highly over-rated commodity, don't you think?"

"You've got a point," I agreed. "Does your work involve stretching the truth as well?"

"It does," he said. "I'm a professional lobbyist. I travel to the capital from Philadelphia once or twice a week and hang around the corridors of the Senate Office Building, buttonhol-ing Senators and their aides and trying to get them interested in my cause."

"Exactly what is your cause?"

"I'm fighting to get legislation passed to protect the Beau-mont beetle," he said. "It isn't the most popular cause on Capitol Hill these days. I have to push past nuclear-waste-control proponents, poverty people, and pro- and antimilitary lobbyists, and all to get some harassed Senator interested in a half-inch-long black beetle that only lives in one Philadelphia stream. Can't be more than a few thousand of the little bug-gers."

"Are they an endangered species, threatening the survival of the entire food chain?" I asked.

"No, that's the problem. They really aren't worth a damn. If they were wiped out tomorrow no one would miss them and nothing would happen. I work for a group of nutty old ladies who live in a town near the stream. They have lots of money and nothing to do all day but drink coffee in each other's houses and discuss the saving of this worthless insect. Strange, isn't it?"

"Not as strange as the fact that you're willing to work for them," I said.

"I have to make a living," he said philosophically, "and getting a job as a lobbyist for some worthy cause these days isn't easy, with charities and special interest groups cutting their budgets. I used to work for heart disease, but they laid me off, and when this came up . . ." He shrugged expressively and divided the last cherry tart. "I'll admit that my motives aren't terribly pure but I do an honest day's work for the money. Today, for example, I'm going to push for a bill to declare the Beaumont beetle the national slug." He reached into his briefcase and handed me some literature and a petition.

"Do you get laughed at a lot?" I asked, looking at the outrageous statements in the three-color pamphlet.

"Not really. The trick is to sound sincere and straightforward even when it's obvious that you're lying through your teeth. Senators respect that."

"As you said," I conceded, "honesty is a highly overrated commodity." I signed his petition and wished him luck.

It was just after two o'clock when my taxi pulled up outside the Madison on the corner of M and 15th streets. Though not one of the new hotels, it is a regular stop-off for political brass and has a reputation for excellent service and unusual decor. I was greeted by the manager, who personally escorted me to my suite, which was furnished entirely in nineteenth-century American antiques. A large breakfront contained an impressive collection of American hand-blown glass flasks, including a rare campaign flask inscribed "*Hard Cider and Log Cabin,*" for William Henry Harrison, and there were some excellent American landscape prints on the walls.

By this time it was 2:45. I had a three o'clock appointment with Army Intelligence and, knowing how cranky the Army can get when their timetables are upset, I asked the manager to phone Colonel Landon at his office and tell him I would be late. I could have gone straight to the Pentagon, but I didn't want to give the impression that I considered this meeting of any importance. I had a maid unpack my suitcases while I showered, then relaxed with a glass of white wine. I dressed casually in a midcalf, brown-tweed soft wool skirt, a hunter-green silk blouse, and brown suede boots. I wore my hooded tan canvas raincoat, which was lined with sable.

At 4:15 I had the doorman at the Madison get me a cab and instructed the driver to take me to the Pentagon. We drove south past the White House, the Washington Monument, and the Smithsonian, turning to circle the Lincoln Memorial where we crossed the Potomac River into Virginia.

The Pentagon, a massive five-story, five-sided structure, is located in Arlington. Each floor contains five concentric circles with ten spokelike corridors. Altogether, the building has almost eighteen miles of hallway. I entered the main concourse and stood for a moment to take in the enormity of the place. Except for certain sensitive areas like the War Room, the file room, the communications room, and the men's room, the Pentagon building is open to the public and hundreds of people, military and civilian, workers and tourists, milled in the noisy hall. There were numerous stores there for the convenience of the workers, including a barber shop, a bank, a florist, a book store, and even a travel agent. There was also an information desk, and that was where I headed. I was greeted with a smile from a very young corporal with a blond crew cut and freckles.

"Yes, ma'am, may I help you?" he said with a Midwest twang. Being called "ma'am" by GI Hayseed made me feel ancient, and I repressed an annoyed wince.

"I have an appointment with Colonel Moses Landon of Army Intelligence," I told him. "Where would I find him?"

The corporal consulted a large bound computer printout, thumbing carefully through the names until he found the one I wanted. "That's room 2E832, ma'am," he said. "Second Floor, ring E, corridor eight, room thirty-two. You can't miss it. If you get lost ask for the Chairman of the Joint Chiefs of Staff. He's right near there."

I made my way through the crowds to the elevators. Colonel Landon certainly seems to rate in this organization, I thought. An office next to the Chairman of the Joint Chiefs wouldn't be handed out to just any bum on the street. Okay, I was impressed, but I still didn't want the job.

An attractive sergeant with thick blond hair and a peaches-and-cream complexion was seated in the Colonel's reception room at a small desk. She quickly checked her book, confirmed that I was expected, buzzed her boss for an okay, and ushered me into his office.

Colonel Landon stood when I came into the room. He was in uniform, a tall handsome man with black curling hair, gray-green eyes and a firm jawline. He greeted me cordially. I could tell he was assessing me as he shook my hand, and I could tell that he was pleased with what he saw. His expression was self-confident, perhaps too self-confident. He was a man used to giving orders. But there was something else too, a kind of personal power—sensual, even sexual—that I found very attractive. Okay, I'm more impressed, I thought. I still don't want the job, but that doesn't mean we can't get to know each other.

"I'm sorry to have kept you waiting," I said as he helped me out of my coat.

"That's perfectly all right," he replied. "Time is irrelevant to women. I expected you to be late."

"Not all women are late," I protested, resenting his arrogance.

"They are when they're beautiful enough to know they're worth waiting for," he amended charmingly. "Would you like a drink? It will take the chill out of your bones." I nodded. "I have scotch, brandy, or some white wine if you'd prefer something light."

"Brandy, please."

He moved toward a small refrigerator/bar near the bookcases and I took the opportunity to glance around the room. Colonel Landon's office like the Colonel himself was a cut above the average. While the colors and furnishings were standard government issue, there were some antique maps on the wall, a lamp made out of a bombshell casing on the desk, and a large framed picture of General Patton inscribed, "To my friend Mo." I picked it up to examine it more closely.

"That's my father," Landon explained, coming toward me. "He served under the General in North Africa." He waited until I sat down before handing me my drink, then pulled up another chair and seated himself opposite me. "My father was a career man and was stationed in Europe after the war. I was born on an Army base, and though I was educated in private boarding schools, I always knew there was no other life for me than the military."

"It obviously suits you," I said, sipping my drink. The phone rang. It was his secretary; Landon assured her that she would not be needed and could go home. "Aren't you putting in overtime?" I asked, wondering when we were going to discuss the real reason for my visit.

"It is pretty late," he said, glancing at his watch. "Let me buy you dinner. We can have a few more drinks and talk. Unless you're on a tight schedule."

"I would love some dinner," I admitted, "but I don't want to accept your offer under false pretenses. If dinner is part of a soft-sell approach to get me to accept the assignment to help Princess Lyapunov, you should know that I really have very little interest in doing the job. I just came here to satisfy the Princess that I had considered all the facts before making a decision."

"You're getting carried away," Landon smiled. "I'm not that manipulative. I asked you to dinner because you are a beautiful woman and I would like to get to know you better. I'm not trying to sell you anything. Quite the contrary; I wouldn't especially welcome your company on this mission."

"Oh?"

"I'll have enough difficulty carrying out my own orders without having to concern myself about your activities as well. You would be in no danger but, still, a careless move or word could endanger the whole mission."

"Then why did you agree to this crazy compromise in the first place?"

"No one asked my opinion," said Landon candidly. "I understand Her Highness had a personal interview with the President. No, Miss van Bell, I don't want to work with you, I just want to eat with you. How about it?"

Though I had had every intention of ultimately refusing the assignment, I was nevertheless disappointed. I had expected the pleasure of fending off repeated entreaties to offer the

government my matchless aid, and now I discovered that the
government was only interested in a little friendly meal.

On the other hand, Colonel Landon was an attractive man,
and I was every bit as interested in his physical attributes as he
obviously was in mine. I would enjoy having dinner with him,
but I couldn't let him hold the upper hand all night. Perhaps
an exclusive French restaurant would take some of the wind
out of his sails. I could show off my French and my knowledge
of fine wines. I smiled as I pictured myself imperiously inter-
preting the menu, and he took this to mean I had accepted his
offer.

"What shall we have?" he asked. "French? Italian?
Chinese? Washington has become more sophisticated these
past few years; we're no longer considered the culinary boon-
docks."

"I'd love to go to Le Faisan Bleu," I said airily. "It was
written up in several gourmet magazines and is supposed to
have one of the most extensive wine lists in the country. But
I'm afraid it might be too expensive for you, military salaries
being what they are."

His mouth twitched into the merest suggestion of a smile. "I
think I can manage it," he said, putting on his overcoat and
handing me my gloves. "Let's go. My car is right downstairs."

You'll be eating canned spaghetti from the commissary for
a month after tonight, you macho moron, I thought wickedly
as I preceded him out.

I had expected the Colonel to be driving a jeep but instead
he owned a mint-condition 1964 dark blue Jaguar 3.8-liter
sedan with tan leather upholstery and right-hand drive.

"This is an impressive piece of machinery," I said as we
drove effortlessly through the early-evening traffic. "Did
some retired general give you a discount?"

"This was my first car," said Landon proudly. "It was new
when I got it, and over the years I've taken every bit of the
engine apart myself and put it back together. Fixing cars is a
hobby of mine."

I stared thoughtfully out the window while I digested this

new bit of information. Landon was obviously no ordinary army brat. A new Jaguar in the midsixties must have cost a cool ten grand, a lot of money in those days.

Nighttime parking in the capital is not a problem, as few people actually live there, and Landon had no trouble locating a space a few paces from the restaurant. The menu in the window was written in French and the prices were comparable with the finest restaurants in New York. I happily anticipated impressing both Landon and the restaurant staff with my flawless French which, along with the right names, always got me a choice table.

The maître d' beamed when we walked through the door, and I was somewhat disconcerted when he embraced Landon with obvious familiarity.

"Moses, mon cher ami," he gushed. *"Quelle agréable surprise. Comment allez-vous ce soir?"*

"Bien, bien, Marcel," said Landon, squeezing his hand. *"Comment vont les affaires?"*

"Business, as you can see, is booming," replied the little man, switching politely to English and including me in his smile.

"Christina van Bell, Marcel Vauquer," said Landon, introducing us. "I know we don't have a reservation . . ."

"Reservations are for tourists," said Marcel indignantly. "For my friend Moses and the lovely mademoiselle there is always a table. Come with me."

By now I was beginning to suspect that Colonel Landon was pretty well known in Washington society, despite his rather modest profession, and this frustrating realization made me order a double scotch on the rocks.

"Would you like me to interpret the menu," he asked, "or shall I order for both of us?"

"I can read the menu for myself," I said irritably, "but since you've obviously eaten here before, why don't you order."

Landon's smile indicated that he knew he had one-upped me. He had a lengthy discussion with the waiter in French and finally decided on veau Sylvie, which is a roast of veal split lengthwise, stuffed with slices of ham and cheese, then re-formed and tied and served with braised lettuce and buttered noodles. He selected a Lafite-Rothschild 1980 from the wine list, a perfect complement to the veal.

As we settled down to our drinks, I began to relax. My attempt to take Landon down a peg had backfired but I could hardly object to a dinner companion who spoke fluent French and knew his way around a wine list. Beneath the table his knee touched my thigh and my treacherous body responded instantly.

"Tell me," I said to cover my confusion. "Is this entire project feasible? Do we often smuggle people out of Iron Curtain countries?"

"Not often, but Kabalevsky's knowledge of military secrets makes him an important enough man to warrant the attempt. What I can't see is the Secretary of State's decision to get us involved even minimally in removing a large fortune in jewels, just to score points with a President who has been taken in by a sentimental old woman with a title."

"What do you mean by that?" I asked.

"Well," he said, waving his hand. "A man would say it's enough to get Kabalevsky with all his military expertise out of the country. A woman wants to complicate matters by bringing home a bag of trinkets."

"They're hardly trinkets," I interjected.

"They are to me. They should be to you too. Kabalevsky's knowledge might save American lives, but not one American citizen will benefit from the return of these jewels."

"Perhaps the Princess will lend them to a museum."

"Perhaps she will," Landon smiled, "and you can buy a new dress for the opening. Something exclusive."

"You're being a male chauvinist pig!" I snapped.

"I am. But like all women, you bypass the essential and focus on the trivial. That's the reason women rarely hold positions of authority."

"That's not true!" I said indignantly. "I hold a position of authority and I do a damned good job of it."

"What position is that?" he asked seriously.

"I'm the publisher of *World* magazine. That's how I met Princess Lyapunov. I interviewed her for an exclusive cover story. We distribute millions of copies nationwide, and I run the entire operation."

"Your name is on the masthead," Landon nodded, "but I checked on you before our meeting. From what I can see, Malcolm Gold seems to run the magazine. You do an occasional story and only stop in to collect the money, which proves my point."

"You don't have a point," I asserted. "Malcolm works for me. I let him handle the daily chores, but I could run the whole thing if I wanted to."

"I don't doubt it," he agreed readily. "It's what you've chosen to do that I'm focusing on here. Women prefer to let men handle the really important work, the nitty-gritty of our economic, political, and military concerns. That's all I'm saying. Men concentrate on farming and finance and other essentials. Women decorate the world with trivial concerns like art and music and other frills. They're nice, but they're not essential. Find me a big construction project that provides thousands of jobs and millions for the G.N.P. and I'll show you a man in charge of it. Find me a gallery opening for some swish who dabs colors on a canvas and you can bet it's the brainstorm of some woman. I'm not putting down your intelligence, you understand, just your priorities. My ex-wife was the same way: beautiful, charming, and totally preoccupied with trivialities."

"You were married?" I laughed. "And she didn't kill you in bed one night?"

"On the contrary, bed was the only place we got along." Landon smiled. "I was working for the government, dealing with crises around the world that threatened our very way of life. And what was Lila concerned with? Abstract philosophy. She was studying for her doctorate and sat around all day reading Kant and Descartes and Kierkegaard and the rest. Completely worthless. I would tell her that there are forty Russian missiles pointed at Washington, and she would attempt to prove to me that the missiles didn't exist. She once proved to me that Kansas didn't exist. It drove me crazy. But she was terrific in bed—all woman. A face like an angel and a body to match.''

"Apparently that wasn't enough if you're no longer married," I observed.

"Oh, I was content enough. She left *me*," he said fairly. "She ran away with a forty-year-old philosophy professor with thinning hair and a roll of flab around his middle." His face tensed, then became deliberately blank.

"Perhaps she found being a soldier's wife difficult," I said absently, contemplating the large wedge of apple charlotte that Landon had ordered for dessert.

"Boring is more like it," Landon sighed. "She hated military functions, the formal dinners, and cocktail parties. Then, I was away a great deal and she was in school and couldn't travel with me. I gave her anything she asked for, though, an apartment off base, a car . . .''

Everything except respect, I thought, watching him stab at his dessert with his fork. He was not as indifferent as he tried to pretend. He had said he was content, not passionately in love, but a man like Moses Landon would not easily accept his wife's leaving him, especially for someone he considered inferior.

"It's getting late," I said, tactfully changing the subject. "We've talked for hours and you still haven't explained the Russian mission."

"I thought you weren't interested," he said, his eyes narrowing suspiciously.

"Let's say I'm curious," I said. "Women are that way, like cats."

"You said it, not me." There was a glint of amusement in his gray-green eyes. "But I'm afraid I can't discuss classified information in a public restaurant."

I looked across at him, full of conflicting emotions: resentful of his outmoded macho attitude toward women yet respectful of his honesty, his directness, and his considerable intellectual capacities. Above all, though, I was attracted to him. He was very much my physical type and it was clear that the attraction was mutual. I wanted to make love to Moses Landon and at the same time I wanted not to like it. If he was a dud in bed, I could dismiss him. I began to fantasize that he was impotent. Lots of overtly sexual men were. Perhaps his bitterness over his ex-wife's desertion was based, not on his feelings of physical superiority over her pot-bellied lover, but on the fact that he had been unable to perform since she left. Perhaps she had to use all sorts of tricks to get him aroused to begin with, and he hadn't been able to find anyone since who was equally adept with suction hoses or whatever it was she used. Well, even if this were true, he'd rise like the phoenix after ten minutes in my bed.

"How about my hotel?" I purred. "We can have a drink and trade secrets."

"I didn't know you had any to trade," he said mildly as he held my coat.

"All women have secrets," I replied lightly. "Trivial secrets, perhaps, but secrets all the same."

We returned to the car and Moses drove quickly through the now deserted streets to my hotel. Any expectations that my deluxe accommodations might impress him, however, were doomed to disappointment. The manager greeted him by name when I stopped at the desk for my key, asked after his father, and promised to send up coffee and the chef's special dessert, on the house.

Moses unlocked my door, then stepped back to allow me to enter first. Though this was my suite, he did not seem the least bit ill at ease. He hung up our coats, switched on just the right amount of light, and had the waiter lay out our coffee and dessert on the low table in front of the couch.

"Would you mind helping me with my boots?" I asked, flopping into a chair. "I hate wearing shoes in the house."

"You just like to see me kneel at your feet," he teased, easing off each boot, then rubbing my feet gently between his hands to restore the circulation. "Stockings too?" I nodded. He pushed my skirt to the top of my thighs, exposing my shapely silk-clad legs. His fingers touched the elasticized top of a stocking and I stretched out my leg, watching as he slowly peeled off the dark-hued silk to reveal the bronze of my naked thigh. He held my foot in his strong brown hands and kissed each plump little toe in turn. He then repeated the entire procedure on the other leg, sending little electric currents all along my limbs.

"You have exquisite legs," he said, his fingers lingering on the silken flesh. "You could be a dancer." He stood and, holding out his hand, pulled me gently to my feet. I leaned against him as if for support, and he caught my arms and crushed me to him.

I had planned to seduce him, to encourage his initial shy attempts until, with my ultimate submission, he would think himself an experienced Don Juan. I was good at this sort of play-acting. I could have been a courtesan of kings, if I were so inclined. All men like to think themselves in charge, but it was clear from the way he held me that Moses had a different game in mind. His mouth closed over mine, fiercely demanding, his fingers tightening on the tender flesh of my arms. I yielded to his demands, unable to do otherwise, giving kiss for kiss until my knees felt weak and my stomach was a hard knot of desire.

My body betrayed me, and he took this betrayal as consent. Lifting me easily in his arms, he carried me into the bedroom and set me on my feet. Wordlessly he began to unbutton my blouse, kissing my neck and the hollows in my collarbone and the cleavage between the mounds of my lace-covered breasts. He pulled the silk free of the skirt, slipped it over my shoulders and arms, and flung it aside. He reached around to unhook my bra, then drew it off. My breasts are firm and full, the nipples slightly uptilted, and he touched them now with the tips of his fingers. I caught my breath and closed my eyes, trembling as he bent to take first one and then the other into his warm mouth. His tongue flicked over the nipples, tasting their ripeness. His hands moved over my torso to my waist, and I gave a small sigh as he slowly opened the fastening of my skirt. The heavy material fell around my feet and I stepped free, clad only in my silk bikini briefs. I expected him to rip them from my body but instead he held back.

"Take them off," he whispered, making it seem as if this

final gesture were my choice, that in the chaste, pure way of romance novels I was offering myself to him, not begging him to take me.

I felt his eyes on me as my fingers touched the waistband of my panties and my body flushed with sexual heat. I inched the material over the plump mounds of my ass cheeks and down over my thighs, turning so that I presented the luscious curve of my derriere as I moved the briefs along my legs. Behind me I heard the sharp intake of his breath.

"Are you an ass man?" I teased, looking up at him wickedly from between spread legs.

"I am . . . and a leg man . . . and a breast man . . ." He grasped my waist with both hands and tossed me unceremoniously on the bed.

He was still fully dressed. I lay back and watched as he removed his jacket and hung it over the back of a chair. He unknotted his tie and loosened the buttons on his shirt. His movements were confident, but there was a slight bit of restraint about them as if he were deliberately slowing down the pace. Moses was no muscle-bound athlete, but years of Army life had left their mark. He was lean rather than broad, his shoulders and biceps were well-defined, and his stomach was a firm flat slab. There was a dark mat of hair on his chest that formed a V just above the point of his navel. He did not turn away as he took off his pants, and the sight of his cock, already swollen with lust, made my stomach muscles tighten in pleasurable anticipation.

Moses stretched out beside me, propping himself on one elbow so that he could look down at me. He brushed the hair gently away from my face, then let his finger trace a line along the bridge of my nose and around the outline of my lips. I opened my mouth slightly and pushed at his finger with my tongue, then nibbled it playfully. Our eyes met and held. I could feel my heart thudding against my chest as he leaned over me, his lips brushing mine. His tongue snaked into my mouth, sending little currents of excitement along my spine. I slipped my arms around his neck, drawing him closer as his fingers grazed the soft, lush triangle between my thighs. His touch was knowing, erotic, turning my body to liquid fire.

Moving downward, his lips sought again the tender ripeness of my nipples and I moaned helplessly as he sucked each one to a hard point of pleasure. I felt the throbbing hardness of his cock against my thigh, but though he was very much aroused, Moses was clearly focused on my pleasure rather than his own. He did not attempt to thrust himself inside me, but, stretching out between my spread legs, he contemplated my dewy pussy, running his tongue along the fleshy outer lips until I shivered and whimpered with delight.

I spread my legs farther apart, tilting my pelvis upward. I parted my swollen lips to expose the deep-rose membrane of my love-canal and the glistening red knob of my clit. Moses took the hint. His tongue tunneled its way along my steamy passage, his lips nibbling the warm, moist flesh. He sucked hungrily at the warm milky fluid he had helped create, inhaling the perfume of my sex. He was a man who enjoyed oral sex, not just as a hasty prelude to a more conventional coupling, but as a complete form of lovemaking in itself. His tongue and lips made my cunt come alive and I cried out as his tongue touched my distended clit. My thighs began to tremble and I bucked my hips, but he stayed with me, flicking that little button of joy until my spiraling senses peaked and a massive shuddering orgasm rippled over me. Giving me no chance to wind down, Moses exchanged his tongue for his fingers, slipping the fingers of one hand inside my sopping pussy and easing the index finger of the other hand into the puckered opening of my anus. In minutes he had reduced me to a quivering mass of raw feeling, groaning and sweating helplessly as I climaxed a second, then a third time.

When I opened my eyes I was beneath the blankets. Moses was smiling down at me, his hidden fingers lightly stroking my sweat-filmed skin. I felt the warmth of his thigh against my own and I reached beneath the cover to touch his cock and balls. He shivered slightly and I wriggled down into the warm darkness, my lips brushing the damp mat of hair below his pectorals. I kissed the flat hardness of his stomach and the hollows below the protruding bones of his hips. Then, taking his stiffened cock gently in my hand, I ran my tongue along the sensitive underside. He groaned loudly as I took the helmetlike head into my mouth, sliding my lips slowly down the thickening shaft. I continued to move up and down his meaty pole, relaxing my throat muscles to take as much of him into my mouth as I could. I was stretched out between his thighs, the heavy blanket still covering my head. I could not see his face, but I heard the deep moans of pleasure, felt the trembling of his thighs, and inhaled the incredible musk scent of his genitals. I felt my passion rising as I made love to his cock, my body growing warm and my pussy juices flowing freely. I wanted to give him pleasure in the totally unselfish way he had satisfied me, but when he flung off the covers and drew me upward, I did not protest. Holding me tightly, he rolled on top of me, easing his cock swiftly and surely into my aching cunt.

Here too, he put my needs foremost, gauging my response to his thrusts and adjusting the rhythm and tempo of his lovemaking accordingly. As we melted against each other in the unique dance each couple makes of this universal act, I felt myself pulled down, engulfed in the surging currents of our lovemaking. I wrapped my legs around his waist, my fingers raking his back as I tried to absorb his flesh, his fluids, his very essence into me. We were not just fucking, we were making love, giving and taking equally. My breath was coming in short rasping gasps as my trembling body spiraled toward climax. His hands bruised my flesh for a single instant, then I shuddered and cried out as the warm burst of his semen poured into my throbbing cunt to mingle with the honey-hot juices of my own orgasm.

He held me tightly against him for one final moment, then with a deep sigh let me go. I lay back against the pillows as he drew the covers over us both, then nestled contentedly against his warmth and fell asleep.

CHAPTER SIX

I have always believed that sex is the best form of exercise. There are people who rise at dawn, take a cold shower, run miles along some godforsaken beach, eat berries, and drink pulverized vegetables just to keep from gaining a pound. If they would spend a strenuous couple of hours between the sheets with an active and imaginative lover, they would never have to worry about getting fat. They'd work off those extra calories and enjoy themselves at the same time.

Based on the night I had just spent with Moses Landon, I felt confident that I had had my exercise quota for the week. He was a tender, passionate, creative lover, demonstrating un-flagging energy and a confident, masculine technique. I found it hard to understand how his wife could willingly give this up for a man whose greatest asset was his library.

To enhance these euphoric feelings, I discovered to my delight that, like myself, Moses was a late sleeper. Many's the time I have awakened at noon to discover my partner in a sweaty jogging suit, consuming his third cup of coffee at a breakfast table littered with dirty dishes. However, Moses was still breathing peacefully beside me. A man after my own heart I thought, snuggling companionably against him.

The only thing that still irked me was Landon's blatantly chauvinistic attitude toward women. I don't mind being considered a sex object—at times I rather enjoy it—but I like a man to acknowledge my intellectual credentials as well. I dug my elbow into Landon's side and he stirred reluctantly.

"What time is it?" he mumbled.

"Almost noon," I said. "I just got up."

"Only noon? You didn't tell me you were an early riser."

"Me? I thought the Army got its men out of the rack at dawn for cold showers and the ol' hup-two-three-four."

"They do. I had years of that crap, and I swore that when I got a desk assignment I'd sleep late at every opporutnity. I also swore that I'd kill my sergeant at boot camp. I'm still working on that one."

"I'm hungry," I moaned. "I need a shower and some breakfast."

"So? Go ahead." He pulled the covers up to his chin and closed his eyes.

"I hate to shower alone," I murmured, rubbing my toes along his naked leg and tickling the hairs on his chest with my fingers. He growled softly. I moved my hand lower and he caught his breath as I began to caress the flaccid length of his cock. "Are you sure you don't want to join me?" I teased, licking around the outer edge of his ear. "Nice hot shower? This suite has a Swiss shower and I'm just itching to try it out." I pushed my tongue into his ear canal and he shivered slightly, his cock beginning to swell against my hand.

With a sudden swift movement he grabbed at my hands, flipping me onto my back and pinning them on either side of my head. I struggled playfully beneath his weight, my breasts rubbing against his chest. My entire body grew warm and my pussy tingled pleasantly. He kissed me roughly, then with growing passion as I relaxed under the pressure of his lips and stopped fighting him. I could feel my temperature boiling upward and for a moment I thought I was going to pass out. I was nearly breathless when he finally let me up.

"Okay," he said, looking straight into my eyes. "But no push-ups."

The gleaming white-and-silver bathroom was in sharp contrast to the more traditional furnishings of the rest of the suite, with a huge sunken tub and a separate Swiss shower. We turned on the special steam attachment and adjusted the multiple showerheads whose temperature and pressure valves ran the gamut from a gentle flow to pulsating water massage. I closed my eyes and let the water flow over my shoulders as the hot clouds of steam filled the cubicle. Moses soaped my back, then began to massage my tight muscles with a loofah. The rough surface of the sponge made my skin tingle. He moved over my shoulders to the upper part of my chest, pressing his body against me in a pleasantly sensual reminder of his previous lovemaking. The hot steam and the warm flowing water slowed our senses as he took me in his arms. He kissed me, a long lingering kiss. I trembled against him and reached down to fondle his semi-erect organ as his lips moved along my neck, searching out my pulse and the little hollows in my collarbone. Time seemed to stand still as I took Moses' cock and guided it into my aching cunt, arching my back and thrusting my pelvis upward. Moses gripped my buttocks, pulling me against him, and, trusting him not to let me fall, I wrapped my legs around his hips, letting my upper body swing free. I fantasized that we were Siamese twins welded together by our genitals, cock in cunt. I closed my eyes again, concentrating on this single point of contact, on the sensations of his thrusting tool beating against the hard little knob of my clit.

As my excitement increased, Moses speeded up the tempo of his thrusts. I rotated my hips, tightening and relaxing my vaginal muscles to give him maximum pleasure as my own body raced toward orgasm. Then, with a final thrust, Moses exploded inside me, his hot cream filling my cunt. My buttock muscles tightened and with a loud cry I came too, my throbbing cunt milking the last drops of cum from Moses' retreating cock.

We turned off the steam and rotated the showerheads to "massage." The needlelike jets of water brought us back to life as we playfully washed and massaged each other, using loofahs and scented soap. Touching and caressing each part of Moses' body once again awakened my passion and by the time we emerged from the bathroom wrapped in thick heated towels, I was ready for another session between the sheets. I looked at Moses and saw my desire reflected in his eyes.

Wordlessly he dropped his towel to reveal the proof of his readiness, long and full between his legs. I knelt before him and took his swollen offering into my mouth. I let my tongue and lips slide slowly along the steellike shaft as I relaxed my throat muscles and swallowed him to the hilt. I let his cock rest in the warm cavity of my mouth, feeling it tremble against my tongue. I dug my fingers into the firm flesh of his buttocks, then raked my nails slowly downward. He tensed and cried out as the searing pain on his ass and the warm pressure of my mouth on his cock spiraled his senses upward. I wanted to hurt him and make love to him at the same time, to take control and to surrender completely. Sensing my ambivalence, Moses slowly withdrew his cock, then eased it back into my mouth, teasing my senses until I relaxed and opened myself to him. He was once more in control. I was all his. I reached out and cupped his heavy balls in my hand and he moaned softly as I massaged the pliant flesh. My own pussy was heating up and my body began to tremble as I sucked that delicious stalk of flesh. I felt him approach orgasm but with a sudden fierce cry he thrust me away, pushing me back against the thick pile of the carpeting. With one swift motion he thrust his stiff pole deep into my hungry cunt. Towering over me he alternated long thrusting motions with shallow, teasing ones, bringing me to the brink of orgasm again and again while refusing me the ultimate release. I gasped for breath, arching my hips and straining toward him. I wrapped my legs around his waist and ran my hands over the hard muscles of his back and arms. He held his torso suspended above me, using all his strength where our genitals fused together in a dizzying dance of pleasure. Moses' body tensed suddenly, then exploded in orgasm, and jets of hot creamy cum squirted deep inside me, triggering my own mind-blowing climax.

At this point most men would have climbed back into bed, pulled up the covers, and gone to sleep but Moses was an energetic as well as imaginative lover. For the next several hours we tried a number of positions and techniques until, totally exhausted, we fell asleep in each other's arms.

It was midafternoon when I opened my eyes. There was a growing emptiness in my stomach and I realized that I had not eaten since the previous evening. I am a creature of appetites, physical as well as sexual. The feel of Moses' warm naked body against my own stirred my senses, but this time hunger won out.

"Hey GI Joe, wake up," I said, poking him in the ribs.

"Lemme alone, I don't have any more chocolate bars," he grunted, not opening his eyes.

"You don't have any chocolate bars, period," I said grumpily. "And this isn't boot camp. I want a proper breakfast, not K rations, though how we can get the kitchen to send one up at this hour is beyond me."

"Breakfast is no problem," said Moses, struggling to a sitting position and squinting at the clock, "but I'm going to need another shower first."

"Great," I said enthusiastically. "I'll scrub your back."

"No, please, I'm only human. We'll never eat if we get started again. Let me go first, okay? You women take forever in the shower." I was about to devastate him with a snappy comeback to that sexist remark, but he sprang to his feet and bounded into the bathroom before I could say a word.

The Army must train its men to do everything on the run because Moses emerged from the bathroom in just under four minutes. He was still damp from his shower, his dark hair clinging in wet ringlets around his face and his towel slung low enough to display his washboard stomach to my appreciative gaze. I gave a long low wolf whistle and smiled at him suggestively. He flushed slightly. Ha, sexism is only supposed to be for the sexist, I thought wickedly.

"Why don't you shower while I dress and order breakfast?" he said, trying to ignore my appraisal of his half-naked body. "You have about twenty minutes." He sat down on a chair and began to put on his socks.

"See if you can get them to send up something besides Froot Loops and cold toast," I said, heading for the bathroom. "If I'm not out of the shower by dusk, just shove it under the stall door."

I deliberately took my time, hoping to find Moses fuming over congealing eggs, but when I reentered the sitting room an hour later, he was at the front door talking to the very young bellhop who had just delivered our food.

"Just remember what I told you," he said, handing him a bill. "You haven't seen me and you don't know anything. Got that?"

"Yes, sir! Anything to help the government, sir!" the kid stammered. He made a clumsy salute, which Moses smartly returned before closing the door.

"What was all that about?" I asked.

"I told the manager that we were interrogating a spy up here and that it would be a great service to national security if the hotel could send up some breakfast, as we had worked right through the night."

"That's the silliest thing I ever heard. The suite's in my name. The manager showed me the rooms himself and I had him phone you at your office to say I'd be late for our appointment."

"That's what made him believe me when I told him you were a front," said Moses complacently. "I ordered breakfast for three. Judging by your appetite at dinner last night, I thought an extra portion wouldn't be overdoing it."

"How can you tell such outrageous lies?" I scolded.

"It'll give the staff something to talk about for the rest of the afternoon," he shrugged, "and it got us a special breakfast at three in the afternoon."

"I was hoping to stay here a few more days," I sighed, peering under the covers of the breakfast tray, "but I'm too hungry to complain."

It was a first-class breakfast. There was orange juice, eggs Benedict with a side order of asparagus, soft rolls, fresh fruit salad in champagne, and coffee with hot instead of cold milk in the pitcher. We spent the next half hour concentrating on the serious business of staving off impending starvation, dividing the third portion between us. Things slowed down around the fruit salad and second cup of coffee, and we sat back with satisfied looks on our faces.

"I do like a woman who enjoys her food," said Moses, smiling across at me. "You like to eat, you like to make love, and you are the most beautiful and most sensual woman I have ever met."

"You're not so bad between the sheets yourself," I said. It was not an exaggeration. Moses Landon was a solid ten in sexual technique. He also had a life-style that perfectly matched my own. Princess Lyapunov had been right. I was very much attracted to him.

"I'd like to see you again," he said, looking at me in a way that made me flush. "May I call you when I get back from Russia?"

I frowned slightly. I'm an extremely self-centered, hedonistic woman. I don't like to defer my pleasures and I didn't like the idea of not seeing Moses again for several weeks while he carried out some idiotic government mission.

"Why don't you get someone else to go?" I said petulantly. "Pull rank. You must have some subordinate with masochistic tendencies who would like to further the cause of democracy and earn your undying gratitude at the same time."

"I'm afraid not," Moses said. "I was the natural choice. My mother was from Kiev and I learned Russian at home. I also visited Moscow several times as a tourist in my student days, which gives me a working knowledge of the city. But even if I wanted to back out, I couldn't. The Army isn't like private industry; I have to follow orders."

"What exactly is the plan for smuggling the Princess' nephew out of Russia?" I asked.

"What's the difference? You've wisely decided not to participate."

"I'm going to miss you," I said, "and I'd just like to know what you'll be doing. It would make you seem less far away if I could picture you going through the days while I wait."

"Flattery will get you anything," he laughed. "Can I trust you to keep your mouth shut?"

"I'm the sphinx."

"Well, it's a pretty simple plan," he said, pouring himself another cup of coffee and settling back in his chair. "Things have loosened up considerably since the depths of the Cold War, and despite Reagan, both our country and the Soviets continue to make at least a token effort to communicate, especially in the area of cultural exchange. As it happens there's a group of American journalists, representing well-known newspapers and magazines, traveling to Moscow to participate in a Soviet-American conference on the media. You know, a few of our journalists and a few of theirs sit around and get drunk and trade views about what it's like to be a working newsman in each country. It's as much a social event as anything else. Gives some working stiffs a chance to escape their desks and spouses for a few days and soak up some culture. There'll be a great deal of sightseeing, trips to the ballet, that sort of thing. I'll travel with the group, carrying a phony passport listing me as a newspaper reporter. According to the itinerary, there's a big farewell banquet scheduled for the last night. Kabalevsky will arrange to be at that affair, disguised as a waiter. At the last minute we will switch places, probably as we leave to board the bus.''

"Won't they notice the switch?" I asked.

"The bus will go directly from the banquet to the airport to catch a night flight back to Paris, which is the first leg of the journey. It will be dark and late and hopefully everyone will be drunk. Kabalevsky's absence will not be noticed until he fails to show up for work the next day. By the time they figure out what's happened, he'll be safely in Washington.''

"What happens to you?"

"Well, after the bus leaves, I sneak out of the banquet hall and make my way to the American Embassy. I will be hidden there until the fireworks die down and then be smuggled out of the country.''

"What if you're caught making the switch or picked up on the way to the Embassy?"

"Then the Americans deny they ever heard of me, and I end my days in a gulag in Siberia.''

"Makes you sound pretty expendable," I said.

"I guess I am. That's the name of this game. But I have a better than average shot at it. My Russian's good, not textbook stuff, and I look like my mother. I could pass as a Soviet citizen if I were stopped or if I needed to ask directions.''

"I thought you said this assignment wasn't dangerous?"

"For you, not me. You would have also traveled with the group, using your own passport and your credentials as the publisher of *World* magazine. You would have worn expensive clothing, which you obviously own, and a great deal of jewelry that would look as close to Kabalevsky's as the paste artists could manage. At some time during the stay, the fake jewels would be exchanged for the real ones and you would simply carry them out. You would not be personally involved in the switch and there would be no reason for the Russians to suspect that the jewels weren't actually yours, since you would have been wearing various pieces all week. It's just . . . well . . ."

"Well what?"

"Listen, Christina, even if there were no jewels, if you were just an ordinary journalist like the rest, this trip isn't for you. You're a wealthy, pampered woman, used to the best of everything. Just look at this hotel room." He waved his hand to indicate my suite. "The Russian idea of deluxe is a room the size of your closet and a hot shower, if you're lucky. The heating is sporadic, the beds are lumpy, and the blankets are scratchy. And it's cold there. This is February, not July. The people can be very warm when you meet them as individuals, but they lack Western sophistication and social graces. Service in hotels and restaurants is haphazard and you wouldn't be treated with the special deference you're used to. A silly old woman and her pile of rocks are not worth the sacrifice of either your time or your creature comforts. Believe me, I think you show remarkable good sense in refusing."

I picked at the remains of the fruit salad as I considered his remarks. I had to admit that the factors Moses had just ticked off had crossed my mind a number of times since the Princess first proposed that I undertake the mission. In fact, they were the very reasons I didn't want to go. However, having Moses agree in his smug, patronizing way that being spoiled and self-centered was acceptable, even expected, because I was a woman made me angry. He clearly didn't think I could handle the assignment and this, perversely enough, caused me to suddenly change my mind. Even as a child I had resented being told that others could do things I couldn't. When I was fourteen years old I had driven my aunt's station wagon through the side of our neighbor's house in an effort to prove I was old enough and capable enough to handle a car.

"I'm not solely concerned with my physical comfort," I said defensively.

"You could have fooled me," he shrugged. "Your shower has a steam attachment. There is a heated rack to warm the bath towels, your bed sheets are one hundred percent cotton, and your comforters pure down. The rooms have three-inch-thick carpeting to cushion your feet and double-paned thermal windows to keep the temperature at a perfect seventy-two degrees. Despite the fact that there's eight inches of snow on the ground and the wind-chill factor makes it minus seventeen degrees, you are wearing a thin silk robe that barely conceals your tan.

"I'm not complaining, you understand. When I'm shivering in some badly heated Russian hotel room, it will give me great pleasure to think of you snuggled under piles of down quilts, eating Godiva chocolates, and reading the latest French fashion magazines."

"Listen, Colonel Smartass," I snapped, "I'm as rugged and stoic as any woman, or any man for that matter. I probably have pioneer blood somewhere in my veins. And just to prove you wrong, I'm going to accept that assignment. I'll show you who's a cream puff."

"I didn't say you were a cream puff, Christina," he said, looking worried, "but once we're actually in Russia I'll have little time to listen to your complaints about the lumpy beds or warm your cold hands or even be romantic. I'm going to have to keep a very low profile if my exchange with Kabalevsky is to go unnoticed."

"I can take care of myself," I assured him haughtily. "We pioneer women are used to minor hardships."

"This isn't a Wild West soap opera . . ."

"Forget it, I'm coming along. The Pentagon has okayed this idea so you have no choice but to take me."

He sat back and glowered at me. I glared back. I was tempted to stick my tongue out at him but refrained. We pioneer women have great personal dignity.

Then a triumphant smile broke out on his face.

"You don't speak Russian," he crowed. "All of the journalists on this cultural-exchange junket have learned some conversational Russian. It was required for the trip. An interpreter will be used for the actual conferences, but it was felt that some ability to exchange social pleasantries over dinner was important. If you can't speak for the entire week you'll stand out like a sore thumb. It might put you in danger if anything were suspected.''

"I speak French and Italian fluently and a smattering of at least a dozen other languages, including Hindustani," I boasted.

"We're not going to India."

"I can learn Russian. I'm a natural linguist."

"You're a cunning linguist," he retorted but I ignored his pun.

"It's the beginning of a new college term," I continued. "You find me a course in some local college and I'll bet you that after a few sessions of learning the accent and some nights with the old textbook, I'll speak the language as well as anyone else in the group."

"It isn't that easy," he laughed. "Russian is a difficult language and we leave for the Soviet Union in less than two weeks. But if you want to fall on your face, that's okay with me. It will give me a viable excuse to leave you behind."

"You just find me a course," I told him, "and reserve a place for me on that junket. I'm going to dent that male chauvinist armor you wear if it's the last thing I do. By the time this mission is completed, you'll be grateful to have had me along."

CHAPTER SEVEN

The next afternoon a messenger dropped off a bulky package at my hotel. Inside was a note from Moses, written in his firm, neat hand, informing me that Professor Mylar Klementsky of Strachey University had agreed to allow me to sit in on the first few sessions of his freshman Russian course. Demonstrating what I felt was an uncharacteristically puckish sense of humor, the package also contained a gray Strachey U. sweatshirt and a copy of their freshman handbook, along with careful instructions on how to reach the campus.

I thumbed through the handbook while I was eating breakfast on the morning of my first class. The University was located on a spacious campus, just over an hour's drive from Washington. It was a small private college, named after the biographer Lytton Strachey, who was much in vogue at the time the college was founded. The school offered degrees in foreign-language studies, political science, and prelaw, all useful for students who hoped to enter some branch of the government foreign service. They had a hockey team that was notorious for its inability to win a game, and the numerous fraternities and sororities attested to an active campus social life.

I had never gone to college, having started work when I was seventeen, but I feel that life is the best teacher and that my experiences have taught me far more than any formalized curriculum could have. Still, I looked forward to the next few weeks. It would be a pleasant change from my frenetic, pleasure-centered existence, a time to recapture the wide-eyed innocence of my adolescence.

I wanted to fit in with the rest of the students and decided to forgo my usual French designer clothing. I dressed in layers: Strachey U. sweatshirt and jeans over silk long johns to keep out the cold, a navy-and-white down vest and yellow waterproof hiking boots. When I surveyed the result in my mirror, I was satisfied that I could easily pass for a young college student.

Washington was experiencing a week of unseasonably pleasant weather for early February. The morning air was clear and the temperature a balmy thirty-eight degrees as I stepped into the rented car that was waiting for me just outside the hotel. In keeping with my college-freshman image I had called Rent-A-Heap instead of my usual executive car-rental service and the result was a light blue 1963 Chevrolet four-door sedan with a stick shift, cracked brown vinyl upholstery, and a fox tail tied to the antenna.

Strachey University was a jumble of mismatched buildings, reflecting no single style or taste, connected by stretches of snow-patched lawns and winding tree-lined walks. Clusters of chattering young people crowded the paths, swinging overfilled book bags and consuming hot dogs, slices of pizza, and cans of soda and beer. I approached a group of young men who were enjoying a communal joint, and they stepped back to include me in their circle.

"Excuse me," I said, directing my remarks to a tall blond with a square jaw and an impressive wedge-shaped torso. "Can you tell me how to get to Skivvar Hall?"

"I sure can," he said, passing me the joint. "In fact, this is your lucky day. We were all just going to Skivvar Hall ourselves."

"Terrific, lead the way," I said, inhaling deeply on the joint.

"Are you new on campus?" he asked.

"I'm just here for a little remedial work on my Russian," I

said. "I'll be sitting in on Professor Klementsky's class for a few sessions. My name is Christina van Bell."

"Say, that's a coincidence," he laughed. "We're all in Klementsky's class too. I'm Carl Grey, but everyone calls me Chuck. This," he said, introducing the others, "is Animal, Lumpy, and Groundhog. We're all Juniors."

"I thought Professor Klementsky's class was for Freshmen," I said.

"We all flunked the first time around," laughed the rotund young man named Lumpy, "even Groundhog here and he's our best student."

"You see," Chuck explained, "we're all brothers in Kappa Delta Pi. We had a pretty full social season last term and we sort of neglected our schoolwork. Our float would have won first prize at the winter carnival if the Dean wasn't such a tight-ass."

"He said it was pornographic," growled Animal. "Here's a photo. Would you call that pornographic?"

I studied the small color snapshot of an impressive ice sculpture depicting, rather graphically, an uncommon carnal experience.

"I'd say it was a prizewinner for sure," I assured him.

We had now arrived at Skivvar Hall, and the frat brothers led the way to Professor Klementsky's classroom on the third floor. It is customary for college students to sit as far away from the professor as possible on the theory that this will prevent their being called on during class, but unfortunately these coveted seats were already taken and we were forced to take seats near the front. Professor Klementsky arrived a few moments later. He was a large, round-shouldered man with thinning white hair and rimless spectacles. His rumpled brown suit was patched at the elbows and covered with a dusting of white chalk. He placed his belongings on the desk at the front of the room, picked out his lecture notes, and walked to the lectern. He surveyed the class with a wary, suspicious glare.

"Good morning, my eager young minds," he boomed, looking over the student roster. "Miss van Bell, are you with us?"

"Here, Professor," I said, raising my hand.

"Your situation was explained to me by Colonel Landon," he said, favoring me with a brief glance. "If you need any extra help while you are with us, please let me know." He looked down again at the list. "Bless me, do I see Mr. Grey and his traveling circus here?" He scowled at the fraternity brothers, who squirmed nervously. "I hope your efforts this term will be more rewarding than last year's, gentlemen," he rasped. "Perhaps you can learn to conjugate a few verbs before favoring us with more frozen interpretations of the Kama Sutra."

"We regret our lack of concentration, Professor," Chuck piped up. "Our artistic endeavors last term distracted us from our studies."

"Leonardo da Vinci engaged in artistic endeavors," the Professor said mildly. "You four engaged in misdemeanors." He took a deep breath, letting it out through his nose with a weary wheeze. "Now then, my Slavic baboons, let's start with a little elementary vocabulary, shall we? Some words people like you can use such as: *tyoormah*, the prison, and *soodyah*, the judge."

We spent some time working on a basic vocabulary list, then listened to an explanation of Russian grammar and sentence structure. I had not exaggerated when I boasted to Moses that I was a natural linguist and I quickly assimilated the various rules.

"Now then," the Professor said finally, "I think we should make an attempt at a bit of conversation." There was an anguished groan from the members of the class. "I realize that simple conversation is a daunting prospect for you, even in English," the Professor sighed. "However, onward and upward is the motto here at Camp Samovar. Miss van Bell, Mr. Bonk, step up here, please."

Animal, blushing furiously, stumbled to the front of the room while his mates chuckled gleefully. He was a huge, bulky youngster with very wide shoulders and a short, thick neck. He stood rigidly, shifting his weight from one foot to the other in a nervous little dance. I gave him an encouraging smile and he grinned back, obviously pleased that I was sharing his agony.

"You've both met at a party," the Professor said, setting

the scene. "You'll conduct a typical first conversation, exchanging pleasantries and so forth, and I will make corrections and translate your talk into English." He nodded, indicating that we should proceed.

"*Zdrahstvooite,*" I said, smiling.

"Hello," the Professor translated.

"*Mozh na preeglaseet vas trantsavaht?*" Animal asked.

"May I have the pleasure of this dance?" the Professor translated, nodding his approval.

"*Nyet, va khachoo sest, tak kak ya nenmo'ga oostahl,*" I said.

"No, I wish to sit down as I am rather tired."

"*Vy predpacheetah'yete blandee'nak ee'lee bryoone'tak?*" I asked.

"Do you prefer blondes or brunettes?" the Professor said, obviously somewhat startled at the turn the conversation had taken.

"*Ya zhenah't,*" Animal protested.

"Um," the Professor swallowed, "I am a married man."

"*Kakee'ye eenfektseeo'nny ye bale'znee vy pereneslee?*" I asked innocently.

The Professor's face reddened. "I hardly think that a discussion of this gentleman's infectious diseases is appropriate for party talk," he scolded.

"Just checking," I said, smiling sweetly as the class hooted with laughter.

"I can see that this is going to be another term to remember," the Professor sighed. "And though it breaks my heart to say it, as much as I've enjoyed our little sojourn into the land of bilingual carnality, our time is up for today. I would suggest that you review your vocabulary lists, my eager little linguists, for I may be tempted to spring a pop quiz on you." There was a moan of pain from the back of the class and the Professor dismissed the assembly with a mute wave of his hand.

As the students rushed out of the class, Chuck and Animal stopped to speak to me.

"Listen, Christina," said Chuck, "we're having open house at the fraternity tonight. Why don't you join us? There'll be plenty of beer, and Animal's girlfriend makes a great dip with instant onion soup mix.''

I repressed a slight shudder.

"You have the makings of a first-class Kappa Delta Pi," Animal urged. "All the prettiest girls on campus come to our parties. You'll have a terrific time, I promise."

"Perhaps I will," I said noncommittally. "I've never been to a fraternity party. It might be fun."

"Great!" said Chuck. "We'll see you about nine. Our house is right on Fraternity Row. It's the one with the purple door."

The frat brothers left the room and I confronted a morose-looking Professor Klementsky.

"I'm sorry about that exercise," I told him. "I don't know what got into me."

"At least your accent was correct. You have a good ear, Miss van Bell. Which is more than I can say for those lurching members of the Brotherhood of Beer-Barrel Drainers or whatever it is they call themselves."

"Come on, Professor," I chided. "All kids act up a bit. I'm sure their little club is perfectly harmless."

"That's what they said about the Hitler Jungvolk. Still, you have a point. When I was a student I belonged to a group called the Future Linguists of America." He sighed nostalgically. "And let me tell you, we were no bunch of stuffed shirts. No indeed, we were quite a bunch of hell-raisers. We were known all over the campus. I remember one Halloween we scribbled Latin graffiti on the walls of the Common."

"Sounds simply riotous," I said, picking up my books and walking beside him to the front steps of the building.

"Some condemned us as wicked pranksters," he said, waving a finger at me, "but I assure you, Miss van Bell, graffiti though it may have been, our Latin grammar was impeccable!"

I smiled and waved at him as I left.

It was a beautiful afternoon and I wandered around the campus noting the curious and unaesthetic mixture of architectural styles. Gothic, neoclassic, and stark modern buildings stood beside each other, a testimony, the freshman handbook pointed out, of the University's dedication to the individual creative spirit. As I crossed the athletic field, a long low metal building painted in the school colors attracted my attention. I opened the door and peered inside. There was a huge ice rink, and the school's infamous hockey team, the Whippets, were stumbling through another practice session. I always enjoy watching young men with good bodies jump all over each other, so I took a seat on the sideline bench next to an old man with a bulbous red nose and a grizzled, weather-beaten face. He was wearing a faded baseball cap and a grimy sweater with the word "COACH" in block letters on the front. He was watching the practice with a look of deep depression on his face.

"That's a fine-looking team, coach," I said, admiring the narrow waist and well-formed buns of a blond youngster who seemed to be having difficulty managing his stick and his skates at the same time. The old man turned slowly and squinted at me with an expression similar to the one the captain of the Titanic might have had just before the iceberg hit.

"How long have you been blind?" he rasped. "That's the biggest collection of stumblebums and assholes ever assembled on one rink! We haven't had a winner since I started coaching here, and that was before Roosevelt was president."

"You mustn't lose hope," I said optimistically. "This might just be your year."

"Next year will be my year," he said. "Next year will be my year 'cause next year I can retire. I'm going to get the hell out of this place, go fishing in Florida, and forget that I ever had anything to do with this disaster." He stood up and cupped his hands to his mouth. "Flotsky, for cryin' out loud, if you can't move the puck, at least skate aside and leave it for someone who can!" He sighed and sat down again. "On some campuses the coach is a revered and beloved figure," he muttered. "He brings honor and glory to the name of the university. He helps young men make the transition from childhood to manhood by teaching them the value of good clean competition. How the hell can I do that when those idiots can't even put one foot in front of the other without tripping? Do you realize," he snapped, pointing a finger at my nose, "that I have never, ever, been interviewed on television? Other teams go to tournaments and their coaches are all over the damn networks. I haven't even been interviewed by the damn college newspaper since the end of the Korean War!"

"It must be very frustrating," I said sympathetically.

"Look at that!" he said, jumping to his feet again. "O'Brien, for Pete's sake, keep your hands off that guy's ass! There will be no ass patting on this team until you learn to make a goal. I've warned you guys about that! You have to earn your perversions!" He shook his head sadly. "Kids have no respect for tradition these days," he growled.

By this time I was getting hungry so I said my farewells and made my way back to the parking lot to retrieve my car. I considered giving Moses a call, then remembered he had a late meeting. Washington is not a town noted for its nightlife, so I decided to have dinner, then check out the frat party before returning to my hotel.

It was after nine o'clock when I returned to the campus, and I was grateful for my silk underwear as the temperature had gotten considerably colder. It was rush night on Fraternity Row, a social event whose purpose was to allow new students to compare various sororities and fraternities before making their bids to join. Each fraternity catered to a particular social class or specialized interest group. There was a fraternity for the wealthy scions of the founding fathers, a fraternity for jocks, and a fraternity for students with anarchistic political views. Birds of a feather flock together seemed to be the operative theory here.

As far as I could tell, Kappa Delta Pi catered to the slob contingent.

In contrast to the beautifully kept houses and lawns maintained by the other fraternities, the Kappa Delta Pi house was a sagging three-story affair of indeterminate color. The lawn was littered with empty beer cans and a red neon outline of a pair of lips winked grotesquely from a second-story balcony. Through the broken porch window, I could hear the laughter and shouts of the celebrants rising over the blare of a stereo that was heavy on the bass. I think the song was that college-kid anthem "Louie Louie," though I seem to remember the song having clean lyrics.

I picked my way through the vestibule into the large living room. It was furnished in early Salvation Army, with plenty of flickering candles, disco lights, emergency flares, and other unusual sources of illumination. A makeshift table composed of two sawhorses and a couple of wooden planks held a punch bowl that was filled with a purplish liquid cooled by dry ice which gave off clouds of dense, wet fog. There were plates of soggy crackers and several unidentifiable dips. I tried a Wheat Thin and some green dip but decided to find something more recognizable to drink.

I spotted Chuck behind a painted wooden bar, hammering a tap into a fresh keg of beer, and made my way over to greet him.

"Far out, you made it!" he exulted. "Have a beer."

"Seems you've drawn quite a crowd," I noted, accepting a mug of dark, vile-smelling beer.

"Mostly brothers and their dates," Chuck said. "But there's a few new prospects. You can spot 'em easily. There's something squeaky clean about a new student, as if his mother was still doing his laundry on weekends."

"I like young men," I said, taking a cautious sip of my beer. "I think I'll have a look around."

"We have a rec room downstairs with a regulation pool table. It's the only one on campus. Don't let the brothers sucker you into anything, though. Most of 'em are excellent players."

"I'll remember that," I nodded. I made my way through the kitchen, where five young men were doing something indescribable with six cucumbers and a food processor and walked down the backstairs to the basement.

The rec room amply described the condition of the furnishings, and it included a dart board with a picture of the president of the college, a pinball machine with the serial numbers filed off, and a pool table which, as I arrived, was the center of attention for the assembled crowd. Animal, in a state of advanced inebriation, was giving a demonstration of trick shots to an admiring audience.

"Christina!" he boomed, wrapping his arm around my shoulders. "Hey, everyone, this is Christina van Bell! She's in my class with that twink Klementsky!"

"Is your pool as good as your Russian?" I teased.

"Better," he bragged. "You wanna play? I'll go real easy on you 'cause you're a girl."

I seemed to be a target for sexist remarks these days, but I flashed him a bright innocent smile. "Oooo, do you think a dumb little bunny like me could learn to play a game like this?" I squealed in a high-pitched voice.

"If I teach you, you'll be a champ," Animal boasted. "Better than any other girl." Sarcasm was obviously wasted on him.

"How does it work?" I asked, staring with exaggerated blankness at the stick.

"The object of pool is to hit the colored balls into the pockets without sinking the white ball," Animal explained. "Just hit that white one against óne of the colored ones and try to drop it in a pocket. You have to say what ball you're trying to sink, though. You can't just aim wildly and hope you hit something."

I walked casually around the table, studying the layout. "Nine ball in the side pocket," I announced.

"I don't think you can make that shot," Animal protested. "That nine ball is packed behind three other balls, and the pocket's too far away."

"Could you do it?"

"Maybe. But it's no shot for a beginner."

"I'll just try it," I said. "Red's my lucky color." I let him chalk my stick, then aimed and carefully made my shot. The cue ball bounced off the six, into the cushion, then curved gently around the three blocking balls, nudging the nine at just the right angle to enable it to roll, with millimeters to spare, past the other balls and across the table where it plopped into the pocket.

Animal's mouth dropped open as the onlookers roared their

approval. I handed him his cue stick and pulled the joint he was smoking out of his mouth. I sucked half of it into my lungs and dropped the butt into his beer.

"You've played this game before," he said accusingly.

"When it comes to balls, I'm an expert," I said. "I may not have any but I know how to play 'em." I looked pointedly at the bulge in his pants, then turned and sauntered away.

I stopped in the kitchen for another beer and a joint, then made my way past a group engaged in a beer-spitting contest and went up to the second floor. Between the beer and the hash, I was beginning to feel pretty good. I was also beginning to feel horny, a typical reaction to these indulgences. I wandered around the floor, peering into some of the rooms at the young couples piled on beds and squeezed into dark corners. It brought back memories of the early gropings of my own youth, of a tow-haired boy sprawled on top of me, fumbling with the fastening of my bra. Then as if in flashback, I saw the same shock of flax-colored hair through the half-open door of the next room. I pushed open the door to get a better look and the young man turned toward me.

"Pardon me," I said. "I didn't know this room was taken."

"S'okay," he assured me, flushing slightly. "You can come in. No problem."

"You're a pal," I smiled, crossing the room and flopping onto the bed next to him. "I'm so stoned, I don't think I can stand up much longer. My name's Christina."

"Mine's Rick," he mumbled, flushing even more deeply. He glanced at me, then down at his feet, twisting his fingers together nervously. I turned and studied him in the half-light. He was very fair with alabaster skin and fine, sensitive features. His lashes and eyebrows were the same pale wheat color as his hair, and his eyes were hazel, flecked with gold. He had on new black jeans and a clean plaid shirt that smelled faintly of detergent. I smiled, remembering Chuck's comment about new students, and Rick smiled shyly back.

"It's a great party, Rick," I said, companionably offering him my half-empty beer can. "Why aren't you downstairs with the rest of the crowd?"

"I'm not a very good dancer . . . and I don't care for pool or darts."

"There are other activities," I said, waving my hand in the direction of the other bedrooms.

"I've given up women," he said defensively.

"Oh?"

"I'm not gay, you understand. It's just that . . . well . . ."

"You haven't met the right one," I said helpfully.

"I haven't met anyone," he said sadly. "Oh, I know I'm as good-looking as the next guy and I see the way girls stare at me, but I'm eighteen and . . ."

"You've never slept with a woman," I finished softly.

He nodded miserably.

"It's nothing to be ashamed of," I told him. "There's a first time for everybody. All you need is someone to show you the ropes."

"If you're volunteering, I would like that more than anything," he said with a sly trace of humor.

"I'll just close the door then," I said, slipping off the bed and doing as I said, "so we can be more comfortable." I unlaced my heavy hiking boots and took off my socks, then pulled my sweatshirt over my head. I heard the sharp intake of Rick's breath as, divested of the loose-fitting garment, the lush mounds of my breasts became visible through the thin silk of my body suit. I unfastened the belt on my jeans and slowly unzipped the fly front. I peeled the tight pants over my hips and pushed them along my thighs, making the most of this sensuous striptease. My beige silk thermals fit like a second skin, revealing the curves of my body and hinting at more intimate treasures.

Rick had removed his shoes and socks but had stopped there, mesmerized by my performance. I moved toward him now and, urging him back against the pillows, began to loosen the buttons on his shirt. My hair brushed his lips as I bent over him and he caught the shimmering waves, then lifted my head with his hands so that we faced each other.

I smiled reassuringly, then leaned forward and gently pressed my lips to his. He trembled slightly and I deepened the kiss, my tongue exploring the inner recesses of his mouth. The bed was narrow and I stretched out on top of him, pressing my body against his. There is a pleasure in petting—there's no better word for it—that belongs to early sexual discovery. As we wriggled half-clothed against each other, I pretended that for me, too, this was the first time. I sighed and moaned, grinding my pussy against the hard bulge in his jeans. His shirt was open and when his hands fumbled with my thermal top, I helped him pull it over my head. His skin was warm against my own, but his rough fondling of my breasts made me wince.

"They're not made of rubber," I whispered gently. "You have to stroke, not squeeze them." He followed my directions, first brushing his fingers lightly over my ripe mounds, then teasing the nipples with his tongue. My skin tingled pleasurably, sending currents of excitement to my hot little twat. I reached down to unfasten his pants, drawing his throbbing pink erection from his shorts. He had an adolescent's lean body but his cock was man-size and, straddling his legs, I crouched hungrily over it.

I put my lips over the helmetlike head, then took him comfortably into the warm pool of my mouth. I began to suck him slowly, hugging his shaft with my mouth and working his jeans and shorts over his hips so that they pinned his thighs. Thus further restrained, he was at my mercy and my flicking tongue tip teased the underside of his glans, then traced the swollen vein on the underside of his shaft. I could feel his body trembling as I worked and I had to stop several times to prevent his ejaculating prematurely.

I took his balls in my hands and began to lick his scrotum like a mother cat with a newborn kitten. His breathing quickened as I worked, his body squirming beneath me.

"Relax," I whispered. "This is just the appetizer." He took a deep breath and lay still, gazing at me in an erotic trance. Totally in control, I returned to the head of his prick, running my tongue around the small aperture, then inserting it in the tiny hole. Rick gasped and cried out and I quickly swallowed him again, gulping the entire length of his magnificent erection until my nose nudged his pubic hair. I relaxed my throat muscles, deep-throating his virgin cock and enjoying every minute of it. I was crouched over him, fanny wiggling in the air. I felt his hands on the waistband of my silk long johns, and he stripped the material to expose my burning buns. He ran his hands over my half-moons, inserting a finger tentatively into my sopping cunt. My stomach muscles tightened convulsively and my body responded as if it had been electrified.

"I want your beautiful hot cock in my pussy," I said hoarsely. "I want you to shoot your cream into my aching cunt."

He was ready now. We tore at the remainder of our clothing, then I lay back against the pillows, spreading my legs and parting my pussy lips invitingly. Rick stretched out between my thighs and, sensing a slight hesitation, I guided his now massive cock into the entrance of my slippery pussy. I sighed lustily as he entered me, closing my eyes and thrusting my pelvis upward.

He began to move, a bit awkwardly at first, then with growing confidence. Our foreplay had eased his shyness and I let him take the lead, adjusting my body to his rhythm. I wrapped my legs around his hips and pulled his head down to mine. Covering his face with kisses as we fucked distracted him just enough to increase his staying power without verbal instruction, and by this and other such tricks I made him feel like an experienced Don Juan and brought my own senses to fever pitch.

"That feels so-o-o good," I crooned. "Fuck me harder, darling. I want to feel your cock against my clit." My nipples tingled and my cunt throbbed. I was a racehorse and Rick the jockey on a winning ride to fulfillment. I did not hold back or distract him again. As he burst into orgasm I let go too, transported by the mutual feelings we had created.

We lay side by side on the narrow bed. Rick, no longer shy, looked at my naked body as if committing it to memory.

"You're perfect," he whispered, "like one of those models in the *Playboy* centerfolds." Like many young men his walls were papered with airbrushed beauties in various erotic poses. "I used to fantasize about fucking them," he continued, "but it doesn't compare to the real thing."

"Which is your favorite?" I asked.

"Monique," he replied promptly, pointing to a blond beauty in a lilac lace bra and panties bent over the foot of a satin-covered bed. Her panties were pulled down to her thighs so that her beautifully rounded buttocks were totally exposed. She was looking over her shoulder invitingly. "She has the greatest body. She really turns me on. I have only to look at that picture to get a hard-on."

"What do you fantasize when you masturbate?" I asked softly.

"I . . ." He hesitated, flushing slightly.

"There's nothing to be ashamed of," I told him. "Everybody has fantasies. They're an important part of sex and by sharing them sexual partners can get to know each other better."

"I fantasize about Monique," said Rick, shyly avoiding my gaze. "I've always been an ass man. I think about . . ."

"About fondling a woman's ass," I said, finishing his sentence. He nodded. "I would like it if you touched mine," I continued. "Shall I pretend to be Monique?"

"Don't pretend to be anyone," he said softly. "You're the woman I want."

We were both totally naked. Placing a pillow on the edge of the bed to heighten my fanny, I spread my legs and bent over, resting my head on the mattress. Rick took full advantage of my invitation to act out his fantasy. He began to stroke and squeeze my buttocks, kneeling behind me and rubbing his cheek against the satin of my skin. As my bottom warmed to his touch, he used his lips and tongue and teeth in a way that raised goose bumps on my fleshy posterior. There was no need of instruction or guidance, for fantasy is a natural teacher. Taking one cheek in each hand, he parted my half-moons just a bit, tracing the dark furrow with the tip of his tongue. My stomach muscles tightened and my body trembled as he plunged deeper and deeper, lapping up and down.

I cried out as his tongue tip pushed at the tiny pink hole of my anus and I felt a sticky wetness between my legs. Rick stood and replaced his tongue with his finger, pushing gently at my opening as if to test its capacity to accommodate him. I could feel his shaft, long and hard, against the back of my thigh, and the thought of it reaming my rear end made me hot with desire. I took a wider stance and thrust my fanny higher like a cat in heat. I parted my ass cheeks with my own hands, begging him to take me anally. He positioned himself between my thighs and guided his cock to the entrance of my tiny love-hole. My hands scrabbled at the sheets and I gave a low moan, pushing back as he penetrated my tight canal. While Rick guided his cock, his hands on my hipbones, I reached beneath myself, easing my fingers into my dripping cunt. As his prick glided in and out between the fleshy cheeks of my ass, my fingers strummed my clit until my legs were trembling and my body was filmed with sweat.

Rick climaxed with a roar, pumping warm jets of cream into my clasping anus and I kneaded my pussy wildly, climaxing almost immediately.

Exhausted and breathless, we stretched out on the narrow bed, letting our senses return to normal. It had been a night of sexual discovery for Rick, and for me too, for no two men are ever exactly alike. I hoped that Rick would make love to many women from now on, but first experiences are special and I hoped, also, that he would not forget me.

CHAPTER EIGHT

I closed my eyes and gripped the arms of my seat as the plane struggled to rise above the stormy skies that had dropped an unexpected eight inches of snow on the nation's capital. Our flight had been delayed for well over three hours, but at last the runway had been cleared and we were allowed to take off.

I usually make the transatlantic crossing in the first-class cabin of the Concorde, but this trip was rather less extravagant. I was crammed three across in the tourist section of a 707 surrounded by a group of cranky, hungry journalists bawling for their prelunch martinis.

Moses was sitting to my right. I had barely recognized him in his civilian clothes, nondescript in color and loose-fitting to obscure the trim, fit lines of his body. At my briefing in his office at the Pentagon he had stressed the fact that, as the success of the mission depended on the other members of our group not noticing his switch with Kabalevsky on the return flight, it would be necessary for him to keep a low profile during our stay in the Soviet Union. He had kept apart from the group during the delay at the airport and was now slumped in his seat, his face buried in his newspaper. He wasn't reading, though. He hadn't turned a page in ten minutes. I looked at him over a corner of the paper, and he smiled and gave me a sly wink. There was an amused twinkle in his eye, and I knew he was waiting for me to complain about the somewhat spartan conditions under which we were flying. He had been visibly disappointed when I had shown up at his office speaking Russian like a native after a week at Strachey University, and he had made one last attempt to dissuade me from going along. He had played up the lack of creature comforts we could expect in a melodramatic tone with grand sweeping gestures, and it was only my stubborn determination to win his approval in some area other than sexual expertise that kept me from throwing in the towel. So here I was on the economy flight to Paris, a jarringly noisy sardine can with two disinterested stewardesses and a cash bar. The trip, which was the first leg of our journey to Moscow, would take eleven hours, including a three-hour delay at the airport, but I was determined to keep my peace and not let him gloat later about how I had cracked after less than an hour into our assignment.

Most of the other twenty-four members of our party seemed to be enjoying themselves. Freed of the pressures of deadlines and editors, unshackled from their spouses, children, and mortgage payments, they were relaxing and getting into a holiday mood, aided by frequent refills from the bar. The only person besides Landon who didn't seem inclined to join the festivities was the representative from one of our country's most influential papers, the New York *Institution*. A small bald man with rimless eyeglasses, he was seated behind me and to the left, and was spending his time fretting over the timetable.

"A most regrettable delay," he muttered, scanning the paper in his hands. He consulted his wristwatch and made some hasty calculations on his air-sickness bag with his pen. "Even with a tail wind, we shall miss our connecting flight to Moscow."

"I'm for that," said the man on my left. "It'll give us a chance to stretch our legs and get a decent meal and a good night's sleep, courtesy of Air France."

"We could hit the town and have some fun," I said. "It will be only nine P.M. New York time when we land, much too early to turn in."

"You're right," he said enthusiastically. "I haven't seen

Paris since I covered the peace talks. My name is Dave Stackhouse, political correspondent, *Texas Daily*."

"Christina van Bell, *World* magazine," I said, shaking hands. I accepted his offer of a drink and we settled comfortably back in our seats.

"This is my third cultural-exchange junket to Russia," he said, handing me a plastic cup of wine. "Have you ever been on one of these before?"

I shook my head. "No, this is my first time. What usually happens?"

"A lot of posing and backslapping, mostly," he sighed. "We sit with the Russians and we all pretend that we're brother journalists, interested in truth and justice and so forth. In reality, we think the Russian journalists are a bunch of liars and dupes for the slave masters in the Kremlin, and they think we're liars and dupes for the capitalists who own the papers. We tour their newsrooms and national monuments and cultural sights, and they make sure we never see anything they don't want us to see. Then we have a few seminars where we extol the virtues of a free press and they tell us what a glorious institution *Pravda* is, and we swap phony stories about working conditions."

"Doesn't sound very productive," I said.

"All window dressing," he assured me. "The real reason for this trip is to get drunk and act like animals and have a good time. Believe me, the Russians are terrific once the formalities are over and they have a few drinks under their belts."

"Well, I'm just glad to get away from my husband and the kids for a while," said a *Mirror* columnist. The group murmured their general agreement with this sentiment.

"My wife wanted to come with me," said a sportswriter from the *Journal*, "but I painted such a bleak picture of lumpy beds and leaking faucets that she decided to visit her mother in Florida instead."

"That's women for you," a tabloid photographer laughed. I shot a glance at Landon, but his eyes were closed and he seemed to be asleep. Still, there was the faintest trace of a smug smile on his lips that suggested he was faking.

We arrived in Paris just past midnight their time and were summarily passed through customs by a sleepy agent working all alone in the deserted terminal. Air France personnel had been aware of our late departure from New York and had arranged for the group to be housed in a small hotel near the airport until the following morning. We were shuttled to the hotel on a minibus, and most of the group retired to their rooms to catch up on their sleep. Landon disappeared almost immediately, apparently anxious to maintain his low profile.

I took a bath, smoking a joint in the tub as I let the hot water soothe my aching muscles. Then I put on some clean clothes and went downstairs to the lobby, hoping to find the bar open.

The airport hotel catered to a transient population, and both the bar and the kitchen were open round the clock. Dave Stackhouse and Pete Ludlow, another member of our group, were downing brandies at the bar and they greeted me cheerfully.

I ordered a cognac and Dave moved over so that I could have the seat between them. "I never saw a group disperse so fast," he commented, refilling his glass. "What a bunch of deadheads."

"It's one-thirty in the morning and we have a nine A.M. flight to Moscow," Pete said mildly. "After three hours in the Washington airport and eight hours on the plane, you can hardly blame them if they want a bit of shut-eye."

"Nuts to that," I said. "From all I've heard there'll be plenty of time for sleep when we're in Russia. Paris is one of the greatest cities in the world for late-night action."

"I'm game," Dave nodded. "Any suggestions?"

"I thought *you'd* have one."

"It's been a long time since I was in Paris," Dave shrugged. "Most of the places I knew about were probably closed down by the gendarmes a long time ago."

"If you want the lowdown on after-hours action, you have to ask a native," said Pete. "I suggest we try the desk clerk."

We trouped out into the deserted lobby and found the night clerk seated behind the registration desk reading a copy of *Le Monde* and smoking foul-smelling French cigarettes. Since my

French was the best, I was elected to speak to him.

"It's a lovely evening," I said conversationally, leaning forward on the desk so that he could see down the front of my blouse. I was not wearing a bra and this enticed him to put down the newspaper and flash me a wide smile.

"It is all the lovelier when graced by your presence," he assured me. "What can I do for you, mademoiselle?"

"My friends and I have just arrived from New York," I told him, "and we have only this one night in Paris. My friends insist that everything will be closed in the city at this hour, but I feel sure that there must be someplace where we could go to have some fun. Now, you look like the sort of fellow who knows how to have fun."

"The nature of fun varies according to one's tastes," the clerk said impassively. "You could, for instance, visit the Eiffel Tower and admire the lovely lights. Or you could tour the various monuments and marvel at their great nocturnal beauty. Surely that would be fun for a visiting American."

"I had something a little more unusual in mind," I murmured suggestively. "You know, maybe something indoors."

"There is a place . . ." he said hesitantly, "but is is not for Americans. You are too easily shocked. I could not possibly . . ."

"Perhaps this will persuade you," I said, slipping three hundred-franc notes into his shirt pocket.

"It will, mademoiselle," he said pragmatically. "I will give you an address. When you get there tell the doorman that Pierre from this hotel sent you, and he will let you in." He scribbled an address on a piece of paper and handed it to me.

"What did he say? What's on the paper?" asked Pete, who had been vainly trying to follow our conversation.

"He says that we will be positively shocked out of our primitive minds if we go to this address and tell the man Pierre sent us. It's probably some kind of after-hours club with a stage show."

"You mean he didn't elaborate?" Dave asked.

"Don't you want to be surprised?"

"The last time someone said that to me, I wound up married," Pete lamented. "Let's see if we can get a taxi."

We snared a taxi just leaving after a late trip to the airport, and the driver was happy to have a return fare to the city. I gave him the address Pierre had written on the piece of paper, and his eyebrows shot to the top of his head.

"That is a rather rough neighborhood," he protested. "Are you sure you want to go there at this late hour?"

"Don't worry," I told him. "My friends here are American gangsters. They can handle any problems that come up."

"Ah, James Cagney, bang-bang," he nodded enthusiastically. He threw the car into gear and we lurched off toward Paris.

The night air was bitterly cold, and a light snow was falling as we rumbled through the near-empty streets, but the city's lights blazing through the darkness gave the old buildings and monuments a fairy-tale charm that is unmatched by any other city in the world.

Montmartre is a seamy neighborhood on the Right Bank of the city. It is a peculiar mixture of historical churches like the Basilique du Sacré-Coeur, perched on a hilltop high above the city, and numerous bars and burlesque shows located in the small side streets. It attracts hoards of tourists during the early evening, all of them anxious to catch the show at the legendary Moulin-Rouge, but at this late hour the visitors, their voyeuristic desires satisfied, had all scurried back to their hotels, leaving derelicts and sailors and members of the underclass to roam the darkened streets. It was here that our driver headed, rolling to a halt in front of a small, narrow building mere steps from Place Pigalle. A yellow neon sign that read "Chez Maurice" illuminated the doorway, which was blocked by a rough-looking man in a dark green uniform.

"Pierre sent us," I told him and he stepped aside to let us enter.

Chez Maurice was a typical after-hours club, a dim, smoke-filled room with a mirrored bar along the back wall, a small stage at the front, and tables and chairs crowded in between.

We were seated at a small round table near the front, and as my eyes became accustomed to the gloom, I looked around at the clientele and realized the peculiar nature of the club. Though some of the patrons seemed straight, many were overtly homosexual. I spotted one or two obvious drag queens lounging at the bar chatting happily with men in business suits, and a young man with a severe punk haircut and leather jacket was, on closer inspection, of the opposite gender, but in many cases I had difficulty telling which sex a person actually was. Occasionally a couple would disappear up the stairs at the far end of the room. I figured that there was an upper level to the club, possibly someplace where two people could get some privacy.

The stage show was in progress and a can-can chorus line of male transvestites were just finishing their routine. They tore off their wigs to thunderous applause, then moved off the stage.

Their place was taken by a slim young man in dark blue tie and tails with a husky voice and slightly effeminate gestures. He introduced himself as Jean Bedier and sang a song about "gay" Paris with clever references to the sexual makeup of the audience that had them laughing and stamping appreciatively. He moved among the tables as he sang, and when he stopped before our group I found myself attracted by his fresh good looks, which seemed so at odds with the tawdriness of his surroundings. I flashed him a smile and he smiled back before turning and remounting the stage for the final refrain.

"Looks like Pierre didn't steer us wrong," said Pete as the show ended and people began to move about more freely. "Shall we step up to the bar and join the ladies?"

"Only if they really are ladies," Dave grunted, getting to his feet. "Coming, Christina?"

"I'll join you later," I said as over his shoulder I saw Jean moving through the crowd toward me. "I want to finish my drink."

Jean waited politely until the men moved away, and then he approached me.

"May I sit down?" he asked, and when I nodded he slipped into the chair next to mine, sitting so close that his knee brushed my thigh. I caught my breath as his touch aroused my senses. He was shorter than he had appeared on stage, pretty rather than handsome, with dark blond hair combed straight back and piercing blue eyes fringed by thick dark lashes.

"You're new here," he said. "I would have noticed if you'd been here before."

"I'm just in Paris overnight," I told him.

"Then we must make the most of our meeting," he said, smiling. "Have you had dinner? Would you like to go out?"

"I could use a meal," I said, "but it's three o'clock in the morning. I don't think many restaurants are open at this hour, even in Paris."

"You are right," he laughed. "We will cook in. I have an apartment upstairs. It will be more intimate and we can get to know each other."

It occurred to me that he might be gay—most of the actors and patrons were—but I dismissed the idea that he might think I was a man in drag. Curves like mine can't be imitated and there are many bisexual men who are equally ardent lovers with both sexes.

I stood up and allowed Jean to lead me across the room to the flight of stairs I had noticed earlier. Paris buildings are traditionally long and narrow, and Jean occupied the small back apartment on the third floor. There were two rooms, painted white and connected by a short narrow passage that contained the kitchen. The place was sparsely furnished, the pieces functional rather than decorative, but the windows were curtained with antique lace and there was a hand-embroidered coverlet on the bed.

Jean set a pot of water on the stove and poured out two glasses of wine. I sat on a high stool, sipping my drink and watching him work, and in no time at all he had served up linguine with clam sauce, hot French bread, and a small tossed salad.

We chatted as we ate, but there was a sense of anticipation in the room that had nothing to do with food or polite conversation. I slipped off my shoes and let my silk-clad foot stroke Jean's thigh beneath the table. I felt him respond, but as I moved my leg upward toward his crotch he shifted his chair suddenly so that he was beyond my reach.

"Is something wrong?" I asked.

"No . . . nothing," he said, flushing, but I could tell that something was.

"That was a wonderful meal," I said lightly, "but I'm stuffed."

"Why don't you lie down in the other room?" he suggested. "I'll clear the table and join you in a few minutes. Make yourself comfortable."

I took his offer in its most literal sense and when he did join me, I was stretched out naked on the bed, my fingers in my pussy, masturbating lazily.

"You look good enough to eat," he said huskily. "Better than any dessert."

"Would you like a taste?" I teased, spreading my legs and holding my pussy lips apart so he could see the glistening red cherry of my clit.

I was thoroughly aroused and without preliminaries Jean knelt at the foot of the bed. He grabbed my thighs, pulling me forward so that my legs were hooked over his shoulders and my yawning pussy was on a level with his mouth. He was an expert in the art of cunnilingus and my fleshy little nub quivered with joy as he bathed it in long, swirling laps. I moaned with pleasure, tossing my head from side to side as Jean closed his mouth over my whole vagina, sucking lustily. My hips bounced in response, my fingers clawing at the sheets and my breath coming in short sobbing gasps.

Without stopping his oral ministrations, Jean took one hand from my thigh. The next moment I felt something long and hard pushing into my vagina, and I gasped as it stretched the walls of my pussy, reaching to the very entrance of my womb. Jean pumped the dildo in and out and within seconds I was climaxing wildly, groaning and whimpering with pleasure.

"That was incredible," I whispered as I slowly came back to reality. "You have almost a gift for oral sex. It's as if . . ."

"As if I were a woman," Jean finished softly.

I hesitated, not wanting to hurt his feelings, then suddenly it all made sense: the feminine decor, the use of a dildo, Jean's apprehension when my toes approached his crotch.

"Why didn't you tell me?" I said, sitting up.

"I didn't know if you'd like it," she replied, sitting on the edge of the bed so that we faced each other. "Many women are squeamish about lesbianism."

"I'm not strictly gay," I said, "but I like the change of pace. You're a very special woman, Jean, and I would like to make love to you."

She nodded almost imperceptibly, her eyes burning into mine, then she stood and began to undress. Her slender body had not an ounce of extra fat. Her stomach was almost concave, her hips narrow and hard like a boy's. Her tiny breasts stood in proud little peaks and her dark blond pubic hair was close-cropped. She was almost a hermaphrodite with both male and female characteristics present, and my excitement at the thought of possessing her made the blood pound through my veins. She stretched out beside me and opened her arms. Our mouths melted together in a long passionate embrace. I moved my hands over her smooth skin, rolling her nipples between my fingers and grinding my pussy against her tight little twat. Her ass fascinated me and, turning her over, I massaged the sculptured flesh of her buns and the backs of her thighs. She sighed softly, her body relaxing, almost dissolving into the softness of the bed. I gently raised her hips, kneeling behind her on the bed. Separating her cheeks, I licked all along the dark crevice between, flicking her puckered anus and slipping between the folds of her succulent cunt. I heard her gasp and she buried her face deeper into the mattress, thrusting her ass even higher. I continued to explore her sopping cunt, my probing tongue searching out the hard little knob of her clit. Jean's eyes were shut tight and her breath was coming in short, sobbing gasps.

"Fuck me, baby, fuck me!" she cried, bucking her hips wildly as I licked greedily at the sweet juices of her honey-pot.

Suddenly I remembered the dildo. I pushed her quickly onto her back and sucked the soft plastic tip before inserting it into her vagina.

I moved it slowly at first, then increased the tempo. Jean let out a low moan of pleasure, raising her legs and thrusting her hips upward.

"That feels so-o-o good!" she cried. "Fuck me harder, baby. Really let go!"

I applied the dildo more vigorously, massaging her breasts and belly as I worked. My own pussy was steaming now, hot and wet with desire. As she reached the pinnacle of pleasure, she let out a hoarse cry, her body wracked with the vibrations of her orgasm. I quickly parted my pussy lips, thrusting the protruding end of the dildo deep inside. Our pussies fused together, connected by that slick pole of pleasure. We sat up and held each other, playing with each other's breasts as we bucked our hips, our pussies sliding on the dildo, then grinding together in orgiastic pleasure. We climaxed wildly, our juices soaking the sheets as we made final thrusting moves along the dildo inside us. I had scarcely regained my senses when Jean pushed me onto my back and, removing the plastic toy, lowered herself on top of me so that we were head to toe. Jean's pussy was moist and open, her clit a prominent ripe bud. I savored the flavor and aroma of her sex as my own hips gyrated, pushing hard into Jean's face. She was tonguing me like an expert, probing deep into the recesses of my steamy passage until my head reeled. I never knew that anything could feel so good or last so long. I felt Jean climax violently and I cried out as my own orgasm exploded in a rush of heat that turned my body to a fiery inferno.

I let Jean down easily and she turned and took me in her arms. I tasted my own sex on her lips as we pulled the covers over us, our sweat-filmed bodies cuddled against each other. Jean drifted off to sleep, but though I was totally exhausted I was not able to do the same. Cursing Moses Landon, Princess Lyapunov, the weather, French taxis, and my own egocentric stupidity, I barely managed to shower, dress, and make it to the airport in time to catch the nine A.M. Aeroflot plane to Moscow.

I hadn't seen Dave and Pete since we separated at the club and was glad to see that they too had managed to get to the airport in time.

"Did you have a good time last night?" I asked as we struggled through the narrow aisle to our seats.

"Not bad," Pete yawned. "We drank too much, though. Dave struck up a conversation with a gorgeous woman, but that didn't last long."

"She excused herself to powder her nose and I saw her go into the men's room," Dave laughed. "I'm afraid that was just a bit more than I was ready for. That was a nice-looking man you met, though."

I nodded in agreement but refrained from further comment. Why kiss and tell?

"Hello, all Americanski journalists," said a jovial voice over the plane's intercom. "This is Captain Brodvoske, and you are welcomed on Flight 104 to glorious city of Moscow. We are nine o'clock flight and will be leaving on time at ten-fifteen. You will have good time and will find complimentary copies of English *Pravda* in seat pocket next to vomit bag."

"In case you can't tell, *Pravda*'s the one with the picture of the Premier on the cover," Dave grunted sourly as he sat down.

I had drawn an aisle seat in the last row, a penalty for being late, but I smiled when I saw Moses next to me at the window working the crossword puzzle in the international *Herald Tribune*. There were only two seats in this row and, as the noise of the engine muffled our conversation, we could talk without drawing attention to ourselves.

"Have a good time last night?" I asked cheerfully as I sat down beside him and buckled my seat belt.

"Passable," he replied. "I watched the French version of *Bonanza*, read a little, and went to sleep. I wish you had done the same."

"What do you mean?"

"I heard about your nocturnal sojourn into the land of the demented," he said as the plane lurched off the ground. "I can't say I'm very surprised, but in future I wish you'd delay the immediate gratification of your egocentric needs long enough to get some sleep."

"What's the difference? I can catch up on my sleep when we get to Moscow. We don't have any official functions until tomorrow. They canceled this afternoon's luncheon because of the delay in our flight. I heard that little geek from the *Institution* moaning about it. If you think getting to bed early and sleeping with your right hand tied to your side makes you such a hotshot, go right ahead. If you explode from an excessive backlog of semen, that's your problem."

"That's the trouble with you women," Moses said. "You

never plan ahead. I need you on your feet for the next few days, not on your back.''

"Don't worry about me," I snapped. "I'm at my best when I'm exhausted and hung over. You just do your job and I'll do mine, okay?"

"You're beautiful when you're angry," he teased, and it was such a typically chauvinist remark that I closed my eyes and refused to talk to him for the rest of the trip.

It was late afternoon in Moscow when we straggled off the plane four hours later and were greeted by two Intourist representatives who had been assigned to act as interpreters, guides, and nursemaids to our little group. Boris Nikolayevich Doshchenko was a blond giant with piercing blue eyes and a wide, friendly smile. His coworker, Svetlana Ivanova Osypovych, was a thin, serious-looking woman with dark skin and jet black hair. She had a list of our names in her hand and counted us three times, comparing her number to the number on the list.

Unlike American airports, there was no covered passageway between the plane and the airport terminal, and we huddled in the freezing cold while Boris and Svetlana conferred with the ground crew and supervised the loading of our luggage onto an open trailer.

"They do one thing at a time," Dave said in answer to my whispered complaint about having to wait in the subzero temperatures, "and they do it in the order that they've been instructed by the Central Committee, no matter what the extenuating circumstances. First a head count, then the luggage, then the welcoming speech."

"It would be nice if they did the welcoming speech inside," I muttered. "I'm freezing. Have you noticed that they haven't cleared the snow off the walk?"

"There is no walk," David replied as Boris clapped his hands for attention.

"On behalf of people of Soviet Union, I make you all welcome," he said in English, spreading his arms expansively in a symbolic gesture of embrace. "We are honored to have so many members of American press as our guests and hope that your visit to our country will be instructive and enjoyable.

Now, I know there have been many delays because of terrible weather and you are all very tired, so we will go quickly through customs to hotel. Please follow me."

"I need a drink," I said as we trudged after our luggage into the drafty airport terminal.

"I hope you mean tea," said Dave as he helped lift my suitcases onto the table in front of a solemn-looking customs agent, "because the bar at the National won't open until after dinner."

Our luggage was given a rather cursory going over as the customs inspectors checked for pornography and political or religious material, all of which is forbidden under Soviet censorship rules. I had nothing like that, of course, but my ten pieces of custom-made white-leather luggage, monogrammed in gold, caused quite a stir and the contents were examined with barely concealed curiosity.

When he came to my jewel case, my inspector couldn't repress a slight gasp. Though the jewels were all fakes, they were expertly done and only a practiced eye could have told them from the real thing. The average Russian had never seen such wealth except in a museum, and all activity stopped as the other inspectors, our Intourist guides, and even the airport security officers were called over to have a look.

"Is there any problem with bringing these into the country?" I asked in Russian.

"*Nyet*, there is no problem," the inspector said. "I was just admiring them. They are very beautiful, though of course they are thoroughly decadent and completely useless in a glorious socialist state where all workers share equally. I will note that you have brought them in, so there will be no question of your taking them out again."

"You're very kind," I said, smiling at him.

We were loaded onto an ancient bus with our luggage and bounced from the airport to the city where I had my first glimpse of the gold and silver domes of the Kremlin's three churches, standing boldly against the leaden winter sky.

At the National, Moscow's deluxe tourist hotel, we had another protracted delay while our passports were collected and our rooms assigned. A relic of Czarist days, with heavy

Victorian furniture and gold-painted figures of Grecian women entwined around lamps, it commanded a magnificent view of St. Basil's Cathedral with its nine brightly painted onion-shaped cupolas crowned with golden double crosses of the Orthodox church.

There was a shabby elegance about my room despite the sagging mattress on the bed and the almost primitive (by my standards anyway) bathroom facilities. However, my exertions in the past thirty-six hours had finally caught up with me and, vetoing the idea of a bath, I crawled beneath the covers of the bed and fell instantly asleep.

CHAPTER NINE

After breakfast we were assembled in the shabby lobby of the National, then herded across the street to the Kremlin. It was nine A.M., far earlier than I was used to functioning, but I carefully refrained from commenting on this fact. The world is divided into day people and night people, and I noticed that several other members of our group were heavy eyed and surly, so I felt better.

The Kremlin is the heart of Moscow, surrounded by redbrick battlemented walls one and a half miles in circumference and in some places sixty-five feet high and ten to twenty feet thick.

"Our destination is Palace of Congresses," Boris told us as we crossed Red Square and entered through the large wrought-iron gate into the Alexandrovsky Gardens which stretch along the northwestern wall. "It was added to Kremlin complex in 1961 and much of it is underground to avoid clash with old Kremlin architecture and ruining skyline. It is here we will hold meetings with Soviet journalists." He took my arm as the road climbed steeply and I flashed him my sexiest smile. He was definitely the handsomest man in the group, and I could tell by the way he returned my smile that he found me equally attractive.

Our conference room held two dozen carefully selected, solemn-looking men and women seated on one side of a rectangular conference table. Behind them were more members of the Russian working press—these armed with cameras and note pads—who would cover the events at the conference for *Pravda* and *Izvestia*. Two men in identical gray suits, white shirts, and narrow black ties stood on either side of the door. They were there ostensibly to provide security, but in reality they would make a complete report of the meeting to the KGB. I was pleased to note that when I entered the room all cameras turned my way and the flashbulbs started firing. Politics never affects male hormonal activity. I gave them my best Yankee Doodle smile and flashed a healthy expanse of leg before taking my seat at the center of the table.

"Ask the comrades if I can get some copies of those," an Iowa newsman called out.

"What would your wife say?" Dave laughed, pretending to wrestle Pete for the empty seat next to me.

"Let her get her own pictures," the newsman grumbled as the meeting was called to order.

A minor functionary from the Ministry of Information began the proceedings with an extensive and extremely boring speech of welcome. He was a short, beefy man in an ill-fitting blue suit, and he kept clearing his throat and fiddling with his tie as he talked. I was directly in his line of vision and I amused myself by quietly opening the top few buttons of my blouse so that the rich bronze of my breasts was clearly visible over the lace edging of my bra. His eyes widened and a thin film of sweat broke out on his forehead as he struggled to keep his mind on what he was saying. There was a polite spatter of applause when he finally sat down, then the floor was opened for questions.

"Mr. Mitosova of *Pravda* wishes to know how you find Russia," said Boris, translating the first question.

"We turned left at Paris and followed our noses," one American quipped.

"They are enchanted by the workers' paradise," Boris told the reporter in Russian. The Russians nodded their approval of this sentiment and pencils dashed madly across pads.

The round-table discussions weren't much to write home about, and I wasn't too interested in participating in verbal tennis games. It was mostly nonpolitical shop talk because the Russian journalists, under the watchful eye of their government, were careful not to say anything that did not adhere strictly to the Party line.

"You see what I meant about these conferences?" Dave said to me as the group broke for lunch. "It doesn't matter what you say. It all gets translated into official bureaucratese and everyone is happy."

Lunch was a bit more informal. Both Russians and Americans were on their own as far as table conversation went, and in most cases this limited the discussions to polite generalities. Service in restaurants was slow by Western standards, but the food was always worth waiting for. The Russians have a saying (as they usually do about everything): *Shchi da kasha, Pishcha nasha:* Cabbage soup and gruel are our food. I'm happy to say we did better than that. The Russians rolled out the culinary red carpet for their guests, and I always took seconds of everything. Being a world traveler, I was of course familiar with most of the foods served, but some members of our group were a bit more provincial.

I was seated next to a reporter from the Alabama *Standard*, who first watched me fill my plate, then took the exact same foods for himself. He waited patiently while I poured myself some mineral water, and I realized that he had probably never seen *blini* before.

"These are *blini*," I told him. "They're a sort of do-it-yourself first course. Would you like me to show you how to eat them?"

"Please. This is a far cry from ham steak and collard greens, but we were warned we'd have to rough it."

"I wouldn't argue if you meant the showers," I laughed, "but I would hardly call this food roughing it. *Blini* is served in one of the finest restaurants in New York. Now, watch closely. You take one of these little pancakes and pour some melted butter on it like this . . ." I demonstrated as I spoke. "Then you put on a layer of this nice thick sour cream, and you top it off with a big blob of caviar. Then you roll it up into a tube and pop a little more sour cream on top. See? That's a *blini*."

He took a cautious bite but found it to his liking and quickly mastered the art of making them.

"What I wanna know," he said, chewing happily, "is what's this caviar stuff? Never had any of that down in 'Bama."

"Fish eggs," I said. His mouth stopped in midchew and a pained expression crossed his face. He swallowed with difficulty, then quickly poured himself a glass of vodka and took a large gulp.

"Did you say fish eggs?" he croaked.

"You eat hen's eggs, don't you? This is the same thing, just served differently."

"What kind of fish?" he asked unhappily.

"Sturgeon."

He nodded, but I could tell that he wasn't convinced.

Boris was seated on my other side, obviously enjoying this interchange. "Have you ever been to America?" I asked him.

He shook his head. "No, but of all tourists, I like best Americans. You are most like Russians, generous, emotional . . ."

"Why don't you spend a little more time with us then?" I asked. "We're all together in one wing of the hotel on the top floor and it's usually party time at night." I lowered my voice. "We could get to know each other better."

"I should like that," he said, smiling, "but unfortunately Intourist guides are not allowed upstairs in hotels for foreign guests."

"Rules are made to be broken," I shrugged, "though Svetlana looks as if she sleeps with the rule book under her pillow." I nodded toward the other Intourist guide, who was seated at the end of the table silently eating her meal. "Is she always so formal?"

"She is very serious about job and commitment to State," Boris nodded. "It is easy to laugh but someday she will be high-ranking member of Communist Party. Here such loyalty is rewarded."

"There are many kinds of rewards," I said suggestively, my

fingers lightly stroking his thigh beneath the protective covering of the tablecloth. "It just depends on what you want." Our eyes met and held and a quiver of anticipation raced along my spine.

Our Russian hosts were anxious to show off their capital city, and each day after lunch, several hours were devoted to a tour of the principal sights. Russia is the largest country in the world, and the Russians have a Texan's love for exaggerated bigness. The rule seems to be that if something is big it must be good, and if it's twice as big it will be twice as good. Moscow has some of the biggest squares in the world. The size of the squat ugly apartment complexes and mock-Gothic, sandcastle skyscrapers erected in the capital by Stalin is overwhelming and seems totally out of proportion with the pea-sized humans who inhabit them. There is a numbing uniformity to these structures that fails to charm, unlike the more human-sized but enchanting sidewalk cafés of Paris or the small parks of London.

Though the average Soviet citizen may live in a cramped, poorly designed apartment and own few personal or household items, all citizens can enjoy the Lenin Stadium, the permanent Exhibition of Economic Achievements, or the Moscow Metro. These are symbols of the richer life that each Soviet citizen may expect when communism reaches fruition. The subway in particular is a showplace for foreign visitors. Each station is individually designed, with gold chandeliers hung from vaulted ceilings and walls of mosaic designs depicting the triumphs of the Soviet army or the art and culture of the U.S.S.R., and all were spotlessly clean.

"Moscow subway is fastest way to travel through city," Svetlana told us proudly. "Under capitalism only few may enjoy grand apartment, but under communism all can enjoy splendid subway."

We were standing at the Paveletskaya station with its eighty snow-white marble pillars and its polished granite floor that was fashioned to resemble a gigantic carpet.

"I've never seen anything like this," the *Institution* representative sighed. "Look at those paintings. And in a subway too!"

"Aren't the New York subways just as nice?" I asked. "I've always heard that they're the best in the world." The little man's mouth dropped slightly and he gave me an incredulous stare.

"Are you kidding?" he said. "Have you ever been in the New York subway?"

"Well, no, actually I haven't," I admitted. "But I've heard . . ."

"A New York subway station is about as elegant as the bottom of a bedpan," he snapped, cutting me off. "The only art you'll find on the walls down there is of the four-letter crayon variety."

"Graffiti have been found scribbled over frescoes in ancient Roman caves," I told him. "It's been around since the dawn of mankind."

"So have roaches," he said shortly, "and I don't want them in my subways either. However, if you ever do decide to view our subway art, make sure you leave those rocks you're wearing behind."

"These aren't really my best pieces," I said modestly, adjusting the long emerald and sapphire pin that secured my sable hat. I took off my gloves so that the large emerald ring and matching emerald and gold bracelet flashed conspicuously. "I just wanted to add a bit of class to our group. I didn't want the Russians to think we Americans had no fashion sense."

"They stay up all night worrying about it," he sighed.

Moses, who was traveling under the terribly creative pseudonym of "Joe Smith," had suggested that I wear several pieces of the paste jewelry each day so that our traveling companions would be accustomed to the idea of my having them with me. That way, should a customs agent cast a suspicious eye on their real counterparts upon our departure, I would have more than his coworker's scribbled entry in some lost file to prove that I had indeed entered the country with them. Though Moses had hardly said ten words during our entire trip, nobody in our group seemed to care much. Both Russians and Americans spent their time looking at me, and I did nothing to discourage these attentions.

Despite our hosts' repeated assurances that we were free to see or do anything we wished, we were left little time to be on our own. Though it was bitterly cold and the streets were blanketed in white, we were fortified with hot tea and, packed in a creaking, overheated minibus, taken to monuments, statues, parks, public buildings, and museums. The Square of the Cathedrals at the Kremlin have been converted into a series of museums, just four of over 150 in the city devoted to military, revolutionary, and scientific achievement in the Soviet Union. My favorite was the Museum of Russian Folk Art on Stanislavsky Street, with its vast collection of objets d'art in glass, metal, pottery, lace, wood, and bone.

When the *Institution* representative asked where he could purchase a postcard, the entire group was taken to the huge post office at Komsomoskaya Square. Russian postage stamps are gorgeously printed masterpieces of color art and I impulsively sent a postcard to Malcolm Gold in New York.

"I'm sending a postcard to my ex-wife," Pete laughed, dropping it into the wall slot. "I told her I was defecting and that if she wants her alimony she'll have to sue me in the people's court."

Our evenings, too, were planned for us. There were tickets to the Moscow Circus, a year-round attraction in the city, a Stravinsky concert, and a wonderful performance of *The Seagull* by Chekhov at the Moscow Art Theater. The company was founded by the famous actor-director Konstantin Stanislavsky, who developed his famous method of teaching acting within its walls.

After the evening's entertainment ended, our bus returned us to our hotel where our Intourist guides bid us good night. I was used to a meal and several rounds of drinks after the theater, but in Moscow they rolled up the sidewalks and tucked in the edges before midnight. There are no real night spots in the city and the only place to get a drink was the late-night bar at the hotel, which closed at two A.M. This left us to make our own entertainment after hours and presented us with a logistical problem.

Russian decorum frowns on its guests carousing in their rooms at all hours of the night. A good Russian goes home, reads *Pravda*, eats dinner, and hits the sack. This wouldn't have stopped us, of course, except that we had Natasha to deal with.

Guests in Russian hotels are required to turn their room keys over to the key lady stationed on each floor whenever they leave their room and pick them up from her again when they return. This allows hotel staff access to the rooms at all times and provides an informal means of watching the comings and goings of the guests. In case of any unusual disturbance, the key lady can call hotel security.

Natasha was the night key lady on our floor. She was a short, stout middle-aged woman with a sour look on her face, probably the legacy of her many years at an incredibly boring job. I decided to alleviate her tedium to our advantage by slipping her a friendly bottle of vodka—the economy size—each evening as we left the hotel to see the circus or the theater or whatever that evening's activity was. By the time we returned to our rooms, Natasha was peacefully snoring at her post, and no amount of noise could wake her.

Moses did not participate in these nocturnal festivities, but no one seemed to notice his absence. There were several other women in our group and, while I was the favorite, no one objected to swinging with any willing partner or trying more daring combinations to compensate for the disproportionate number of men. If our Intourist guides noticed our haggard, glassy-eyed looks as we trooped down to breakfast each morning, they never commented on it.

One thing I did each night was to carefully examine the contents of my jewel case to see if the fake jewels had been replaced by their valuable doubles. As of our next-to-last evening in Moscow, the exchange had not been accomplished, and I began to worry that our plan had become known to the authorities. Before leaving for the performance at the Bolshoi, I placed the unlocked case prominently on my night table.

No matter who dances, there are always lines at the Bolshoi Theater and every performance is sold out. The Bolshoi is Moscow's Metropolitan Opera House or La Scala. The word *bolshoi* means big, or great, and true to its name the pink-hued stucco building is huge with eight Grecian columns and a portico crowned by a heroic horse-drawn Roman chariot cast in bronze.

The interior of the theater was a blaze of red velvet and gilded ornamentation. A massive glass-tasseled chandelier suspended from a dome painted with pictures of the Muses dominated the auditorium and our privileged status as foreign guests of the Soviet Union had commandeered us center-orchestra seats.

Like everything else in Russia, the ballet is produced with elaborate and realistic stage effects that can at times over-shadow the actual dancing. The evening's performance of *Romeo and Juliet* was no exception. In one scene 150 Montagues and Capulets dueled ferociously across the vastness of the Bolshoi stage and in another there were three complete musical groups performing. While the Bolshoi symphony played in the pit, an entire brass band appeared on simulated stone steps leading to a street on stage and a mandolin group entered from the wings.

During one of the long intermissions, I contrived to have a hurried conversation with Moses in one of the private cur-tained boxes on the third tier. It was the first time we had been alone since leaving Washington, and Moses gathered me swiftly into his arms, crushing his lips hungrily to mine until my knees grew weak and my head started to spin.

"This is torture," he murmured savagely. "Having you so near, yet unable to touch you, to even speak to you alone . . ."

"I want you too," I whispered, pressing myself against him, "and as you pointed out on the plane several days ago, I'm not used to delaying the gratification of my egocentric de-sires."

"Just a few more days," he murmured, kissing me hotly. "Tomorrow night is the banquet. In less than a week I'll be back in Washington and I promise you the best dinner ever to celebrate our success."

"What if something goes wrong? The jewels haven't been exchanged. What if someone suspects?"

"There's still plenty of time," he assured me. "It would make sense to exchange the jewels at the last possible moment. But if anything does happen, if the jewels aren't exchanged or if Kabalevsky isn't on the bus after the banquet tomorrow night, get on that plane and go home. You are in no danger if you leave with the group as planned.''

"What about you?"

"You don't know me. We never met. Don't try any phony heroics, either here or back home, understand? Promise me, Christina." I tried to pull away, but his hands gripped my arms, bruising the bare flesh. The lights dimmed, indicating the end of the intermission, and there was the sound of footsteps and the murmur of voices outside our box. "Promise," he whispered hoarsely, his eyes searching my face in the darkness. I nodded and, pressing me close for a moment, he reluctantly let me go. We slipped out of the box separately and went back to our seats. I did not speak to Moses for the rest of the evening, but our conversation had upset me, and my tears when Romeo and Juliet died in their subterranean tomb were not entirely for the beauty of the performance or the doomed lovers on the stage.

It was just past midnight when our group arrived back at the National and crept stealthily past the snoring Natasha to our rooms. I had used my afternoon shopping time to purchase vodka and snacks for the evening's festivities, and the bottom of my small closet harbored several bottles of flavored and colored vodkas, for which I had developed a taste since coming to the Soviet Union. Russians never drink vodka without eating something, and I had also purchased several packages of imported Polish crackers and a tin of beluga caviar at GUM, Moscow's main department store, that afternoon.

We had been playing musical beds all week, and it was Dave Stackhouse's turn to host the party. I was rather elaborately dressed and, wishing to be more comfortable, I took off my jewels and slipped out of my black satin gown. Luck was with me that evening and there was plenty of hot water, though I missed my luxurious shower back in New York. I slipped into a white silk peignoir with full, slashed sleeves and plunging neckline that revealed tantalizing flashes of tan skin. The material clung softly to my figure, hinting at the roundness of my hips and the long tapered lines of my legs.

Reentering the bedroom, I poured myself a drink and sat

before the mirror on my dressing table. As I ran a comb through my damp hair, I still could not get my meeting with Moses out of my mind and was feeling depressed and apprehensive. I was also horny, and though it was Moses I wanted in my bed, I was not averse to the idea of a substitute. Dave Stackhouse had proved a diverting and versatile lover the other night and, taking a healthy swallow of my drink, I resolved to drown my fears in an orgy of sexual excess.

I heard a series of taps outside my window, as if someone was deliberately rapping on the glass. My room was on the top floor and there were no trees or TV-antenna wires that could account for the noise. The raps were repeated, more sharply this time, and after turning down the light I parted the heavy drapes to take a look.

The sight of Boris holding onto a stout rope and dangling outside the window gave me a shock, but I quickly recovered and hurriedly unlatched the window and helped him inside. I started to speak but he put his finger on his lips and shook his head to silence me, then carefully closed and relatched the window.

"Do you have radio?" he whispered. I pointed to the night table and he switched it on, turning the volume up. The Soviet news was being broadcast and a bored-sounding newscaster was praising the exceeding of production quotas at a Sverdlovsk factory. "All rooms are wired," said Boris softly. "They do not listen all the time, but periodic checks are made." He took off his hat and coat and laid them carefully on a chair.

"So, you decided to break the rules after all," I said, pouring him a drink.

"Is great risk," he said, smiling, "but worth it." His eyes traveled from the graceful line of my neck to the more obvious symbols of my sex beneath the transparent silk of my gown. I did not blush or turn away. I am proud of my body and like to have it admired and I felt a quiver of excitement as I pictured his next move.

"*Na zdorvie*," he said, raising his glass, then swallowing the vodka in one gulp. "To your health."

He was still in his evening suit, the blue almost shiny with wear, the collar and cuffs of the shirt badly frayed. He was a giant of a man and the suit fit badly. It was typical of the dress of most Muscovites, who look as if they're all going to a "hard times" party, but Boris carried his shabby clothes in a way that many much wealthier men would envy. Though not a classically handsome man, he had the handsomeness of people who are at ease with themselves. His soft blond hair and deep-blue eyes reflected the subdued light in the room, and he exuded a masculine, sensual power that drew me to him.

"I'm glad you came," I said, not caring how or at what risk, but only that we were together.

"And I too," he nodded, putting down his glass and taking me in his arms. He bent his head to mine and kissed me gently and correctly, then slipped his hands into the plunging neckline of my gown, baring my shoulders and breasts. He took one in his hands and covered it with his mouth, teasing the nipple until it stiffened against the roughness of his tongue. I slipped my arms around his neck, pulling him closer and savoring the feel of his lips and tongue on my breasts.

I was wearing nothing beneath the thin silk of my gown and, dropping my hands to my sides, I slowly began to gather up the folds of material, exposing my calves, then my thighs, then the golden triangle of my sex.

Boris knelt before me and I spread my legs, holding the front of my gown against my waist and thrusting my pelvis forward invitingly. His hands grasped my buttocks and he buried his face in my fragrant bush, planting kisses all around the moist little garden of my mons. My body burned as his hands stroked my buttocks and thighs, his tongue and lips building a little fire inside my cunt.

"You have a beautiful body," he murmured in Russian. "Like cream satin, touched with gold." My hands were on my hips, the material of my gown still bunched in my clenched fists.

"Would you like to see the rest?" I asked in Russian.

Boris nodded and, raising my arms upward, I slowly pulled the gown over my head, stretching my body sensuously like a cat. I knelt on the rug opposite him, tugging playfully at his tie.

"Now you, *lyoobof*," I whispered, and he smiled at my use of the Russian term of endearment.

Lifting me in his arms, he got easily to his feet and, holding me as if I had no weight at all, he carried me to the narrow bed. He watched my face as he undressed, removing each article of clothing with elaborate care. He did not blush or turn away as I allowed my eyes to sweep over his magnificent body—his broad chest, his firm flat stomach, and the dark gold lushness of his pubic hair. I always find the sight of a man's body highly stimulating, and a sudden rush of heat swept over me, leaving me tingling with desire. He had a cock that matched the rest of his proportions and my eyes widened as I took in its massive size. He stretched out beside me, crowding me on the narrow bed, and kissed me with vodka-scented lips. As his tongue penetrated my mouth, I felt myself melting inside. I pressed myself against him, holding back the urgent feelings that made me want to beg for his cock. I wanted to give him more, to experience more than a fast fuck.

I shifted my position so that I was on top, kissing and licking the salt-sweet flesh of his chest and the indentation between the hard mounds of his rib cage. He moaned softly as I moved downward. His obvious enjoyment of my touch excited my animal passions and made me work all the harder to arouse him. He spread his legs and I wriggled down between them. Taking the base of his swollen shaft in one hand, I used my other palm to massage his glans with a slow, circular motion. He groaned more loudly and his hips arched off the sheets. A pearllike drop of moisture appeared at the slitted tip of his organ and I leaned forward to lick it off, cupping his pendulous balls as I did so. They felt good in my hands and, bending my head, I took first one and then the other into the warm cavity of my mouth, licking the loose fuzzy surface until they were thoroughly wet.

I glanced up. His flushed face and labored breathing indicated he was aroused and ready for more serious foreplay. Holding the base of his turgid pole in one hand, I put my lips over the pink helmetlike head. No two cocks are alike and Boris' had an acrid manly taste that really turned me on. I kept my tongue tip moving over his shaft as I swallowed him, then I slowly pulled back, feeling his cock lengthen as I withdrew. I was as turned on as he was, and I threw my entire body into my work. I maintained a firm, steady rhythm, gyrating my hips and making low humming sounds that caused my mouth to vibrate on his cock. Boris' eyes were closed and his hips arched upward to meet my hot hungry lips. Then suddenly he caught his breath and placed his hand on my head.

"You must stop," he gasped hoarsely, "or I will not hold back."

"I don't want you to," I whispered. "I want you to come in my mouth."

With a long sigh, he lay back, giving himself up to the ministrations of my lips and tongue. His hips moved rhythmically as he thrust all eight inches of his cock into my mouth, and I forced myself to relax, swallowing as much of him as I could. Suddenly he stiffened and, taking my head between his hands, he spurted his warm sticky cum deep into my eager mouth. I gulped down as much of his creamy gift as I could, then carefully licked the last drops from his shaft and balls. Boris seemed almost asleep as I wriggled upward along his body and nestled my head against his neck, but as I pressed myself against him, he took me in his arms, shifting so that he was on his side, suspended above me weightlessly.

He bent swiftly and his lips closed over mine with a fierceness that almost took my breath away. His hands bruised my flesh as they moved over me and he forced my head back, his tongue pushing between my lips. I was like a fragile toy in his powerful hands, helpless beneath the sheer size and strength of him. I am usually an equal partner in my lovemaking, but I had unleashed a tiger with my teasing expertise and I found myself swept away by his overwhelming dominance.

Boris moved downward, kissing my throat and my chest and the little hollows in my collarbone. My body burned beneath the roughness of his lips and tongue, stung to passion by the love nips of his teeth. I cried out, yet felt my heartbeat quicken. I pushed at him with my hands, my struggles only serving to excite him further. Despite the harshness of his lovemaking, I was incredibly turned on. My pussy was moist, aching with desire, and the thought of Boris' supersized cock thrusting into my tight passage made the blood pound through my veins.

He moved on top of me now, forcing my legs apart. He parted my pussy lips and with one swift, brutal movement, thrust the entire length of his massive cock deep inside. For a moment I could hardly move. I lay pinned beneath his weight, his swelling shaft filling me completely. Totally ignoring my lack of response, Boris began to move, slowly at first then, as my pussy walls stretched to accommodate his size, with increasing urgency. The narrow bed creaked and swayed with the violence of his thrusts that asked, demanded, a response. I took my cue from them and gave up all resistance, surrendering my senses to the insistent fury of his lovemaking.

I closed my eyes and arched my hips, my fingers searching for a handhold in the broad muscles of his back. Our mouths crushed together and I tasted blood as his teeth cut the tender flesh of my lips. With a sudden upsurge of strength, I moved with him, meeting his pounding thrusts, then falling back as his body beat into mine. I felt him stiffen, then let go, and I gave a wild cry as great hot spurts of cum splattered the walls of my cunt. My buttocks tightened and I dug my heels into the mattress as his throbbing tool triggered my own mind-blowing climax.

CHAPTER TEN

I awoke the next morning with a splitting headache, puffy eyelids, and a fuzzy taste in my mouth. The legend that vodka never causes a hangover is just that—legend—and the three empty bottles on my dressing table were a silent reminder of the night's activities. In addition to the caviar, crackers, and vodka, I had introduced Boris to the joys of hash, though we hardly needed artificial stimulants to heighten the excitement of our lovemaking. I didn't remember his leaving, and I hoped that he hadn't tried to exit my room in the same way he had entered. He had taken quite a risk just to make love to me, but I was used to inspiring such heroics and, reviewing our evening together, I knew he had found it worth the gamble.

I fumbled for my watch. It was seven-thirty A.M. With true Russian efficiency, breakfast was laid out at eight o'clock whether anyone was seated at the table or not. Latecomers had cold tea, congealed eggs, and soggy rolls to contend with, and after the first day I had made it a point to be on time. I am always particularly hungry after a night of lovemaking so, dragging myself out of bed, I headed for the shower.

I staggered into the dining room forty-five minutes later, rather gray around the edges but dressed and ready for breakfast and the day's activities. We were scheduled to have one final meeting with the Russians that morning to sum up our discussions over the past week. That night there would be a farewell banquet in our honor and we would go directly from the banquet to the airport to catch a plane back to Paris, the first leg of our journey home.

"I remind you to have bags packed and outside room before leaving for farewell dinner," Svetlana was announcing as I took a seat. "They will be loaded on bus you will take to airport. You will not be returning to room after banquet so leave nothing behind."

I took a double portion of scrambled eggs and buttered a thick slice of Russian black bread. I poured a glass of hot black tea, adding three heaping teaspoonfuls of sugar. Most Russians drink their tea black, or with lemon and a spoonful of fruit jelly, but I felt the need of a sugar fix to get my metabolism going. I noticed that Boris looked a bit peaked, but he smiled with a special warmth when he caught my eye and gave me a sly wink.

Moses was lingering over his tea, which was uncharacteristic of him. To avoid conversation he usually breakfasted quickly, then adjourned to the lounge where he buried his face behind the morning papers until it was time to leave for the Kremlin. Thinking he might want to speak to me, I took a second cup of tea. I hoped that I didn't look as hung-over as I felt. I was in no mood for a lecture on the virtures of abstinence and a good night's sleep. Svetlana, however, gave us no chance to be alone. She remained in her seat, waiting with obvious impatience for us to finish our meal and join the rest of the group. Moses rose first, holding Svetlana's chair with elaborate courtesy, then moved around the table to do the same for me.

"We have the afternoon to ourselves," he whispered as I stood up. "Stay in your room and leave the door unlocked. I'll meet you there."

The warmth of his breath on my neck sent shivers along my spine. More than anything I wanted the feel of his hands on my body, of his lips on mine, but Svetlana was watching us and I could not risk even a verbal reply. I nodded briefly to indicate I had understood and preceded him out of the room.

I attended our last formal meeting with a profound sense of relief but with a touch of sadness too. Despite the differences in our politics and professional ethics, we had come to like and respect our Russian colleagues as individuals. Though they were reserved, passive, and almost brusque in public, they had proved themselves warm, emotional, and overwhelmingly hospitable in more intimate circumstances. In this respect I found them to be more like us than continental Europeans and, as I became more fluent in their language, I discovered they also possessed a sly sense of humor.

"There was a Georgian peasant who called the Minister of Agriculture a fool," a *Pravda* reporter told me as we exchanged handshakes and addresses after the meeting. "He received a sentence of twenty years—five years for slander and fifteen years for revealing a state secret."

I laughed and told him the one about the three politicians and a light bulb but I could tell from his expression that the joke hadn't translated well in Russian.

We returned to our rooms after lunch, and I faced the formidable task of packing my clothes. Most deluxe hotels have a maid that will perform this service for you, but when I asked the desk clerk how to arrange for this at the National, she looked at me disdainfully.

"In socialist workers' paradise all serve needs of state, not needs of spoiled capitalist who changes clothes three times a day," she said haughtily, eyeing my French designer dress with distaste.

"I'm not running a salt mine up there," I explained patiently. "All I want is someone to help me pack my bags. The maids clean my room and make my bed. Why can't one of them pack my bags?"

"Room and bed are property of people. Making bed in National is like making own bed at home," she replied inflexibly, and no amount of pleading, reasoning, or threatening would change her mind.

So I was left to do the job myself. I emptied the closets, dresser drawers, and night table. I laid out all my belongings on the bed, the chairs, and the dresser top, then opened my ten empty suitcases and lined them up on the floor. This doesn't look too difficult, I told myself. I'll just start throwing things into the first suitcase, and when it's full, I'll move on to the next. When I run out of suitcases and clothes, I'll be done.

Unfortunately, after two hours I was left with a large pile of unpacked clothes and no suitcases. I frowned and glared at the clothes. It just didn't make sense. They had all fit into ten suitcases when I arrived. How could they not fit now?

The door clicked and I stifled a scream as Moses slipped into the room, closing it carefully behind him. He placed his finger on his lips, warning me not to speak, and bent to whisper in my ear.

"The room's bugged," he reminded me. "Don't speak until I say it's okay."

He was carrying a small box that looked like a transistor radio. For a few moments he prowled around my room, looking behind various pieces of furniture until he located the listening device secured to the wall behind a framed photo of Karl Marx. He nodded and connected his little box, placing it beneath the picture on the dresser.

"That's a jamming device," he said. "It will block out any transmissions from your microphone, just in case someone's listening. I would have been here earlier but I had to wait for the key lady on duty to go to the bathroom. I didn't want her reporting to anyone that I had come in here."

"Terrific," I said, barely listening as I glared in frustration at the bulging suitcases. Moses looked over the chaos and chuckled.

"What are you doing?" he asked.

"What does it look like I'm doing? I'm packing. And this damned Russian weather has caused my clothing to swell."

"What are you talking about?"

"All of my clothes fit very neatly into those suitcases when I left New York," I explained. "Then they sat in this lousy Russian weather for a week and grew like sponges in water, and now they won't fit back in."

"That's idiotic. Clothing doesn't swell."

"Then how do you explain the fact that they don't fit?" I demanded.

Moses sighed and unlocked one of the suitcases. The cover sprang open and piles of clothing leaped out, scattering all over the floor.

"Thanks a lot!" I snapped. "It took me half an hour to get that case closed."

"Your stuff might fit if you bothered to fold it and pack it in an intelligent and organized manner instead of just cramming everything inside like this," he noted.

"I don't see what difference it makes. The clothing—"

"Of course," he continued, "*I* was packed in ten minutes. All I had was one suitcase. I guess my years in the military have trained me to travel light."

"I'm not in the military," I reminded him, "but I do have a certain position to uphold. When I appear in public, there is an expectation that I will be stylishly dressed."

"Especially in Russia," Moses laughed. "Lord knows they all know you over here. Your name appears all the time in the society columns of *Pravda*."

"It's even more important here," I snapped. "I have to look as if I can afford these jewels or someone might think they weren't mine. Or have you forgotten the reason for my sojourn into this godforsaken deep freeze?"

"I haven't forgotten," said Moses softly. "I was only teasing. Like all women you're incapable of traveling sensibly but you're a vision at the breakfast table and if ten suitcases packed with clothes helps create that image, I'm for it."

"You wouldn't say that if I were a man."

"But you're not a man and *'vive la différence,'* as the French say. Now, why don't I help you pack? Unless you'd rather spill some gasoline on what's left and light a match."

"Pack away," I said grandly, pouring some vodka into my bathroom glass and flopping down on the bed. "You'll see what I mean soon enough."

He grinned and shook his head, then started to fold some blouses. "Like this, see?" he said, demonstrating. "The sleeves meet at the back, then fold again, then the whole blouse is folded in half and it lies flat in the suitcase and takes up less space. You'll get everything in now."

"Come see me in New York. I'll get you a job as a valet."

"If we can tear ourselves away from the fascinating topic of home economics," he said, ignoring my comment, "I'd like to go over the plan for tonight."

"I'm all ears," I replied, leaning back against the pillows and making myself comfortable.

"Our farewell banquet is at the Kremlin rather than at a restaurant, which means it's a first-class affair," he said, continuing to work as he talked. "We will be attended by a number of waiters, one of whom will be Princess Lyapunov's nephew."

"How will you recognize him?"

"During the cocktail hour that precedes the actual meal, I'll approach each waiter and ask a seemingly innocuous question. Kabalevsky will give me a prearranged answer that will identify him to me. The switch will not be made until the very last moment as the group prepares to board the bus to the airport. Hopefully, everyone will be too tired and too drunk to notice anything amiss. But if anyone starts to speak to Kabalevsky or questions whether they've seen him before, I'm counting on you to cover for him. Kabalevsky will have a passport with his photo on it, so he should have no trouble getting past customs."

"I'll stick to him like glue," I promised, refilling my glass.

"Make sure you don't drink too much at dinner," he cautioned me. "I want you to have a clear head when you leave so that you can cover any emergencies."

"You don't have to worry, O Great Male with the holy dangling phallus," I said tartly. "I won't let you down."

"I know you won't," he smiled as he easily snapped the last of my suitcases shut. "There you are, all your clothes packed and ready to go. See, they do fit after all."

"The swelling must have gone down," I sniffed.

Moses laughed and came over to plant a soft kiss on my mouth. I slipped my arms around his neck and pulled him down to me, closing my eyes as a feeling of warmth flooded through me at his touch. It had been a long time. Too long. Just a few more days, Moses had said last night, but though he had joked about the danger there was a hard look in his eyes that belied the humor of those words. I began to tear at his clothes, pressing myself against him with a hunger and urgency that demanded release. He caught my hands with his, pinning them to the pillow on either side of my head. His grip was like iron. I struggled a few moments longer, then collapsed, tears of frustration stinging my eyes.

"Please," I begged him. "You can't go yet."

"Do you think I don't want you?" he said in a choked voice. "Lie still a moment and don't talk. We must not attract attention."

Obediently I lay still while Moses drew the heavy drapes, checked the jamming device and locked the door. It was late, but there would be time. We hurried out of our clothes and snuggled against each other in the hollow of the narrow bed. I cried out as a protruding spring seared the tender flesh of my naked back, and Moses quickly pulled me on top of him. He rubbed the bruised spot as I sprawled across his body, then moved his hand down to caress the rounded curve of my ass cheek. I lay on top of him, grinding my pussy wantonly against his groin as my lips and tongue explored the planes and hollows of his face and neck. The salt-sweet taste of his skin, the subtle scent of his cologne, sent my senses reeling. Being a woman of extraordinary erotic gifts, I have learned to use all of my senses when making love. The way a man looks and tastes and smells is every bit as important as the way his cock feels in my cunt and mouth. I moved sensuously along his body, bathing him with my tongue, biting and sucking his nipples until he groaned with pleasure. The dark hairs on his chest glistened with my saliva and I moved downward, exploring the concave area of his stomach and the sculptured hardness where his pelvis joined his thigh. I carefully avoided his cock and balls, leaving them for last, but my erotic behavior had turned him on. When at last I approached these essentials of his manhood, he was swollen with excitement, his cock standing in a stiff salute. As I licked around the tip of his cock, he placed his hands on my head. I opened my mouth and he eased his organ into my throat, making soft moaning sounds as I relaxed and swallowed him to the hilt. I began to bob my head, sliding slowly and sensuously up and down his slick pole. I caressed his balls, letting my fingers glide through the dark silky curls of his pubic hair. I could easily have sucked him to orgasm, but I knew there would not be time to arouse him again. My own body was on fire, my pussy aching for his cock. I looked up and caught him watching me with a smoldering intensity that made me melt. I eased my mouth off his cock and, straddling his hips, I guided the tip to my hot, moist opening. I held my breath as I felt him enter me, sliding down his steellike shaft until my ass touched his balls. I stretched out on top of him and his hands grasped my ass cheeks, pulling me more tightly against him. Though I was on top, it was Moses who controlled the rhythm and tempo of our lovemaking. He dug his heels into the mattress, grinding his pelvis against me and bucking his hips so that I was skewered by his cock. I held onto his shoulders, my legs spread and my hips thrust slightly upward, gasping as his man-meat pounded into me. My nails bit into his flesh and I clenched my vaginal muscles as hard as I could, desperate to turn him on even more.

"Jesus," he gasped. "Christina . . ."

"Fuck me," I whispered urgently. "Fuck me hard." I clung to him, my breasts rubbing against his chest, my pussy moving in a frenzy against his cock so that the bed creaked and swayed under us. We climaxed together, holding each other tightly and crying out with unrestrained passion. He rolled over onto his side, his cock still imbedded in my spasming cunt as our breathing slowed and our senses returned to normal.

"Worth the risk?" I whispered teasingly.

"Worth the risk," he agreed, holding me tightly for a few minutes more, then reluctantly letting me go. He sat up and, swinging his feet over the side of the bed, began to pull on his clothes. I lightly stroked his back but he didn't respond. He was all Army now, his mind on the business at hand.

My jewel case was still on the night table and, opening the lid, he studied the contents thoughtfully. He took out a large diamond ring, turning it in his hand and holding it to the light. Then he took it over to the mirror and ran the stone along the glass. I held my breath as I saw the sharp, thin cut, the sure sign of a real diamond. The switch had been made, and I would be carrying the real jewels back home with me tonight.

"Bingo," said Moses softly, carefully replacing the jewel in my case. "Everything is going according to plan." He leaned over and kissed me warmly. "Now cheer up, Miss Worry Wart. Give me a smile to remember, and I'm off."

I did as he asked, not trusting myself to speak. Moses was a sexist pig and he made me angry sometimes, but the touch of his hands could take my breath away and I didn't relish the idea of his freezing to death in a Siberian labor camp. Well, I'll just have to make sure that everything goes without a hitch tonight, I promised myself as I watched him detach the jamming device and slip it into his jacket pocket. He walked to the door and turned one last time. Our eyes met and held, then sticking his head out the door to be sure the coast was clear, he slipped silently out of the room.

I took a leisurely shower and dressed in a pink satin wrap-around sheath that bared my left shoulder and was slit on the right side to midthigh. A thin diamond garter drew attention to my silk-clad legs, and I selected diamond earrings and a pair of diamond combs for my hair.

As I sat before my mirror applying the final touches to my makeup, I pondered the possible ways the substitution of the real jewels for the paste ones could have been accomplished. Though my room was locked when I left, the key lady had access to my belongings at all times and, thanks to my vodka, the night key lady had been out of commission all week. The switch must have been made while our group was at the Bolshoi, I decided. The floor would have been practically empty and anyone could have borrowed Natasha's key, slipped into the room, and switched the jewels. Perhaps it was somebody on the staff, a chambermaid or bellboy. A stranger would have had difficulty getting past the heavy security system in the hotel lobby, and few people would have had the courage to swing themselves over the edge of the roof by a rope as Boris had done. Freud was right, I told myself, as I slipped into my full-length sable coat. Sex, not greed, is man's strongest motivating force.

The dinner was held at St. George's Hall, located in the Grand Kremlin Palace. It was a vast, cavernous space lit by six huge gilt chandeliers casting pools of light on polished parquet floors made from twenty different types of wood. A series of white, damask-covered tables were arranged at one end of the room in an oblong. The table settings were antique Sèvres china, and the dinnerware was gold-plated. In addition to the two dozen Russian journalists who had been with us during the morning meetings, there were a number of other minor political and academic dignitaries, all anxious to practice their English and exchange small talk with the visiting Americans. There is still a hungry curiosity about foreign visitors, especially Americans, that persists despite continuing negative Soviet propaganda about the West. I was immediately surrounded by a crowd of Russians, but I don't think they were interested in swapping opinions about nuclear proliferation. There was an elaborate *zakuska* table, and at least a dozen waiters circulated with trays of drinks, but I could only guess at which one was the Princess' nephew. Remembering Moses' warning, I ate more than I drank while keeping my coterie of admirers suitably entertained with stories of my exploits.

As at all official Soviet functions, the KGB was very much in evidence. There were at least half a dozen agents in identical gray suits, white shirts, and narrow black ties. Moses had been counting on a party atmosphere to cover his switch with Kabalevsky, but I noted anxiously that all of the agents refrained from drinking.

It would have been considered the height of rudeness for us Americans to cluster together at the dinner table, but Moses managed to maneuver a seat opposite me. I wondered if he had identified Kabalevsky, but his bland expression gave nothing away and private conversation was out of the question. Three tables away, Boris caught my eye and smiled. He had total responsibility for seeing us off tonight as Svetlana was confined to bed with the flu.

Dinner began with *bagratin*, a cream-of-veal soup poured over spinach and served with croutons. There followed crayfish soufflé, roast partridge with pickled fruits, and a separate course of vegetables that included white asparagus, tiny peas, and leeks in parsley sauce. In addition to vodka, Abru-Durso champagne, the favorite wine of the last Czar, was served with our dinner.

The food was delicious, but by the end of the first hour it became obvious that if the party continued along similar lines, Kabalevsky would not be getting a flight out of Moscow that night. The silent presence of the KGB put a damper not only on the conversation, but on the amount of alcohol being consumed. Drunkenness is officially frowned on in the worker's paradise with jail sentences meted out for rowdy behavior in public, swearing on the streets, or disturbing the peace in restaurants. Moses was politely discussing the merits of the Soviet agricultural system in fluent Russian with a heavyset man to his right. His face was in profile, and I could tell from the tension of his jawline and the uneasy way he kept glancing at his watch that the situation was beginning to worry him. A diversion was obviously needed, and I decided that the time had come for Christina van Bell to demonstrate to the Russians why she was known as the life of the party on three continents.

I stood up and rapped on a glass for attention. The room fell silent and all eyes turned to me expectantly. I cleared my throat.

"Comrades," I said in a loud, cheery voice, "I think a few words are in order here before the morgue wagon comes to take us back to our slabs."

The Russians looked puzzled and Boris jumped quickly to his feet. "Our Russian hosts have extended themselves to show us a good time, and I would like to propose a toast," he said in Russian, translating diplomatically.

"Hear, hear," the Americans cried, grateful that someone was trying to pump a bit of life into the party. I splashed some straight vodka into a shot glass and held it aloft.

"To the people of the Soviet Union," I cried in Russian, swallowing my drink in one gulp. The Russians scrambled to attention at this mention of the mother country.

"To the people," they echoed, quickly following my example.

A short man in a worn black suit hastily refilled his glass to return the toast.

"To American friends," he said in English. "May they carry many memories of good visit with them home."

"Down the hatch," called an American.

"Mud in your eye," said another.

"So's yer old man," said a third, and we all slugged down a hearty dose of the potent vodka.

Protocol satisfied, the Russians sat down. But Landon had apparently understood my plan, for he quickly rose, glass in hand, and made a speech in his flawless Russian.

"Comrades, I make no secret of the fact that my family came from your glorious country. Russians and Americans have much in common and during the terrible conflict in Europe in 1941 my American father joined his Russian brothers to defeat Hitler's Third Reich." The Russians murmured their approval of these sentiments. If there's one thing the Russians hold close to their hearts, it's the memory of their terrible losses in World War II. "A toast," cried Moses, and the Russians sprang to their feet, glasses filled and ready. "To the memory of the valiant Russian soldiers who died in the great war!"

"To the soldiers of the United States," a Russian returned in English, sentimental tears glistening in his eyes, and we all gulped back another shot of vodka.

"To the armies of the glorious Soviet Union," I said, refilling my glass.

"To the army!" the crowd roared, and more vodka was consumed.

By now the mood of the crowd was considerably more relaxed, but I saw that the KGB agents were maintaining their sobriety.

"You gentlemen haven't been drinking," I called out, pointing an accusing finger in their direction. "Do you have something against drinking to the armies of the Soviet state?"

"Certainly not," said a KGB agent, "but . . ."

"Then drink," commanded a Soviet official, and they all snatched up glasses of vodka and joined in the toasts.

During the next half-hour we drank to the memory of the Moscow Uprising, the October Revolution, the memories of several dozen assorted heroes of the Revolution, all of the allied generals of World War II, the entire Communist Party past and present, the American Congress and members of the cabinet, the Premier and the President, and the good health of all present.

This helped us polish off several crates of vodka and definitely improved the tone of the party. Chairs were pushed back from the tables, jackets removed, and ties loosened. The remains of the dinner had been cleared, and as we waited for dessert, several members of the Soviet delegation broke into a hearty and off-key Russian folk song.

Despite Moses' warnings, I was pretty drunk myself and I climbed onto the table and began to parade up and down as if I were on a runway at a burlesque theater. I am something of an exhibitionist and I especially enjoy displaying myself before strangers. I caught the looks of expectation on the faces of the men and women seated below me and I felt a shiver of excitement race through me. When the boisterous folk song ended, one of the Russians began a slow, rhythmic clapping that was picked up by the others until the room echoed with the sound.

One by one, I began to unfasten the hooks that held my dress. As I moved from my arm hole, down along my waist to the rounded curve of my hip, I was aware of being watched and kept my pace deliberately slow. I had to crouch to reach the last hook and when it was unfastened, I held my dress together with my hands. I smiled lasciviously, then stood and slowly unwrapped the heavy satin to expose the front of my body, clad in complementing pink satin underwear.

The audience cheered and applauded, urging me on and I stepped from the concealing sheath and tossed it away.

All eyes were fastened on me now and even the KGB agents had left their posts for a closer look at the action. I strutted and posed as the clapping became more sensuous, and several of the men began to openly fondle their groins. From the corner of my eye I saw Moses slip from his seat and edge toward the back of the room. One of the agents started to turn around but I quickly distracted him by unhooking my bra and flinging it in his direction. Boris began another song with a rousing chorus. As the group joined drunkenly in, I began a randy bump-and-grind, tossing my head and playing with my succulent breasts. I slowly snaked my panties over my hips, bending over and flashing the luscious mounds of my half-moons and the glistening thatch of my pubic hair. If you have it, flaunt it, I always say, and I have more to flaunt than any other woman I can think of.

I began to groan softly, closing my eyes and running my

tongue wetly over my lips. I flicked my nipples and ground my steamy mons against the palm of my hand. All eyes in the audience were focused on my crotch, and many of the men and women mimicked my actions. The sharp, pungent smell of arousal filled my nostrils as I slipped my fingers into my vagina, whipping my pussy to a froth.

"You like me like this?" I called in Russian. There was a roar of affirmative replies. "Would you like a little more?" The cries grew louder.

I lay down on the table, bending my knees and parting my thighs to reveal the rich, moist center of my sex. I held my pussy lips with graceful fingers. I could feel the sexual tension in the room as I postured wantonly, my burning body begging for release. A moment later, I felt a steellike erection nudge the swollen lips of my vagina. I arched my hips upward as two hands grabbed my buttocks and a powerful thrust drove deep into my aching cunt. I cried out as he pounded into me. He was still fully dressed, and I found the roughness of his clothing against my naked flesh turning me on even more. I was stretched out on the table, my head thrown back. Through sweat-filmed eyes I saw Dave Stackhouse behind me, his massive hard-on in his hand and a wicked look in his eye. I opened my mouth and he fed his tool into it, almost forcing me to swallow him completely. I sucked it with sluttish abandon, aware even now of the presence of the others, their eyes watching avidly. I was in heaven, my mouth and cunt totally, wonderfully filled with cock. I closed my eyes and let myself go, overwhelmed with passion. I came three times before the stranger between my legs blasted his love-milk into my steaming tunnel. Seconds later, Dave filled my hungry mouth with his spurting seed, causing me yet another climax.

I was not satisfied. I was turned on by being the center of attention, by giving my body wantonly to a roomful of clamoring strangers, and I called lustily for the next round. Pete Ludlow buried his face in my sopping cunt while two of the Russian journalists positioned themselves on either side of my head, pants down around their ankles and cocks in their hands. I turned my head from left to right, sucking first one delicious cock and then the other while my hands cupped and fondled their dangling balls. All the while my pussy was being gobbled wildly and I writhed with pleasure as my body again raced toward orgasm. As I reached the pinnacle of pleasure, the man I was sucking exploded in my mouth. I was unable to swallow any more, so I turned my head and the warm, gooey liquid spattered my neck and chest. I spread it over my body, massaging it into my breasts as if it were the most expensive lotion. The man on my left now demanded his turn and I easily brought him to orgasm, allowing him to cover my face with his cum.

Pete Ludlow raised his face from between my thighs and licked my own cream from his lips.

"Now that's what I call a beautiful sight," he said, "a woman bathed in cream. You know, baby, you're a real turn-on." He loosened his pants and, looking down the length of my body, I saw his meaty erection, rock-hard and ready for action. He flipped me over on the table and pulled me toward him until my feet touched the floor and the rounded curve of my ass was on a level with his cock. I thought he was going to do it doggie-style but instead he separated my ass cheeks and positioned the tip of his penis against the pink, puckered hole of my anus. I love being sodomized, and I spread my legs as wide as I could and pushed back against Pete's advancing cock, sighing happily as he stretched and filled my anal passage. He started thrusting slowly and I moved with him, moaning with pleasure at the sensations he was creating. I reached back and held my ass cheeks apart so that his hands were free to play with my breasts and probe my steaming cunt as his cock plundered my rectum.

I was like a bitch in heat, and the more Pete drilled my ass and thumbed my clit, the more I wanted it. I writhed and moaned, my stomach muscles tightening as Pete's swelling manhood stretched my tight passage. I was crying out, begging him to fuck me harder, to ream my ass until it hurt. By the time he erupted in my asshole I was coming also, tightening my anus around his spasming cock until it shriveled and grew limp inside me.

I staggered to my feet and looked around. A vast orgy was taking place in the sedate dining hall, with no one holding back. Russians and Americans in various stages of undress were sprawled on top of one another, hell-bent on proving that the Cold War was just a figure of speech. My jaw and ass and pussy ached, but I threw back a rejuvenating shot of vodka and joined in again. Within minutes I was crouched over a woman's fragrant cunt while a *Pravda* reporter did me doggie-style from behind. I lost count of the number of times I was penetrated, of the number of pussies and cocks I sucked, and of the number of orgasms I had. I just kept sucking and swallowing and coming until, too exhausted to move, I pillowed my head on my arms and fell asleep on the floor.

I was awakened by a gentle shaking of my shoulder. I opened one eye and saw Boris' handsome face inches above me.

"You must get up," he whispered urgently. "Is time to catch plane home."

"Don' wanna fly, wanna sleep," I muttered, trying to turn over, but Boris lifted me in his arms and set me on my feet. I leaned heavily against him, closing my eyes.

"Here, drink this," he said, putting a glass in my hand. The ice-cold vodka shocked me awake and, taking several gulps of air, I managed to stand on my own.

The dining hall was a shambles. Chairs were overturned, damask cloths pulled from tables, and empty vodka bottles rolled crazily over the polished floor. Naked journalists, dignitaries, and KGB agents were sprawled everywhere. Boris crisscrossed the room, rousing the drunken, protesting Americans and forcing them into their clothes, coats, and hats. Several waiters were still on their feet, and Boris called to them to help herd the guests to their bus. I managed to dress and make my way outside where I leaned against the building, trying to regain my sense of balance. Several of our group straggled past me unaided, then a waiter who was escorting a staggering form in a bulky overcoat and fur hat stopped beside me.

"Please, can you help me?" he asked in Russian. "This man is very drunk."

I started at Moses' familiar voice, but there was no time to talk. I grasped Kabalevsky's other arm, and the three of us made our way across the ice. Moses-the-waiter pushed the hulking figure up the darkened stairs of the bus, then turned to take my arm. For one final moment, Moses and I faced each other across the frozen darkness. I felt his lips bruise mine, then he thrust me up the steps. I turned quickly, but Dave Stackhouse had moved behind me and in the dark I could not see past him. There was no going back. Thanks to my sexual diversion the switch had been made and it was Kabalevsky, not Moses who was on his way back to the States.

Most of my fellow passengers were too drunk and exhausted to do much besides fall asleep in their seats and no one paid the least bit of attention to the silent figure huddled against the window next to me.

A freezing rain had started as our bus lumbered toward the airport, and icy road conditions slowed our pace to a crawl. By the time we arrived, we had only minutes to spare before our plane took off.

An impatient crew of men, who had expected our arrival an hour earlier, rushed from the terminal and started to load our luggage onto a waiting trailer. The journalists roused themselves and started straggling off the bus. Kabalevsky and I were in the last pair of seats. I stood and let the old man go in front of me, following him shakily down the aisle.

I was still somewhat drunk and I had my eyes on the lighted doorway of the terminal building, so I wasn't looking carefully when I stepped off the bus. The rest of the group were almost at the terminal door, and as I hurried to catch up, my foot hit an icy patch hidden in the darkness. I felt my feet fly out from under me and heard a workman cry out a warning. Unable to regain my balance, I fell heavily, my head striking the ground. I gave a low moan, then blackness overcame me and I lost consciousness.

CHAPTER ELEVEN

I opened my eyes slowly, wincing at the strong light. I was staring at a cracked whitewashed ceiling with a naked bulb screwed into a plastic fixture. My head ached painfully and my mouth felt dry. I turned my head slightly, taking in my surroundings.

I saw a row of identical narrow white wrought-iron beds. Women wearing shapeless white cotton gowns shuffled about the room, which smelled strongly of disinfectant.

"Feeling better?" asked a voice in Russian. I followed the sound. The speaker was a wizened old lady who was propped up in the bed opposite to mine. She had a gnome's face, all wrinkled and sunken and crowned with tufts of white hair. She smiled a wide toothless smile.

"What happened?" I croaked in Russian, struggling to a sitting position.

"They brought you in very late last night," the old lady said.

"Woke me up too," said a high-pitched, querulous voice from the bed next to mine. "Didn't they, Tanya?"

I turned and saw an almost identical old lady hooked up to an intravenous device.

"You weren't asleep," said Tanya, across from me. "You

were calling for an extra blanket right before they brought her in.''

"I was cold," said the old lady in the bed next to mine, "and the nurse wouldn't come."

"There was no nurse," sighed Tanya, "and no extra blankets either. You can see for yourself all the beds are full.''

"I could have had her blanket," whined the old lady, pointing at me.

"Where are your manners?" snapped Tanya. "The young lady is sick too. All must share equally."

"No, take the blanket. I'm not cold," I said hastily. I pushed it from me and was horrified to discover that I too was dressed in a backless, wrinkled hospital gown. "This won't do," I muttered, swinging my legs over the side of the bed and standing up cautiously. My vision blurred, then refocused. I walked unsteadily to the next bed and tucked the worn blanket around the old woman's feet. No wonder she was cold. The room was positively frigid. "Where are my clothes?" I asked her.

"They take all your clothes. It's the rules. But the coats they hang there." She pointed to a metal wardrobe.

I had no trouble identifying my coat among the others and quickly replaced my hospital gown with the full-length sable. Then I climbed back on the bed, tucking my bare feet under me as I considered my next move.

"Nelzyah!" I looked up and confronted the ugliest head nurse I had ever seen. Her small black eyes glared down at me and her wide mouth was twisted into a disapproving frown. *"Nelzyah!* It is not allowed," she repeated.

"What's not allowed?" I asked in English.

"You cannot wear coat."

"I'm cold—*khalod'nee*," I shrugged.

"You have blanket," she said, but I ignored her remark.

"Where are my clothes? I want to leave."

"Clothes are safe," she assured me. "You cannot leave until doctor examines you. Is hospital policy. Like wearing gown."

"Nuts to that," I spat. "I don't need a doctor to tell me I have a lump on my head. I can feel it for myself. And I'll be damned if I'll put on that idiotic gown. If I parade around in that, I'll catch pneumonia in my ass and be stuck in this ice palace till spring."

The head nurse's blank expression told me that she hadn't understood a word I'd said. She picked up my gown from the floor. "Doctor will be here soon," she said. "I will help you change." It looked as if I was going to be forced to obey her. Sizing up the odds, I decided that while I had youth on my side, she definitely had bulk on hers. I'm no wilting violet, but comrade nurse looked like she juggled tractors for fun. I considered making a dash for the door, figuring that she wasn't agile enough to stop me. Fortunately, Boris suddenly appeared and intervened before any blood was spilled. My blood, for instance.

The nurse started talking volubly in Russian, and I caught the words "pampered American capitalist" and "decadent fur coat" before Boris held up a hand to stop her.

"Thank you, comrade nurse," he said in Russian, flashing her a warm smile. "You have done a fine job. The doctor has just told me that due to your excellent care, Miss van Bell has recovered enough to be discharged. I have her papers and clothes right here so we need not take up any more of your valuable time."

The nurse blushed, embarrassed by Boris' effusive praise. She took the papers from his outstretched hand and studied them carefully.

"Everything seems to be in order," she nodded. "Thank you, comrade. You may leave as soon as she is ready."

"Prince Charming to the rescue," I grinned as the nurse left the room.

"How do you feel, Christina?" he asked anxiously. "You gave us quite a scare at airport."

"No permanent damage," I assured him. "What happened to the group? Did they leave without me?"

"It was terrible scene," Boris replied. "Your accident made us late for boarding plane because everyone must make sure you would be all right. Plane cannot be delayed without special permission from Central Committee. Central Committee cannot be reached so all passengers must board immediately. Customs inspectors could not properly check baggage and passports due to lack of time and all Americans being drunk and incoherent from farewell banquet.''

"What happened to my baggage?" I asked, suddenly remembering the jewels.

"That was one of the things causing such confusion," Boris said. "You had so many suitcases they could not fit in ambulance. I took smallest one and Mr. Joe Smith of your group promised to check rest, which included jewelry, at airport in America and leave key with Air France security police. He even took jewels you wear to banquet."

The irony of the situation did not escape me. The Princess' nephew had slipped out of the country carrying his family's jewels after all, despite all of Moses' worries about the danger of such a move. Even Boris had not questioned the old man's identity though he had been with our group all week and should have been able to recognize "Joe Smith" by now. Boris must have been drunk, I decided.

"What happens now?" I asked.

"I have arranged for you to leave on another flight later today." He looked at his watch. "It is only eleven o'clock so we have plenty of time. I have been charged by Intourist with your safe departure, so we can spend rest of day together. Then I will drive you to airport and put you on plane personally."

"Very gallant," I said dryly, "but I'm going to create quite a sensation when I turn up at the airport with nothing on but this damned fur coat." I pulled it open to flash him.

"A lovely sight," he said approvingly. "Pilot may even let you sit up front."

"I might be willing to try it if it wasn't so damn cold," I laughed. "I hope the suitcase you rescued wasn't the one with my underwear. Where's my gown?"

"I have in here also," said Boris, placing a monogrammed suitcase on the bed. I selected a gray wool sweater and skirt and a pair of gray suede boots, silently blessing Moses for packing so efficiently. Boris politely left the room while I dressed, and after saying good-bye to the two old ladies, I joined him outside.

"Are you hungry?" he asked as we took the ancient elevator to the lobby. "I could take you to lunch."

"Now you're talking," I said, brightening at this mention of food. I suddenly realized that I hadn't eaten since the banquet the night before and that I was ravenously hungry.

The temperature was well below freezing as we stepped out of the hospital into the early-afternoon sunshine. It had snowed during the night and there were piles of white against the curb. Women wearing cloth overcoats over layers of sweaters shuffled about in front of the building, diligently shoveling the walks. Despite official propaganda of equal opportunity, I'd noticed that it was women who did most of the menial labor in the workers' paradise.

"I have use of official car," Boris said proudly, leading me to an ancient, dark blue Moskvitch. It is against the law to drive a dirty or dented automobile in the Soviet Union, and like all Russian cars this one was carefully polished and spotlessly clean. However, the engine coughed and sputtered when Boris turned on the ignition, and the lack of a defroster and snow tires made winter driving hazardous. Skidding was frequent on the icy streets and Moscow pedestrians added to the danger by entirely disregarding red lights.

"Is better than it used to be," Boris told me when I questioned these suicidal tendencies. "Now most people use crosswalks."

"They have fines for jaywalking where I come from," I said, closing my eyes as a taxi driver sprayed muddy snow on a group of workers when he jammed his brakes to avoid hitting them.

"Is law here too," said Boris, shrugging philosophically, "but streets belong to people. Police are reluctant to impose fines so no one pays attention."

A police car with a cluster of loudspeakers on the roof was parked at a busy intersection, and a paternal voice was trying to coax pedestrians to wait for the light.

"The man carrying the toilet seat, get back on the sidewalk," the voice urged. "You may save a minute now but it will be of no importance if you are killed." The crowd laughed as the embarrassed man did as he was told.

Our destination was Gorky Park. It is the oldest park in the city and a sentimental favorite of Moscow residents. It was little more than two kilometers long and one kilometer wide, nestled comfortably between the university and the Kremlin. It had a small river and a variety of warm-weather activities, including a children's playhouse, a Ferris wheel, and landscaped walks. In winter, however, the main attraction was ice skating. The park had four skating rinks linked by special skating paths, but I declined Boris' invitation to try this popular sport.

The park contained several restaurants and cafés, and Boris escorted me to one that commanded a view of the skaters. It was early afternoon on a working day and the place was practically deserted.

Unless meals are preordered for a large group, service in Russian restaurants is so incredibly slow that there's a joke saying that many Russians have read *War and Peace* between courses. However, Boris managed to get our soup course served with minimal delay and, having gotten the chill out of my bones and the edge off my appetite, I was content to relax in my seat and sip my tea.

"Shall we propose a toast?" I asked, holding up my glass.

"I think you've proposed quite enough toasts on this trip," Boris laughed.

"Things did get a little out of hand," I admitted, "but I was just trying to liven the evening up a bit."

"You did that," Boris agreed. "Room was *plo'kha*."

"Bad?"

"Very," he nodded. "In Soviet Union waiters are held responsible for damage and all were detained after party."

The waiter arrived with our food and our conversation was momentarily interrupted. Boris had ordered *pelmemi*, light boiled dumplings filled with meat and served with sour cream, baked potatoes, and a selection of pickled vegetables. Fresh fruit and vegetables were rare commodities during the winter, and it suddenly seemed a long time since I had seen a ripe peach or a head of lettuce. It would be good to get home, I thought, to hot showers, electric blankets, thick pile carpeting, all the things that make life worth living.

Then I remembered that Moses had been posing as one of

those waiters and Boris' remark about the police took on a new meaning.

"I'm sorry about the waiters," I said carefully, spreading sour cream on my dumplings. "Perhaps I can pay for the damage. I can easily afford it."

Boris shook his head. "That would not be allowed. In Soviet Union all must pay own debts. Police checked papers of all waiters and they lost half a night's wages. Was not so terrible . . . for most." He looked directly at me as he said this, and there was something in his expression that caught my attention.

"What do you mean?" I asked, taking a second helping of vegetables. The pickled beets suddenly tasted like sawdust, and I had to force myself to swallow.

"One waiter did not have proper papers and was arrested by police. Not to carry papers is very serious crime in U.S.S.R. so few people forget. Person without papers has usually committed crime in other part of country and is therefore escaped criminal."

My stomach dropped. "What if he's not a Soviet citizen?" I croaked.

"All foreign citizens in Soviet Union are registered with KGB," Boris explained. "Foreign citizen without official permission to be in country can be tried as spy under Soviet law."

I nodded, not trusting myself to speak. Thanks to my clever diversion the night before, Kabalevsky and the jewels were safe, but this same maneuver had prevented Moses' escape. Once his identity was established the United States would deny that he was working for them. They would abandon him to the tender mercies of the Soviet criminal justice system, which bore as much resemblance to justice as glass bore to diamonds. The room darkened suddenly and my fork clattered against my plate. I fought to keep from passing out.

"Are you all right?" Boris asked anxiously.

"It's my head," I lied.

"Was bad fall," Boris murmured. "We will go outside. Air will do you good."

He paid the bill and helped me into my coat. I leaned heavily against him as we went outside, but the cold air felt good against my face and I began to revive.

We walked along the edge of the lake like two lovers, but I could not enjoy the afternoon. Icicles frosted the bare branches of the trees, glistening like diamonds in the sunlight, but their jewellike appearance only depressed me more. Despite Moses' instructions to try nothing daring or clever or noble, I couldn't just get on a plane and leave him to his fate. It was my fault he was in jail. I had to find some way to help him.

"I haven't been in park in long time," said Boris, interrupting these gloomy thoughts. "When I was student at university, I used to come here to skate."

I nodded, barely listening as my mind retraced the events of the past few hours. Though our conversation might have seemed innocent enough, Intourist guides are usually careful not to discuss anything that might show their government in a poor light. Boris' disclosures of the events following the banquet, even his choice of a restaurant in an area not frequented by tourists in winter, led me to believe that he had not merely entertained me with idle gossip. Could Boris have known Landon's identity? Did he know of the switch with Kabalevsky and of my connection to Moses?

At the hospital, Boris had told me that "Joe Smith" had volunteered to safeguard my belongings. But Joe Smith was really the Princess' nephew. Would Kabalevsky have risked exposing himself to the one person most likely to turn him over to the Soviet police for the sake of some jewels, or had Boris, knowing who he was, discussed this emergency move with him?

The pieces of the puzzle were beginning to fit. I remembered the night that Boris had swung through my window on a rope just to make love to me. No one had ever known he was there. Though I had no positive proof that Boris had switched the jewels, perhaps I had been vain in thinking that he had risked his life solely for a night between the sheets. I glared at him through narrowed eyes.

"It was you," I said furiously. He stopped talking and looked at me.

"What was me?" he asked innocently.

"You switched the jewels. You knew about Kabalevsky and Moses and the whole plan. That's why you risked your neck to come to my room, not from some romantic impulse but to carry out some assigned task!" I turned my back on him and started to walk away.

"Christina, please . . ." he said, reaching for my arm. His grip was like iron. I kicked him viciously in the shins, pounding him ineffectually with my free hand.

"Liar! Fraud! Were you well paid?"

"I was not paid at all. If you will calm down, I will explain . . ."

"Explain what, you czarist baboon! That you were playing James Bond, not Romeo? Well, you fooled me. You ought to go to Hollywood. They could use a clever actor like you in those grade-B films!"

He was still holding my arm and he pulled me roughly against him, silencing my protests with a kiss that took my breath away. His tongue forced itself between my lips and a wave of desire washed over me. My body turned to liquid fire, my angry cries to submissive moans.

"Is not acting," he said softly as he let me go. "I love you, Christina."

We were in a small clearing, far from the restaurant and the frozen lakes of skaters. A plain wooden shack with a sagging door frame and a pitched, snow-covered roof was set against the trees. Boris must have known of its existence for he easily opened the door and led me inside. There were several hard wooden benches, a row of hooks on the wall, and a large kerosene heater. A small window covered with a heavy glazed paper filtered the afternoon sun so that the room seemed bathed in a yellow haze.

"Is place for skaters to leave shoes and overcoats," Boris explained as he knelt to light the heater, "but few skate this far, and today I do not think we will be disturbed."

The room warmed up quickly. I spread my coat over one of the wide benches, took off my boots, and made myself comfortable, rubbing my silk-clad feet and legs against the thick fur. Boris took off his own coat and hat and hung them carefully on the hooks. He sat down on the bench and began to warm my cold feet with his hands.

"Why did you switch the jewels?" I asked him. "Why did you help Kabalevsky escape?"

"My half brother is in American hospital," Boris shrugged. "Kabalevsky used his influence to help him. When he goes to America he will send me news." I nodded, remembering the young soldier who had contacted Princess Lyapunov on her nephew's behalf. "My brother is only family, so you understand why I do this for him. In Russia, family is most important."

"You did not have to tell me of the arrest," I said.

"Colonel Landon is brave man. Perhaps American government can use influence to get him released or to trade for Soviet spy."

"He's not important enough," I said. "This mission is not important enough. They won't help him. But I will, if you'll help me."

Boris shook his head. "Colonel Landon understood risk when he took assignment. I am Soviet citizen, Christina. To help smuggle jewels is wrong, but I did for my brother. But this . . ."

"You said you loved me."

"I do, but you are not in prison. This afternoon I will put you on plane and you will be safe. Is all that matters."

"You don't understand," I said desperately. "It's my fault he was arrested. I started that riot at the banquet which caused the waiters to be detained in the first place. If it weren't for me, Moses would be safe at the American Embassy right now. I can't just go home and leave him to his fate. It would be on my conscience for the rest of my life!"

"You have no choice."

"I can get him out of jail. Surely some prisoners escape!"

"I will not let you take such risk. Even with my help you cannot succeed. We would all three end in labor camp."

I started to cry. Tears welled up in my eyes and spilled silently down my cheeks. Boris took me in his arms and cradled my head against his shoulder. His hand stroked my hair and, holding my head between his hands, he kissed me gently on my forehead, then my eyes and cheeks and finally my lips. I caught my breath as his lips reawakened my senses. I closed my eyes and opened my mouth, breathing in the warmth and fragrance of his desire. This was not acting and despite my feelings of helplessness and depression, my carnal instincts responded to the strength and power of his lovemaking. My body grew warm and, slipping my arms around his neck, I pressed myself against him.

"I want you," I whispered against his ear. "I want you to fuck me."

I could feel his cock swell as I said these words, and his hands trembled slightly as he pulled my sweater over my head and loosened the buttons on my skirt. I stretched out full-length on my sable coat, enjoying the feel of the rich fur against my skin. Boris unhooked my bra, exposing my full, ripe breasts. His lips and fingers were like a torch igniting my passion. He took my nipples into his mouth and they stiffened against the rough surface of his tongue. Boris now eased my skirt over my hips, dropping it to the floor. I was clad only in my sheer silk panty hose, which was molded to the curves of my hips and thighs and lent a transparent sheen to my skin. Boris undressed quickly, and I caught my breath as the heater's light bathed his magnificent body in a reddish glow. I could feel the blood pound through my veins as he slowly began to peel off my panty hose.

Naked on our fur pallet, we were like two primitives, our eyes gleaming with desire. I spread my legs as Boris lowered himself on top of me in the time-tested missionary position. Thus Adam subdued Eve, not with delicate foreplay but with pure animal lust. The feel of his long hard cock against my leg sent my senses reeling. I was hot and wet and, arching my hips, I parted my pussy lips invitingly. A second later his rock-hard shaft had plunged through the moist folds of my vagina until it was buried to the hilt inside me. I dug my fingers into the broad muscles of his back as his cock cored so deep that I felt I would be split in half. We moved together, slowly at first, then with increasing speed and passion. We grunted and moaned, our sweat-filmed bodies heated even more by the almost stifling warmth of the kerosene heater and the sable coat beneath us. I wrapped my legs around his hips, opening my mouth to his as my pussy opened for his cock. I urged him on with my tongue and lips and hands, begging for more until I was almost beaten senseless by the pounding rhythm of his thrusts.

Cut loose from consciousness, my mind focused on our bodies joined together in this consummate sensual act. I listened to the sounds of our passion and breathed in the odors of arousal as his manhood plumbed the farthest recesses of my cunt. When Boris exploded into orgasm inside me, I felt as if my entire body were being blown apart. His hot spurting seed filled me completely, triggering a mind-blowing series of orgasms. Sated by sexual excess and lulled by the overpowering warmth of the room, I closed my eyes and fell asleep.

When I opened them again, I was wrapped in my sable coat, my head pillowed on Boris' fur hat. The sun had gone down and the room was dark except for the small circle of light provided by the heater's glow. Boris was nowhere to be seen. I wondered where he had gone and how long I had been asleep.

My first question was answered when the door opened a few moments later, blowing a gust of freezing air into the room. Boris kicked it shut and placed a brown paper bag down carefully on one of the benches.

"I hope that's something to eat," I said, struggling to a sitting position. "I'm starved."

"It is," he laughed. "Is peasant food but was best I could do." He began to set the food out on an empty bench while I hastened into my clothes and combed my hair. There was a loaf of black bread, a small round of hard yellow cheese, a long dried sausage, and a bottle of vodka. Boris divided the food with his pocket knife and in the absence of glasses we passed the bottle of vodka between us. We ate in silence. The subject of Moses was not broached, but it was very much on my mind. Boris, too, seemed moody and preoccupied.

"What time is my plane?" I asked him. "Perhaps we'd better go."

"Do not tease, Christina," Boris grunted. "You know you have won."

"Won?"

"I cannot refuse you. It is madness, but I will help you rescue your American."

I threw my arms around him and kissed him passionately. "I don't know how to thank you," I whispered, my voice choked with tears. "This means a great deal."

"You have thanked me," he said simply. "If I spend rest of life in labor camp, I will remember past few days. Now, we must make plan. There is little time."

"Can we get him a phony passport or papers?" I asked. "It doesn't matter what nationality. I understand American dollars can buy almost anything."

Boris shook his head. "There is not time. Colonel Landon is being held in Moscow police station while investigation is conducted. Right now he is merely Russian citizen without papers, but when police find out he is American, they will turn him over to KGB. He will be transferred to Lubiyanka prison, most secure prison in Soviet Union, and escape will be impossible."

"But even if we get him out of the police station, he can't leave the country without a passport."

"Not true," said Boris. "He cannot leave at legal points of exit. But tonight I have government car. We will drive to Finnish border where, with luck, you can escape. There are many places on border that are not heavily guarded."

"Will you come with us?"

He shook his head. "I have heard much of United States, but I would miss very much Moscow and my friends. I will take you to border by back roads. When you are safe across, I will return. I will have car until tomorrow morning."

"Then we must get Moses out tonight."

Boris nodded. "We can take your suitcase and you can check out of National as if you were going with me to airport. This will not be difficult. Inspector Leskov is in charge of investigation, and I can perhaps get into police station to see him. But I cannot get him to release Colonel Landon or even to tell me where in building he is being held."

"How about a bribe?"

"We could offer only money, but here money cannot buy a

car or a larger apartment. These can be obtained only by long wait or influence. Inspector Leskov is member of Communist Party. In Soviet Union it is this, not rubles, that is main source of prestige and influence.''

I thought about this for a few moments. "Perhaps I could persuade the Inspector," I said.

He shook his head. "Foreigners cannot visit police station," he said.

"Then I'll pretend to work for Intourist. My Russian is good enough. Could you get me some identification?" He nodded cautiously. "Once I get to the man in charge, I'll just tell him we found the waiter's papers after the banquet and demand that he be released.''

"Police will not release him if you cannot actually produce papers," Boris pointed out.

"Then I'll try some other bluff. We haven't time to be clever," I insisted. "We need a direct attack."

"Inspector is not fool."

"I didn't say he was. But he is a man and, believe me, there isn't a man in the world I cannot ultimately get to do what I want. I just have to present my request in the proper way.''

"You are right," Boris sighed. "Is our only chance." Then he smiled suddenly. "Inspector is only human," he laughed. "By the time you are done with him, he will probably drive you to border himself.''

CHAPTER TWELVE

It was late afternoon when Boris and I returned to his car. My flight to Paris was scheduled to leave at ten P.M., which gave us little time to make our preparations for the evening. We drove first to GUM. Here I purchased a plain black cloth coat, several sizes too big, which would be more suitable to my cover as an Intourist guide than my full-length sable, and a pair of knee-high, black plastic boots one size too small. Ready-made clothing is in short supply in the worker's paradise and prices are high. These poorly made, ill-fitting garments would cost the average worker about four months wages.

GUM is Russia's largest store with an arched glass roof running the entire length of its center artery and lending it the appearance of a railroad terminal. Small shops open from a series of corridors and balconies and other counters are recessed in alcoves. In one of these alcoves was a curtained booth where for five kopeks I could have my picture taken three times in the size required for all official government documents. I posed in my newly purchased coat, and Boris slipped the pictures into his pocket.

"I will take you to National while I put together phony Intourist identification," he told me as we again got back in the car. "They have held your room for extra night due to accident, and you can have meal in dining room if you are hungry. We must check out at eight P.M. to make plane on time. I will pick you up then. If you have sensibly changed mind, I will take you to airport."

"I won't change my mind," I said firmly.

"Americans," he sighed. "You all think you are John Wayne risking his life to save white man from Indian camp. We Russians do not tempt fate. There is saying: Hope for best, expect worst and drink to kill pain."

Boris escorted me to the lobby of the National, and after making sure that my suitcase was delivered to my room, he took his leave.

I am always hungry and, not knowing when I would have my next good meal, I took two helpings of chicken Kiev at dinner. I lingered over my food, drinking several glasses of wine to give me courage and scanning the day's edition of *Moscow News*, a free English-language paper intended for the consumption of tourists and the diplomatic community. There was a small write-up about the farewell banquet on page four. It declared the event an unqualified success without mentioning the orgy that followed the meal or the arrest of the errant waiter. To judge from Soviet newspapers, Russia is a land without catastrophes. There was a listing of foreign-language films in the entertainment section, and I noticed that *The Searchers* was being featured at the Yermolova Theater, at 5 Gorky Street.

"John Wayne," I said aloud, remembering Boris' earlier comment.

"*Prastee'te?*" said the waiter who had just arrived with my dessert.

"I said John Wayne," I repeated in Russian.

"Ah, the Duke," he beamed. "His family came from Russia, you know."

"No, I didn't," I said. "I always thought he was of Irish descent."

"An understandable mistake," he replied, obviously pitying my ignorance, "but there was a story about him in *Pravda* when he died and they mentioned the cossack village where he was born."

"Cossack, huh?"

"Anyone who has seen him ride a horse could not doubt that he had cossack blood."

"He probably would have been thrilled to hear you say that," I conceded.

I had showered and changed and was waiting in the lobby when Boris arrived an hour later to collect me. He handled the elaborate checkout procedures, then carrying my suitcase, he led me to the car that was parked out front.

"Is everything taken care of?" I asked as soon as Boris had eased the car into the flow of traffic. He nodded and slipped an envelope from his pocket. I looked over the contents and found it contained an authentic-looking set of papers, complete with picture, identifying me as an Intourist employee. The picture wasn't bad, all things considered, but I frowned when I saw the name in the upper right-hand corner of the ID card.

"Where did you get this name?" I demanded. "Maria Monomakh? What kind of name is that? I don't feel like a Monomakh."

"Is perfectly respectable Russian name," Boris said, trying to keep the car from skidding on the icy streets. He reached out the window and gave the windshield wipers a sharp pull to get them going.

"Also you've got the wrong birth date down here," I muttered. "You made me two years older than I am!"

"I guessed," Boris said absently. He wiped the front windshield with the sleeve of his coat.

"Yeah, well obviously you guess that I look older than I am, is that the story?" I said angrily.

"Christina," he sighed, "I was in terrible hurry. I had to steal papers from storage room, find empty office with typewriter, and fill in papers before anyone could notice what I was doing. Also I had trouble finding glue for picture, so I could not have time to worry about your real birth date."

"Commie bullshit," I snapped. "You didn't seem to think I was this old when you were moaning between my thighs." I waved the papers in front of his nose and he slammed on the brakes as the car skidded dangerously.

"Christina, please! I have to concentrate on traffic."

"And my eyes are not brown," I continued, peering closely at the papers. "Haven't you looked at my eyes?"

Boris pretended he didn't hear me.

We were halfway to Sheremetyevo airport when Boris slowed the car and pulled to the side of the road.

"Is dark enough now," he told me, "and we have not been followed. We will return to Moscow by different route so we will not be noticed. However, if you have changed mind, we can still make plane to Paris."

My stomach churned and I took a deep, shuddering breath. The moment of irretrievable commitment had arrived. Once that plane took off for Paris without me, I would no longer be a welcome guest of the Soviet government. The fact that I had stayed behind to help an American agent escape Soviet justice would only add to the charges against me should I be apprehended. The possible consequences of failure loomed around me like the plot of a Dostoyevsky novel.

"Why don't you get that coat I bought this afternoon at GUM out of the trunk?" I said evenly. "I think it's time I became Maria Monomakh."

It was after ten P.M. when we reentered the main section of the city. It was a dark freezing night that suited our purposes admirably. Boris parked the car a block from the police station. We had discussed the pros and cons of keeping the engine running, but the difficulty of obtaining more petrol should our supply run out made us decide not to keep the car idling.

"Do you know what you are going to do?" Boris asked as I draped a plain woolen scarf around my head the way I had seen Russian women do.

"I have a general idea," I said.

"Don't forget to speak Russian," he cautioned. "Though most Intourist guides speak English, your accent would give you away immediately. And try to work quickly. If I stay here too long, policeman will notice me and begin to ask questions."

"Don't fret, Boris darling," I cooed. "Just try to keep

awake and warm. We'll need to make a fast getaway."

"I have a bottle of vodka in the glove compartment," he said. He put his arms around me and held me close. "One more thing. If you see you cannot make success, try to get yourself away. If you are caught, it will cost three lives instead of one."

"I promise," I whispered, pressing my lips to his. I could feel his heart thudding against his chest, or perhaps it was my own. I took a deep breath then pulled myself away, slipping from the car without looking back.

I walked through the drifting snow toward the police station, feeling the cold for the first time in my thin Russian coat. I wondered if they would let me keep my sable coat in Siberia, then quickly pushed the thought from my mind. I had to think positively. Not only my own life, but those of Boris and Moses as well, depended on my performance.

The main lobby of the station house was a cavernous, dimly lit space, tastefully decorated in decrepit wooden furniture and peeling green paint. A life-size poster of Lenin occupied one wall. A very young policeman was seated at the battered reception desk, frowning over some papers.

"May I help you, comrade?" he asked brusquely, intimating that I was interrupting important business.

I loosened my scarf and my hair tumbled in a blond halo around my face. His eyes widened.

"I am Maria Monomakh," I said in Russian, handing him my papers. "I wish to see Inspector Leskov."

"Monomakh, what a pretty name," he said. "Do you have an appointment?"

"Do I need one?"

"The Inspector is a busy man and it is very late."

"I have something important to tell him about a case he is investigating. Tell him it's about the waiter who was arrested last night."

He picked up the phone on his desk, dialed a number, and spoke rapidly to the party on the other end. I caught the words "young" and "beautiful" and smiled to acknowledge the compliment. He replaced the receiver and returned my papers.

"You can go up, Comrade Monomakh. Room two-oh-four. Second floor, first door to your right."

Christina one, commies nothing, I thought happily as I climbed the short flight to the second floor. Neither my papers nor my Russian had been questioned, and I felt ready to tackle the man in charge.

I rapped on the frosted glass door and a voice called for me to come in. The man behind the desk did not stand when I entered. In the harsh yellow light of the room, he seemed slightly sinister, like a character from a Raymond Chandler novel. He was a tall man, with thick greasy hair and dark opaque eyes. His shoulders rounded slightly and his head jutted forward as a result. I could picture him supervising an interrogation, a blackjack in his broad, hairy hand. I could picture him pulling the trigger of a gun.

His eyes traveled slowly over me, assessing, almost insulting. I returned his look boldly, refusing to be cowed. He was a man used to power, but I sensed that if I were too submissive he would quickly become bored and dismiss me.

The Inspector knitted his fingers and leaned back in his chair. "Officer Peshkov said you wanted to see me," he said flatly. This was not going to be easy.

"I am Maria Monomakh," I said, being careful of my accent and trying to sound official. "I was sent by Intourist to speak to you about a prisoner you are holding here. A waiter named Nicholas Kobylinski. He was arrested last night following an official banquet at the Kremlin."

The Inspector turned his head to one side, staring at the blackness outside his window. An ancient wooden blind hung at a rakish angle, the broken cord knotted like a hangman's noose. Despite the coldness of the room and the thinness of my coat, I began to feel warm. He cleared his throat, then stood up slowly.

"May I see your papers?"

I reached into my bag and handed these to him. He studied them closely, taking the time to compare my face to the photograph.

"We have a prisoner who was arrested last night at the

Kremlin,'' he said, giving me a hard look, "but he said his name was Andrei Radishchev.''

Damn Moses, I thought. Why couldn't he keep his mouth shut. "Nicholas must be his patronym,'' I said hastily, "and I wasn't really sure of his last name.''

The Inspector nodded. He looked again at my papers and my stomach dropped, but he handed them back to me without comment.

"It is very late, Comrade Monomakh,'' he said evenly. "You have come here to talk about a man with no papers, a serious crime in the Soviet Union, a man whose name you don't even know. Why?''

"Like you, Comrade Inspector, Intourist guides do not have regular hours,'' I said brazenly. "This waiter was arrested at a function hosted by our office and my superior felt responsible for the mistake.''

"What mistake is that?''

He was leading me on, giving me enough rope to hang myself, and I began to wish that I had thought out what I was going to say more carefully. He set a chair beside his desk, indicating that he wished me to sit down. He continued to stand, however, placing him in a superior position and making it impossible for me to see his expression clearly. It was the technique of an experienced policeman.

"As you probably know, Comrade Inspector,'' I said, feeling my way, "there was a great deal to drink. Unlike we Russians, Americans cannot hold their liquor.'' He nodded as if digesting what I had said. "There was a great deal of confusion at the end of the meal and the waiters were recruited to help get the Americans into their coats and hats and onto their bus. Comrade Kobylinski—excuse me, Radishchev—must have dropped his papers while carrying out these instructions. They were found outside in the snow this morning by a workman. When our office learned that he had been arrested, I was sent over here to vouch for him.''

"Then you have his papers?''

"They are at my office,'' I lied.

"Comrade Monomakh, surely you see that I cannot release

the prisoner without actually seeing his papers," the Inspector said smoothly. "Why don't you fetch them from your office and bring them here?"

"I can't," I said. "I mean, the office is closed now."

"Tomorrow is another day," the Inspector said, smiling slightly. "I assure you that Comrade Kobylinski or Radish-chev or whatever his name is, will be perfectly comfortable in our third-floor detention cell. In fact, he is in luck. He is our only prisoner at the moment, so he won't have to share the bed."

Boris had been right. The Inspector was no fool. I would have to try another approach, something more personal. I began to loosen the buttons on my coat.

"Are you warm, comrade?" he asked solicitously. "Would you like a drink?" I nodded. He moved toward a metal army locker, took out a bottle of vodka and two glasses, and brought them back to the desk. I stood and removed my coat. I was wearing a black wool jersey dress with long, tight-fitting sleeves and a daring décolletage. The only ornamentation was a long gold zipper that ran from neck to hemline and served as the fastening device as well. The material clung to my body, revealing every curve from the soft swell of my bosom to the outlines of my thighs. I was not wearing any underwear and a small patina of sweat broke out on the Inspector's forehead as he handed me my drink.

"Now, Comrade Monomakh," he said, taking a seat opposite me. "Let us stop playing games."

"Games?"

"Intourist did not send you here, comrade. They did not send a young and pretty woman to plead for a foolish waiter without papers. There are no papers, are there?"

"No. I mean, there may be, but I don't have them," I said lamely, pretending to be confused. My initial boldness had caught his interest, but my bluff had failed and I could see no way to bully him into doing what I wanted. It was time to switch tactics, to crumble before his masterly ability to reveal the truth of the whole sordid situation.

"This is a serious matter," the Inspector said sternly. "Why are you trying to get me to free this man? Is he your husband? Your brother?''

"No," I said in a quiet voice. "I never saw him before last night."

"Then why are you so concerned?"

"You must have heard what happened at the banquet last night," I said. "The little indiscretions?"

"That's one way of putting it," he grunted in an amused tone.

I moved my chair closer so that my leg touched his thigh. I leaned forward so that the swell of my cleavage was clearly visible. I was reaching for the Soviet Academy Award with this performance. "Last night at the banquet," I said confidentially, "we all got a little drunk, the guests, the waiters, even the KGB." He smiled a little. The competition between the regular police and the KGB was legendary. "I allowed myself to be seduced," I continued, lowering my eyes.

"Oh?"

"Yes, several times. I could not help myself." I let my hand fall, as if by accident, on the growing bulge in his trousers. "Ever since my early teens, I have craved the attentions of men."

"You have a high level of desire?" he asked hopefully.

"That's one way of putting it," I confessed. "The doctor said I was . . ."

"A nymphomaniac?"

"That's the word," I sighed. "By the time I was through school I had been to bed with most of my classmates and some of the faculty as well. When I couldn't find a man, I slept with a woman, sometimes going through several partners in a single evening. Even so, I am seldom satisfied. I am like the Flying Dutchman of sex, forever sailing the carnal seas, looking for a satisfactory harbor."

"That's very poetic," he murmured, putting his hand over mine as I massaged his cock and balls through the thin material of his trousers. "This is quite a confession, comrade."

"But last night at the banquet, I met Nicholas. He was

perfection. We made love repeatedly, in every conceivable position, and each time I came and came. You cannot know what it means to me to finally find a man who can satisfy me." I began to fondle my breasts as I continued to masturbate him.

"I see," the Inspector said, his eyes riveted on my bulging mounds.

"I know it was madness to try to fool you, Comrade Inspector. I don't know why I even tried, except that I was desperate to see Nicholas again."

"I cannot release the prisoner simply to satiate your abnormal desires," the Inspector said hoarsely.

"Then let me see him in his cell," I pleaded. "You can do that. Just let me have him for a few hours and then I'll leave and no one will be the wiser. It would mean so much to me, Comrade Inspector. I'm hot and wet just thinking about him. If you refuse, I will drown myself in the Volga." I stood up suddenly, and the Inspector's body convulsed spasmodically, a classic symptom of blue balls.

"I want to help you," he gasped. "See, here is the key to your lover's cell." He pulled the key from his desk drawer and showed it to me. "I could easily do as you ask."

"Then do it," I begged him, clasping my hands imploringly.

"I can't," he said, struggling to his feet. He was breathing heavily, his eyes hot with desire. "The prisoner was up most of the night. He would not answer our questions and I'm afraid we were compelled to try more forceful means to get him to talk. If you went to him now, I doubt he could repeat his stellar performance of last night."

Images of Moses' broken and bleeding body flooded my mind. I had to grasp the chair to keep from falling.

"I don't believe you," I cried. "Nicholas is a man of incredible physical reserves. Once he sees me, he'll be ready for action."

"Nicholas is not the only man in Russia with vast reserves of energy," the Inspector said significantly. "Many women have complimented me on my prowess."

"You're a virile-looking man, Comrade Inspector," I murmured, running my tongue suggestively over my lips.

"I could help you, Comrade Monomakh," he said, gripping my shoulders painfully. "We could . . . help each other."

I forced my body to relax. "Yes," I whispered, looking into his eyes and swaying toward him helplessly. "Yes, I want you to help me."

I had played my role well but I was no longer acting. The tension and excitement, the very real danger of the situation, were an aphrodisiac, and I shivered as he reached for the golden ring on my zipper and slowly began to pull it downward. The dress parted, revealing inch by inch my ripe, full breasts and the long tapering line of my waist. Leskov's hand trembled slightly and drops of moisture appeared on his upper lip. He knelt before me, then slid the zipper all the way down to expose the golden bush of my pubic hair and the satiny smoothness of my thighs.

There was no bed in the small room. The Inspector went over to lock the office door, then stretched out between my spread legs. I knelt so that my knees were on either side of his head and my pussy was positioned over his face. He slipped his hands up under my dress to cup the firm flesh of my buttocks. I could feel his warm breath on my nether lips as he inhaled the fragrance of my crotch, and I trembled in anticipation of his next move.

I pulled the hem of my dress over my hips and held it bunched around my waist, spreading my knees even wider so that the long curving line of my vaginal lips peeked through the close-cropped curls of my mons. My body teased and tantalized, offering itself to my lover like ripe fruit in winter. I could feel the moisture inside me waiting for his tongue, and I could tell by the labored sound of his breathing that he was as eager to taste my honey as I was to offer it. His tongue began to trace the tender pink membrane in slow back-and-forth strokes. His hands gripped my buttocks and I closed my eyes, squatting even lower as his stabbing tongue pushed its way inside my steamy passage. He had a particularly long, agile tongue and it was made wet and slippery by my juices. I moaned softly, then cried out as his tongue tip plunged deeper and deeper until it flicked the swollen knob of my clitoris. I pushed my pussy downward, grinding my hips and playing with my breasts as the Inspector sucked me to a frenzy of desire. I climaxed not once, but several times, my love-juices gushing over his lips and face.

Still fully dressed, Leskov was breathing heavily. He had worked hard to satisfy me, holding his own needs in abeyance. However, even in the Soviet Union turnabout is fair play and, reversing my position, I sat on Leskov's chest. I loosened the buckle of his belt and unhooked the clip on the waistband of his trousers. I unzipped his fly and released his manhood from the tight confines of his underwear. His cock was long and hard and stood straight up in mute testament to my charms. As I stretched out along Leskov's body, I wriggled backward so that he could suck my cunt while I was eating him. I nibbled on his cock head for a moment, then started licking his shaft with slow, rhythmic strokes. The Inspector's body tensed with excitement and he moaned softly as I began to ease my mouth over the helmetlike tip of his cock. His hands gripped my thighs, pulling me toward him. He pushed my skirt over my hips and I shivered slightly as the cool air of the room wafted across my exposed buttocks. The next thing I knew, he had parted my pussy lips and buried his tongue in my leaking hole. It was fantastic! As I sucked his cock deeper and deeper into my throat, he ate me with a passion and exuberance that sparked my desire all over again.

We hovered on the verge of orgasm, yet held back. We wanted to savor our oral pleasures, to cling as long as possible to the sweet edge of preorgasmic bliss.

My own resistance crumbled first, and with a primal scream I exploded into orgasm. As Leskov lapped eagerly at my gushing pussy, I felt his cock convulse in my throat and streams of love-milk flooded my mouth.

I lifted myself from the Inspector's prone form and turned to look at my prostrate lover. Leskov's eyes were half-closed and his cock lay limply against his leg. Though his energy was flagging, he was still conscious and, more importantly, almost fully dressed. The keys I needed were on the desk but I would need time. Time to release Moses, time to escape. Another round was called for, and, throwing off my dress, I knelt beside him and began to undo the buttons of his shirt.

"What are you doing?" he gasped. "This is a public building."

"The door is locked," I shrugged. "We cannot make love properly if we are fully dressed."

"But there is no bed," he protested, "and the room is cold."

"Come, come, Comrade Inspector," I chided him, working his pants over his hips. "The night's young. We will make our own heat, yes?" I began to massage his limp prick, coaxing it awake.

"We will make our own heat," he sighed, moaning softly as my touch again aroused his senses. "You are an amazing woman, Comrade Monomakh."

"And you are a man of iron, Comrade Inspector," I murmured, looking hotly at his burgeoning cock. "I think we are well-matched."

The Inspector proved a powerful if somewhat brutish lover, making up in staying power what he lacked in finesse. He was, however, willing to try anything I suggested, from mutual S&M to fucking doggie-style. I began to despair of ever totally exhausting him until a particularly hot session of tonguing each other's assholes finally sealed his fate. Legs dangling over the edge, he lay sprawled face down across the top of the desk, snoring peacefully. He was temporarily out of commission, and I got shakily into my clothes, thoughtfully gathering his hat, overcoat, and gun to help facilitate Moses' escape. I bundled the Inspector's clothes into his locker, turned the lock, and pocketed the key. As a final precaution, I used his own handcuffs to secure his ankle to the leg of the desk.

Wait till that male chauvinist pig sees me, I thought, as I made my way stealthily down the corridor. I carried the Inspector's heavy coat over my left arm, my right hand gripping the trigger of the gun hidden between the folds. I was prepared to use the powerful firearm if necessary. I had come too far to fail now.

I carefully ascended the ancient staircase, pausing everytime the wooden boards creaked. I feared there might be a guard on duty, but the third floor was deserted. On a freezing winter's night, a single drunken prisoner was apparently not worth guarding. Taking his coat was all the precaution deemed necessary to prevent escape.

The holding pen was a simple iron-barred cell at the end of the dimly lit hall. Moses stood as I approached, and I winced as I caught sight of the bruises on his face. There was dried blood on his left temple and his left eye was half-closed. He did not immediately recognize me.

"Hey, Rocky, I come to bust ya out," I hissed, slipping the key into the lock.

"What the hell are you doing here?" he demanded angrily as I pulled open the door to the cell. It was not quite the warm reception I had anticipated.

"What do you mean, what am I doing here? What do you think I'm doing here? Having a guided tour? Here, put on this hat and coat. I have a getaway car parked a block away. If we can get out of the building, I think we'll be home free."

"You must be out of your mind," Moses snapped, pulling on the coat. It fit pretty well, all things considered, and with the collar turned up and the hat brim pulled down, his face was effectively shielded. "I told you to take the next plane home. You deliberately disobeyed my orders."

"If you don't shut up," I growled, "I'll turn the key and leave you here and you can rot in a subzero labor camp for the next ten years." I thrust the pistol into his hands. "Here, you're probably better with these things than I am. Let's go while we still can."

Moses released the catch, ejected the magazine, looked at it, and reinserted it into the pistol. He worked the slide to insert a round into the chamber. He grunted in satisfaction. "Eight rounds," he muttered. "Let's hope we don't have to use it." He slipped the gun into the right-hand pocket of his overcoat, keeping his hand on the weapon. I took his other arm and we made our way quickly down the stairs. The young policeman was still on duty in the lobby and he sprang to attention when we entered.

"Good night, comrade officer," I said, flashing him a triumphant smile as we walked by. He flushed slightly.

"Good night, Comrade Monomakh," he stammered. "Good night, Comrade Inspector." Moses touched his hat brim and nodded, then held the front door open to allow me to slip outside.

CHAPTER THIRTEEN

We walked carefully down the front steps of the building. The small police station was set back from the wide street on a tree-lined quadrangle. It was a lawn in summer but now my foot felt ice beneath the soft snow. A slip could spell disaster.

"Where's the car?" Moses asked as we came to the foot of the stairs.

"Across the street and one block left."

"Okay, let's move. They could raise the alarm any minute." He held my arm firmly, half pulling me along.

"I left the Inspector handcuffed naked to his desk," I gasped. "He won't want his subordinates to see him like that. We should have time." We had reached the lighted street where a passing car forced us to slow our pace. I heard footsteps behind us and voices calling for us to stop.

"On the other hand," I said, "I could be wrong."

"Get behind me!" Moses commanded, whirling around and pulling his gun. "We're sitting ducks in this light!"

I turned and peered into the darkness of the quadrangle. There was a volley of shots. I closed my eyes and held my breath but the bullets went wide. Moses didn't fire back as the shadowy figures in the quadrangle didn't present a clear target, and with only eight rounds of ammunition, he couldn't afford to waste bullets.

"Move back toward the car," Moses said over his shoulder. "It's our only chance. I'll cover you."

Too frightened to protest, I did as he asked, crouching behind him as we moved backward. The policemen showed themselves now—three uniformed men with their guns drawn. Keeping a wary eye on Moses' gun, they began to fan out, making it harder and harder for him to cover them all.

I was breathing heavily, my heart pounding so hard I thought I would faint. Then suddenly there was a savage yell to my left. Boris threw himself on the largest of the three men, a black-haired brute with fists like hams.

"Get back, you fool!" called Moses as the other two policemen turned on the new intruder. I screamed as they fired, but again they aimed wide. Moses fired at the man nearest Boris, and he went down, clutching his knee and rolling on the ground. Red drops spattered the white snow. Moses turned, covering the third man, who prudently held his fire as Boris and the remaining policeman grappled for his gun. They were locked together, then the policeman's knee came up. Boris crumpled, loosing his hold, and in that instant the policeman fired at point-blank range. The shot took Boris in the chest and he stumbled backward.

"Christina, no!" Moses shouted as I started toward my Russian lover. "Get to the car!"

There was another explosion and Boris spun around, blood pouring from a wound in his head. With an oath, Moses fired at Boris' assailant and the man went down, emptying his gun into Boris as he fell. I felt something rip through the sleeve of my coat and I started to run away from the scene slipping on the icy street. From the corner of my eye I saw Moses drop to the ground and fire, then roll over and fire again. He was wasting his ammunition, keeping the last man occupied to give me time to escape. With a stifled sob, I pulled open the door of the car and jumped in behind the wheel. I turned the key in the ignition, cursing as the engine made a grinding noise, then stalled. I pushed the gas pedal down, released it, then tried again. The engine roared to life. I bit my lip and watched the temperature gauge, racing the engine to let the car warm up. I glanced in the rear-view mirror. Not fifteen feet away, Moses and the policeman struggled furiously on the ground, the policeman trying to pull away and shoot, and Moses desperately trying to disarm him. Then I saw that the man who Moses had shot in the leg earlier had raised his head and was aiming his gun at the combatants.

"Watch out!" I screamed as the gun went off. The two men collapsed and I held my breath, praying that both had not been killed. Then, with a powerful shove Moses pushed the policeman's body off his own. He stood up cautiously, his eye on the wounded policeman who had killed his fellow officer. The gun was pointed, shook, then dropped from nerveless fingers as the man fell forward in a spray of snow.

I took a deep breath and my heart started beating again. I heard the sound of a siren in the distance. Reinforcements were on the way, but Moses made no move toward the car. He knelt beside Boris' body, then shook his head and turned away. He retrieved one of the fallen guns, emptying the policeman's pockets in a search for extra ammunition. The sirens were getting louder and the revolving flash of a high-beam light appeared in my rear-view mirror. I couldn't see Moses and I panicked. Putting the car in gear, I pulled away from the curb, pounding my fist on the horn and frantically calling Moses' name. He pulled open the door on the driver's side and grabbed the wheel. The car spun wildly as I moved over and he took my place, but he managed to regain control. Pressing on the accelerator, he raced us away seconds ahead of the police cars speeding toward the scene.

I sat hunched in my seat, too numb with fright and shock to talk. Moses, too, was silent. His expression was tense, eyes straining to see down the darkened streets. We were driving too fast. The car skidded dangerously, wheels spinning on the icy roads. I was grateful for the silence, for not having to think or make a decision. The heater in the car was not working well. I snuggled against Moses' shoulder for warmth, reassured by the sheer bulk of his physical presence.

"Where are we going?" I asked through chattering teeth.

"Out of Moscow, I hope," he replied grimly. "Then to the Finnish border. It's the closest. We'll have to risk sneaking across."

"Boris had the same plan," I said. "He . . ." My eyes filled with tears and I started to cry.

"He was a brave man," Moses said as I fumbled in my bag for some tissues. "This is going to be a lot tougher situation to get out of without him to help us. Why don't you see if there's a map in that glove compartment?" *I understand how you feel, but don't go to pieces*, was his unspoken message.

Moses was right. If we were caught, we might envy Boris' quick death. I pulled open the glove compartment and tumbled the contents into my lap.

"What have you got there?" said Moses, still distracting me.

"A flashlight . . . no batteries. Pencil . . . broken. Bottle of vodka. No map," I said. I opened the bottle and took a large gulp. "Don't worry, Moses, I'm not going to fall apart. You have enough to think about without my adding to the problem."

"I know that," said Moses softly. "You're a good soldier, Christina." Coming from Colonel Male Chauvinist Pig Landon this was high praise.

It was a terrifying two hours. Sirens and flashing lights were everywhere as Moses drove in a crazy-quilt pattern, evading roadblocks and police patrols in his efforts to avoid capture. In the end our luck held and we managed to reach the outskirts of the city. I gave a sigh of relief as the sound of police sirens receded and total darkness closed around us once again. The worst was over, I thought, but then the car suddenly stopped and Moses let out a muted curse. He made several attempts to restart it, but though the engine caught, the car wouldn't move.

"What's wrong?" I asked in a strained voice. As long as we were in the car and moving, I had felt optimistic about our chances of escape. Without the car, however, we would certainly freeze to death before we could get far.

"The hamster died," he snapped. "Don't ask stupid questions. I have to take a look." He got out of the car, and I made a face and stuck out my tongue at his retreating back. He left the engine running, turning the headlights and the interior car lights on. "I think I see something," he said after poking around under the hood for several minutes, "but I need more light."

"I have a cigarette lighter," I said, rummaging through my handbag, then getting out of the car to hold it for him.

"I thought you didn't smoke cigarettes," he said ungraciously as I snapped the flame on.

"I said I didn't smoke tobacco, and if you don't stop carping at me right now, I'm going to stop playing Bonnie and Clyde with you and go home to my aunt."

"I bet you would too," Moses laughed, "but you're right. I'm tense and I'm taking it out on you. My apologies."

"Apologies accepted," I said grandly.

I have never had the slightest interest in auto mechanics and I was impressed by the way Moses lifted the various wires and tapped the various parts of the engine.

"Here it is," he announced finally. "The cotter pin in the throttle linkage has snapped."

"Is that very bad?" I asked, not understanding at all what he had said. "Can we get another throttle pin?"

"Cotter pin," he corrected. "That's a mechanism that links the accelerator pedal to the carburetor, and it's broken. The car will idle, but we won't go anywhere. We'll have to jury-rig it somehow. Do you have a safety pin?"

"I don't think so," I said.

"Any sort of strong pin, something with a good solid clasp that can take a little abuse."

"I have a suitcase in the trunk," I said, suddenly remembering its existence. "We could have a look." Moses carried it to the front of the car where we examined its contents by the glare of the headlights. "How about this?" I asked, unpinning a piece of jewelry from a tweed jacket and holding it up. It was one of the paste pieces, a small circle of diamonds. The pin was straight, stout, and strong.

"Perfect!" said Moses. "Hand it over."

I again held the cigarette lighter while Moses worked on the car, keeping one ear cocked for the sound of approaching traffic. The loaded gun lay on the front fender. We had three clips of ammunition, twenty-four rounds. It was better odds than we had when we left the police station, I thought, hoping that the butane in my lighter held out. Moses had some difficulty accomplishing his task without tools, but he finally managed to reassemble the linkage, holding it together with the pin.

We got back in the car and headed north. The North Star was faintly visible, and in the absence of a map Moses was using it as his guide. It was his hope to connect with the Finnish border somewhere outside of Leningrad. We were driving through a wooded area when Moses suddenly cut off our headlights and drove off the road, deep into the trees. He turned off the engine and took the gun from his pocket.

"What's the matter?" I whispered.

"Cars coming," he replied. "It's a good thing I heard them. Just sit tight till we see who they are."

I held my breath, every muscle tense. Minutes later, a large military truck rumbled by. Several soldiers were perched on the flatbed in back, manning a large searchlight which they swept carefully over the road and nearby trees. I bit my lip as the powerful light passed less than ten feet in front of us, missing the car completely. A moment later the truck had passed us and they were soon out of sight.

I let out my breath and took a second shot of courage from the bottle in the glove compartment. It had been hours since I had eaten and the potent liquor hit my empty stomach, causing my head to spin. Dutch courage, I thought, taking another swallow, but it's better than none at all. Moses had restarted the car and was frowning at the dashboard. Then with a soft sigh, he shut the engine off again and slumped down in his seat.

"Have a drink," I said, thinking he was tired. But he shook his head.

"I haven't eaten since the banquet," he said, "and I need a clear head right now."

"The sooner we reach the border, the better," I agreed. "Why are we waiting?"

"We have less than a quarter of a tank of gas left," he said, "and I'm not sure where we are. I don't relish the idea of getting lost out here and then running out of fuel."

"What other choice have we?"

"We could wait until it gets light, at least we might find a road sign. We might also find a gas station though they're few and far between."

"The car would be recognized," I pointed out. "They must have some sort of all-city alarm out for us by now."

"Probably, but a bribe could get us some fuel and a map," he insisted. "A bribe . . . or a threat." He patted his right-hand pocket. "It's our best chance. In the meantime we can seek out some shelter and get some rest."

I nodded slowly. It was two A.M. We were both tired and hungry and a few hours' rest would be welcome.

"Perhaps we can find a government grocery store," I said wistfully. "I'm starved."

Moses guided the car back onto the road and we continued our journey. I took frequent sips from the bottle of vodka to keep warm, and though my total intake of alcohol was small, the lack of food and my state of nervous exhaustion soon had me half-dozing against Moses' shoulder. I was content to let Moses take charge and offered no further comments or suggestions. Suddenly I felt the car swerve sharply. Moses pulled off the road, cutting the motor and turning off the headlights.

"Wake up, sleeping beauty," he said tartly. "Yonder lies the castle."

I peered through the inky darkness. A ramshackle wooden house and a long low shed were barely discernible.

"Doesn't *look* like a castle," I muttered darkly.

"It's better," said Moses. "I think we've found a small collective."

"What do we do?" I asked. "Knock on the door and ask the farmer if we can spend the night with his beautiful daughter up in the attic?"

"I think we'll leave the good farmer undisturbed and spend the night in the barn," Moses said, opening the door and getting out of the car.

"Oh, goody," I sighed. "A night in a barn."

We tramped through the snow toward the mud-and-stone building. There was a wooden outhouse between the barn and the house and a stone well which told me all I needed to know about the rustic pleasures of Soviet farm life. Besides a share of the crop from the collectivized fields, each family is entitled to cultivate a small plot of land and raise some livestock for itself. The deep personal interest the farmers have in this tiny vestige of private ownership was evidenced by the condition of the barn, which was dry and not unpleasant smelling. There was an old cow, a couple of pigs, and half a dozen chickens sharing the small space, and they accepted our presence silently.

Moses found a lantern and placed it in an empty stall, shielding the light with his coat. He piled some extra hay on the floor for warmth and comfort, but a thorough search of the premises failed to turn up anything to eat. I took off my coat and snuggled into the sweet-smelling hay. I tried to ignore the hollow feeling in my stomach but I was miserably aware that my grandiose plans of rescue and escape had gone awry and that the cost had been high.

"It's about three hours till dawn," said Moses, blowing out the light and sitting down next to me. "Why don't you try and get some sleep."

"What about you?"

"I'll keep watch. Don't worry, I'll be fine. A good soldier learns to adjust to the circumstances. Man can live on a good deal less food and sleep than most of us are used to."

"Moses."

"Ummmm."

"This espionage business of yours isn't glamorous like they show in the movies. It's a damned dirty affair all around. I'm hungry and cold and I'm sleeping in a barn and I have half of the Soviet Union on my tail for killing three policemen."

"You left out the fact that we have a stolen car held together by costume jewelry, that we're out of gasoline, and that we really don't have any idea where we're headed," Moses added.

"Thanks," I muttered. "Now I feel much better."

Moses lay down on his side and propped himself up on his arm so that he could look down at me. The first rays of murky gray light were sifting through the chinks in the barn wall. Moses' hair was uncombed and there were streaks of grime on his hands and face. His shirt was open at the throat and I noticed a darkening bruise below his collarbone. It had not occurred to me that there might be bruises elsewhere than on his face, and I wondered if he were in pain. He had not complained of any but, given the kind of man Moses was, I could not find this behavior unusual. In our Western chauvinist culture real men don't complain or cry or show any emotion that might be construed as weakness. As Boris had pointed out, in America every man was John Wayne, but while most men I knew subscribed to this philosophy, few had the physical or emotional courage of Moses Landon.

"This has been a hard experience for you," said Moses softly, "and I shouldn't be flippant. You saved my life."

"You don't have to be grateful. You'd have done the same thing if the situation had been reversed," I said gruffly.

"Nevertheless, I am grateful. You've taught me a lot in the last few days, Christina. After my marriage I stereotyped all women and I thought of you as just better packaged than most. But you're more than beautiful and sexy. You've proved yourself intelligent, resourceful, capable, and brave. I wasn't lying when I said you were a good soldier. There isn't a man I can think of that I'd rather have beside me."

"That's because you're not gay," I quipped.

"I'm not. But I love you, Christina. Your hair is tangled and your makeup is smeared and you look like an orphan in that coat, but I don't care. No one will ever love you like I do. No one has ever known you as I do. If we get out of this mess alive, I want to marry you."

I have received many proposals, and though I always ultimately say no, the fantasy of two doomed lovers swearing undying fidelity was an appealing one. I was somewhat inebriated, and without giving a verbal answer, I slipped my arms around his neck and pulled his head down to mine. There was a warm glow in the pit of my stomach and my pussy was wet with anticipation. He kissed me hungrily, snaking his tongue inside my mouth. I was still wearing the black wool jersey dress with the long gold zipper. Moses' hand went to my breasts and the sharp intake of his breath told me that he had guessed that I was naked beneath the thin wool. His dark eyes blazed into mine as he opened the zipper. It might be the last time he would see me this way with my feminine treasures spread out for his enjoyment. He removed my dress and the cheap plastic boots, then his eyes traveled slowly over every inch of my body as if to remember it for all time. I reached for his pants, unzipping the fly and reaching my hand in to feel the long hard bulge of his cock. I rubbed it, caressed it, my free hand working on the buttons of his shirt. He stiffened and pulled slightly away.

"I don't care what you look like," I whispered. "I want you. Not just your lips or your cock. I want your whole body naked against my own."

He nodded briefly and began to undress. His body was a mass of cuts and bruises marring the smooth flesh, and I bit my lip to keep from crying out. I began to trace a jagged cut along his rib cage with the tip of my finger, but he caught my hand and pressed it to his lips.

"It's nothing," he said gruffly. "Don't look at them. It's over, and what's over doesn't matter."

"You're right," I said softly. "Only tonight matters. Having you in my arms. Tomorrow will take care of itself."

He did not kiss me or fondle my breasts. Our raw, urgent need for each other was too great for delicate foreplay or tenuous romantic buildups. Forcing my legs roughly apart with his knee, Moses entered me with one swift, clean motion. I arched toward him, my fingers sinking deep into the muscles of his shoulders. I tightened my vaginal muscles around his welcome invasion, drawing him deep into my slippery sex.

He moved his legs apart, forcing mine wider and withdrew slowly, achingly, causing me to cry out as if in pain. Then he slammed back into me with a terrifying force, his cock head pushing at the hard little knob of my clit. His strokes were powerful, angry, and demanding all at once and I shuddered as his strength overpowered me. I squeezed my inner muscles to offer a tight wet resistance, wanting to turn him on more, wanting to drive him wild. Tomorrow we could be captured or shot or imprisoned without hope of escape. But tonight we had each other, and as I arched to meet Moses' powerful thrusts, we held nothing back. Like two desperate animals we lost ourselves in the intensity of our lovemaking.

His mouth covered mine, his tongue snaking between my

lips. His long hard pole coring my sex and his tongue probing deep into my throat made me gasp and buck almost out of control. My fingers clawed at the flesh of his back, and, wanting to give him even more of myself, I encircled his thighs with my legs. He took advantage of this position, thrusting even harder and deeper. I savored the raw, bruising sensation of his cock pounding my pussy. I wanted him that way, faster, harder, deeper, my flesh an aching, quivering receptacle for his lust. My body was attuned to his in a way that I had never experienced before. I let myself go in a way that I never had before.

Suddenly I had a wildly impulsive idea. I stuck my forefinger in my mouth and wet it liberally with my saliva. Then gently separating the cheeks of his ass, I found the tight puckered hole of his anus and plunged it into the opening. His reaction was electric. His body stiffened and arched, his cock pushing hard against my clit. Then he pushed back and began pumping harder and faster than ever. I kept my finger pressed against his anus, gasping and whimpering as his maddened thrusts drove me into orgasm. The wild, sweet sensations washed over me, drenching my senses in a sexual high. I had still not come down when I felt Moses' anus tighten around my finger and his swollen prick erupt into the deepest recesses of my vagina. His hot milk poured into me. He continued thrusting, slow and deep, until with a final shuddering lunge he collapsed on top of me. Pushing all else from our minds, we made love over and over. Our world narrowed to the perfect physical union of our bodies, the give and take of fantastic sex. The tides of our passion swept us away and we fell at last into an exhausted, dreamless sleep.

CHAPTER FOURTEEN

The cool cotton of the sheets felt good against my bare skin. I half dozed, thinking of breakfast. My housekeeper would have set the table and laid a copy of the paper and my morning mail beside my plate. I hoped she had remembered to heat the milk for my coffee and to bring the butter to room temperature so that it would spread easily on my roll. A horn blowing in the street below disturbed my senses. Sounds like a cow, I thought, turning over and burying my face in the pillow. But the pillow was scratchy. Too much starch. I opened my eyes. The sights and smells of the small barn assailed my senses and I sank back into the straw with a loud oath.

"Shhhh," Moses whispered. "Someone's coming." He was fully dressed and was gripping the gun in his hand. I held my breath, pulling some straw over my body and making myself as inconspicuous as possible.

I heard footsteps in the snow outside, then the door creaked open. Gray shafts of light streaked through the opening and a gust of frigid winter air made me gasp.

Several men and women entered the barn, looking about them cautiously. They obviously expected to find someone, for each held a stout stick or a farm implement in his hand. Moses thrust the gun into my hand and, standing, went forward to meet them.

"Good morning, comrades," he called in Russian. "I hope you will forgive our intrusion. We were lost on the road late last night and feared that our low supply of gasoline would strand us in the cold."

"The collective belongs to all of the people. You are naturally welcome to use it," one of the farmers replied politely. He was the oldest of the group, a stocky man in his late fifties. In the dim light his expression was not discernible.

A younger man stood behind him, a shock of black hair falling over his forehead. "Is that your car in the woods?" he asked.

"Yes, that's the car," Moses replied easily. "We didn't wish to alarm you by driving up in the middle of the night."

"You did not wish to be caught driving a stolen government car!" said the young man belligerently.

Beneath the straw, my hand tightened on the trigger of the gun, but Moses maintained his cool.

"That's enough!" the older man said angrily. "What has the government done for you that you should worry about their car? A description of the car and of you both was on the radio this morning," he continued. "There are police and army patrols on all roads between here and Leningrad. If you attempt to go farther, you will be apprehended."

"Will you turn us in?" Moses asked. "There must be a reward."

"There are no rewards in the workers' paradise," the farmer spat, "except for those in power. No, comrade, we will not turn you in." He looked around at the others and each in turn nodded his or her agreement. The young man who had asked about the car seemed about to object, but the older man met his angry gaze with a hardness of his own and at last he, too, consented.

"Thank you, comrades," said Moses humbly.

"The young lady must be cold and hungry," the farmer said gruffly. It was the first sign any of them had given that I had been noticed, shivering naked beneath the straw of the stall. "If you will dress and come to the house, we can talk there."

I perked up immediately at this mention of food. The farmer politely left us alone to dress and Moses put on his overcoat and pocketed the gun and extra ammunition while I scrambled into my clothes.

"Do you think they'll help us escape?" I asked, running a comb through my hair.

"I'm counting on it," said Moses. "We can't do it without some assistance. There's little love lost between the average farmer and the government."

"I don't think they'd promise to feed us if they planned to turn us in," I said philosophically.

"Right now I think you'd give yourself up if the police promised you a meal," Moses said teasingly.

"I am very hungry," I sighed. "But we'll have to be careful not to overeat. Food seems to be in short supply here."

"You're right," said Moses. "Eat slowly and drink a lot of tea. It will fool your stomach and make you feel full sooner, and on less food."

"I'll remember that," I promised.

The main room of the wood-frame house contained an ancient wood-burning stove and a long table cheerfully laid for breakfast with a mismatched collection of earthenware plates and cheap glasses. I noticed a large tin tub and a number of pallets and blankets stacked neatly against the wall. The family obviously lived in this room during the long winter, as the stove seemed to be the only source of heat.

We didn't exchange introductions. The women laid out a plate of cheese, a loaf of very coarse, very black bread, and bowls of a thick gray lumpy cereal sweetened with sugar. It was a far cry from the breakfast served at the National, though we had been told by Boris and Svetlana that our meals were the same as those eaten by the average Russian family. My eyes misted at the thought of Boris, and I busied myself by taking a glass of tea from the samovar. Though not gold and silver it made me think of the one Princess Lyapunov had in her lemon-colored drawing room and I smiled, remembering the last time I had seen her.

"This is the best tea I've ever tasted," I said in Russian, not trusting myself to comment on the quality of the food.

"Have some more bread and cheese," the woman next to me urged. "We have heard that in America there is not much food. It must be true, you are so thin."

"But look at her dress," said the woman on my other side, touching the soft wool reverently. "I would not care about food if I could own such a dress."

"Women!" one of the men snorted. "They think only of trivialities. Men worry about enough wood for the fire and food for their families. Women worry about how they look."

"Come, come, comrade," said Moses. "Women have proved themselves to be every bit as competent as men in all areas of work. Especially here, where women are given more opportunity, many rise to positions of leadership and power."

I nearly choked on my bread as the women beamed their approval of this sentiment, but Moses' expression was sincere. It seemed that our conversation last night had not been the calculated flattery I had taken it for. Nothing I had accomplished in the last weeks, not the successful completion of the mission or the rescue of Moses himself, meant as much to me as this simple statement.

After breakfast we exchanged our clothes for the shapeless, ill-fitting garments of the average Russian and allowed the farmers to hide us beneath the hay of an oxcart. The farmers would dispose of our car and arrange to sell the contents of my suitcase on the black market. The proceeds would provide clothing for all of the children on the collective, the women told me gratefully, but I assured them that I considered it a small payment for all they had done.

Now as the cart bounced and jolted over the icy roads, I allowed myself a small sigh of longing for my sable coat. Despite layers of clothing, I was miserably cold, my bones bruised and aching from the roughness of the ride.

"When we get back to civilization," I said through chattering teeth, "I'm going to spend a month doing nothing besides pampering my body with soft beds, warm clothes, and perfumed baths."

"I know what you mean," said Moses. "I think I'm allergic to this damned hay. My nose has been running since last night."

There was a crowd of people at the station, and in our bulky peasant clothing we were indistinguishable from the others. I clutched a small lumpy bundle containing the last of our vodka, half a loaf of bread, and some cheese. Other women held similar bundles. Some cradled infants in their arms or had small children clinging to their skirts. Crates of live chickens or geese, stray dogs, and frightened horses added to the noise and confusion which swelled as the train from Irkutsk pulled into the station, white clouds of steam billowing from the underside of the engine.

There were two almost empty first-class cars and several second-and third-class cars. The country station of Chvojnaja was small and only the first three cars stood beside the short platform. Soviet trains start up suddenly without warning whistles or final calls of "All aboard." We said a hasty good-bye to the farmer and crowded into the third-class section along with several dozen other people. Third class, with its wooden berths and no private compartments, is not sold to foreigners. It is the most crowded section of the train and dressed as we were, we hoped to avoid recognition. The train was already in motion when we finally settled in a corner berth in the next to last car. The other passengers had made themselves comfortable, bundling up their coats to use as pillows on the hard berths. They shared good-naturedly, for more seats had been sold than there were actual places. We found ourselves opposite a small sunken-chested, dark-haired man, a student with round rimless glasses, and a plump woman with graying hair knotted carelessly on top of her head. She smiled and nodded as we sat down, displaying several gold teeth.

"It is cold today, comrades," she said in Russian. "Our horse slipped on the ice, poor thing, and we almost missed the train."

"He had too much weight to pull," said the little man, eyeing his wife's bulk meaningfully.

"Why didn't you walk then, and lighten the load?" his wife replied, wriggling her bulk farther back on the hard wooden seat.

"My leg hurt," he said plaintively. "You can't expect a man to walk with a leg like this." He pulled up the leg of his trousers to display a straight wooden shank. Moses nodded sympathetically and the man moved closer. "I had to stand on line three hours for the tickets," he said, producing them from his coat pocket. "Three hours. My wife was afraid there wouldn't be enough seats, that we wouldn't get on the train. Look at that," he waved his hand to indicate the overcrowded car. "Two, sometimes three to a berth if the couple has a child. It's against the rules, you know. One berth per person, the rules say. This doesn't happen in first or second class, too many Party members and foreigners to make trouble. Were you on line long?"

"We were late getting to the station," Moses said. "When will the ticket collectors come through?"

"Not until Leningrad," the man said. "Are you going that far?"

"Just a little beyond," said Moses, watching him carefully. "About a hundred kilometers beyond."

The man gave him a sharp look. "That's the Finnish border," he said. "This train doesn't stop in Imatra, comrade. The Finnish border is closed to Russians unless you have special papers."

"I know that," said Moses simply.

"Then you're a fool on a fool's errand," the man spat, putting the tickets back in his pocket and moving away from us.

"Hush, Vasia Andreievich," his wife said. "Who are you to judge? You were young once yourself, eh? Whatever your reason," she said to us, "I wish you luck."

"We all wish you luck," the young student said, "and we will do all we can to help you." He was sitting on the floor between our two berths and I gave him a warm smile of appreciation. Moses was a good judge of character, I thought. Our lives were in the hands of these workers, as they had been in the hands of the farmers a few hours before. By laying his cards on the table, Moses had disarmed them. They were used to lies. This simple gesture of trust had gained their respect and, more importantly, their cooperation.

The train moved slowly. Our car jolted back and forth and the wheels rattled underneath in a steady clacking rhythm. Fighting the knot of tension in my stomach, I looked out of the bleary window at the gray, wintery landscape. Tracks, fields, houses, everything was blanketed in snow. Ice covered the bare trees, turning distant forests to fairylands of black-and-silver filigree.

When it was time for lunch, the women opened their bundles, laying out their contents on one of the lower berths. It was an odd assortment of food; great crusty loaves of bread, rounds of cheese, slices of boiled beef, and rye pancakes kept warm between layers of linen napkins. I brought out my meager provisions, and Moses produced the last of our vodka. We shared with the rest, alternating swallows of vodka with glasses of hot tea, which could be purchased from a tea wagon for three kopeks a glass. Though the contents of our bottle would hardly float a roomful of hard-drinking Russians, the atmosphere was considerably lightened. The young student had a balalaika and readily agreed to my request for a song. He had a pleasing voice and the rest of the company began to clap their hands and stamp their feet, joining in on the chorus. It was warm and close in the car. The tedious journey had made everybody restless, and the vodka had raised everyone's blood pressure. We had eaten and drunk and sung together. It needed only the barest encouragement to move the party to a more intimate level.

The young student started a *yurochka*, a Byelorussian folk dance, and a number of the younger people in the car formed a circle and began to beat out the fast-paced steps. After watching for two measures, I threw caution to the winds and joined them. I am a natural dancer and quickly caught on to the sequence of steps. As the music quickened, I threw myself into the movements, jumping and turning in a way that brought cheers of appreciation from those on the sidelines. When the dance ended we collapsed breathlessly against each other, pleased at having done so well. The music changed tempo and the slow, measured sounds of the gypsy dance *tsigany* filled the car. I was leaning against a young, blond-haired man, and, snaking my arms around his neck, I began to move my body sensuously against his. Other couples began to dance, swaying sensuously as the mood of the party became more erotic. Jackets were taken off, shirts and blouses loosened. Soft moans of pleasure were clearly audible as couples tumbled into empty berths. My own partner was not a novice in the art of seduction, and I soon found myself naked beneath his hard young body, my yearning pussy begging for his cock. I wrapped my legs around his thighs, arching my pelvis so he could penetrate more deeply. I was pure cunt for him, not wanting to be petted or caressed, just wanting his cock stabbing at the knob of my clit. I shivered with pleasure as he entered me, sinking into the soft flesh. He pulled back, then plunged again. Loud moans and sucking noises emanated from the rest of the room, reminding me that the other passengers were similarly engaged. The smells and sounds of sex heightened my own pleasure as my lover stretched my sex, thrusting into me over and over while my fingers fought for a handhold in the hard muscles of his back. His staying power was remarkable and I reached climax after climax before his hot cum quenched my fire and brought me back to reality.

The next few hours were a haze of cocks and breasts and pussies as we changed partners and positions in a communal afternoon of sensual sharing. I was lying between my last two partners, trying to catch my breath, when I saw Moses coming toward me.

"The next stop is Leningrad," he said in Russian, handing me my clothes. His words, like the striking of the clock in the story of Cinderella, broke the party mood. Leningrad meant a longer stop. It meant ticket collectors and uniformed policemen and the KGB. Alerted by an all-city alarm, they would be watching all points of entrance and exit from the city, checking cars and trains, passports and papers. We hurried into our clothes, pulling on boots and gloves in a mad Marx Brothers scramble. Moses and I hunched in our berth, and as the train pulled into the station, our fellow passengers crowded the berths and aisles around us. They sat passively, their expressions conveying the rude indifference most Russians display in public. Several new passengers pushed their way into the already overcrowded car, fighting for seats and lighting cigarettes. The air was unbreathable. The door opened again. An old, bent ticket collector flanked by two brutish-looking militiamen made their appearance. I pulled my scarf more closely around my face and Moses slipped his hand into his pocket. The thought of the gun did little to reassure me. It would not be possible to shoot in such crowded conditions. The new passengers were at the front of the car and grudgingly produced their tickets and papers, but when the uniformed men tried to move through the crowd, they found their way blocked.

"My ticket is for a berth," said one man rudely in answer to the railroad official's brusque request. "You give me a berth and I'll show you my ticket." He was standing in the middle of the aisle, a giant of a man with powerful hands and a short, thick neck.

"You heard the collector," one of the militiamen said threateningly. "And let's see your papers while you're at it."

"They are with my ticket," the man shrugged, a uniquely Russian gesture of contempt. "The conditions in this car are a disgrace. You have no right to charge the price of a ticket, much less ask for papers. Be off now and let the train move before we suffocate."

There were murmurs of assent from the rest of the car and vaguely muttered threats. The militiaman fingered his club nervously but the crowd did not move.

"We are looking for fugitives, comrades," he said in a less belligerent tone. "A man and a woman. Americans. They are wanted for serious crimes against the state."

"Oh, we are all rich Americans here," the young student called out. "You can see that, comrade officer. All rich Americans in this car."

The crowd hooted their approval of this sentiment and the militiaman blushed furiously.

"They are on the run," he said patiently. "They might ride third class to avoid detection."

"Don't be a fool, comrade officer," said an old woman. "It is getting late. Make your check and be off. Don't hold the train any longer."

Other passengers expressed similar sentiments, deriding the militiamen for thinking American fugitives would be in the group. The officers made a few halfhearted attempts to do their job, then gave up. Third-class passengers were people without rights, without luxuries, without hope. The militia-men were outnumbered and were clearly unwilling to test the mood of the crowd further.

I gave a long sigh when the door closed behind them. My heart was pounding and my hands trembled violently. The train heaved and the crowds on the station slid by. The mood in our car was jubilant as the workers congratulated them-selves on their success.

"Thank you, comrades, thank you," I said over and over as we were hugged and kissed and pounded on the back.

"You are not out of the woods yet," the young student reminded us. "There is a border patrol. It's an arm of the KGB."

"We will not let them catch us," Moses assured him and I thought again of the gun and the extra ammunition.

Moses held me tightly as we stood near the door of the car. "When I tell you to, jump," he whispered. "Don't worry, I'll be right behind you. I won't let you get hurt."

"I know you won't," I said.

"I love you, Christina."

"I love you too, Moses."

I felt his lips on mine, my tears wet on my cheeks. His kiss took my breath away as the sound of the wheels on the tracks pounded in my ears and a blast of cold air washed over me. The train rounded a curve, slowing slightly.

"Jump!" he said urgently. "Jump!"

CHAPTER FIFTEEN

Several months later I held a small private dinner in my apartment. Princess Lyapunov, Moses Landon, and the Princess' nephew, Gregory Kabalevsky, were my only guests.

Moses had been hurt when I had ultimately turned down his proposal of marriage, but he had come to accept the fact that my life-style was not suited to a monogamous commitment, or indeed, to a commitment of any sort. I was still very fond of him, however, and enjoyed renewing our acquaintance whenever our busy schedules allowed us time together. Moses had changed since our adventure in the Soviet Union. He had become a champion of woman's rights in his particular branch of the armed forces, urging that women be given an equal chance at dangerous or top-priority assignments.

"Women are more imaginative than men," he was saying now as we lingered over dessert, a frozen cream flavored with strawberries drowning a cream-filled charlotte russe bordered by ladyfingers. "They are more willing to take risks, depart from the standard script."

"You used to think we were merely icing on the cake," I reminded him, "decorating the world with musical recitals and gallery openings."

"You've taught me the value of a good gallery show," said Moses. "The exhibition of the jewels you brought back from

Russia made a great deal of money for the new wing at Harrison-Sloan that you and the Princess are building in Boris' memory.''

"I am sorry I could not have known him," the Princess said. "He was so much responsible for my present happiness." She squeezed her nephew's hand affectionately and beamed around the table at all of us.

"His half brother is getting the best of care," I sighed. "I think that would have made him happy."

"Very happy," said Moses, kissing me, but he was not speaking of Boris.

"I propose a toast," said the Princess' nephew, refilling our glasses and holding his aloft. *"Na Zdorovie!"*

"To our good health!" we echoed, downing our drinks.

BESTSELLING FICTION FROM ARROW

All these books are available from your bookshop or news-
agent or you can order them direct. Just tick the titles you
want and complete the form below.

☐	THE COMPANY OF SAINTS	Evelyn Anthony	£1.95
☐	HESTER DARK	Emma Blair	£1.95
☐	1985	Anthony Burgess	£1.75
☐	2001: A SPACE ODYSSEY	Arthur C. Clarke	£1.75
☐	NILE	Laurie Devine	£2.75
☐	THE BILLION DOLLAR KILLING	Paul Erdman	£1.75
☐	THE YEAR OF THE FRENCH	Thomas Flanagan	£2.50
☐	LISA LOGAN	Marie Joseph	£1.95
☐	SCORPION	Andrew Kaplan	£2.50
☐	SUCCESS TO THE BRAVE	Alexander Kent	£1.95
☐	STRUMPET CITY	James Plunkett	£2.95
☐	FAMILY CHORUS	Claire Rayner	£2.50
☐	BADGE OF GLORY	Douglas Reeman	£1.95
☐	THE KILLING DOLL	Ruth Rendell	£1.95
☐	SCENT OF FEAR	Margaret Yorke	£1.75

	Postage	_____
	Total	_____

ARROW BOOKS, BOOKSERVICE BY POST, PO BOX 29,
DOUGLAS, ISLE OF MAN, BRITISH ISLES

Please enclose a cheque or postal order made out to Arrow Books
Limited for the amount due including 15p per book for postage and
packing both for orders within the UK and for overseas orders.

Please print clearly

NAME...

ADDRESS...

....

Whilst every effort is made to keep prices down and to keep popular
books in print, Arrow Books cannot guarantee that prices will be the
same as those advertised here or that the books will be available.